DIESEL'S KEEPSAKE

Celtic Demons - Book Three

JILL SHANNON

Published by Blushing Books
An Imprint of
ABCD Graphics and Design, Inc.
A Virginia Corporation
977 Seminole Trail #233
Charlottesville, VA 22901

Jill Shannon
Diesel's Keepsake

eBook ISBN: 978-1-64563-976-3
Print ISBN: 978-1-64563-977-0
v1

Acknowledgments

I hope you all enjoy Diesel's Keepsake. I put a little about myself in this book, although, only my family will know which parts. I want to thank my family and especially my husband. Without their patience and support, I wouldn't be able to do what I love to do and that's writing.

I would like to thank my beat readers, Marie Vayer and Sharon Graham-Ellis, for taking the time to read my book. Your opinions, advice, and editing skills are always so helpful. All of which I humbly accept.

I want to thank Vinny Varden once again, my model for this cover, and Steven Timms, the photographer who took the photos. Here we are again, putting together another beautiful cover. Vinny, you are an incredibly special person. During 2020, with Covid-19 shutting everything down in the UK, you lost so much. And yet, you still took the time to help me put this book cover together, something I will always be grateful for.

Steven, your ability to capture the perfect photograph of Vinny in the right light and the exact position brought this book cover to life. You have an extraordinary talent and I'm so thankful to you for your charitable heart and time to make this book cover possible.

Finally, to the amazing staff at Blushing Books, for having faith in me to deliver a book people will want to read. Without all of you, none of this could be possible. And to my editor, Anna, who finds and fixes all my mistakes, you have my deepest thanks.

I love you all, thank you,

Jill

Chapter 1

Ciara O'Malley tossed her cellphone on her desk, frustrated with her online search. Since moving to the Myrtle Beach area three months ago, all she had been doing was organizing her new condo and working. She had had no time for herself. Now that she had the time, she couldn't find a BDSM dungeon accepting new memberships.

Glancing at the paperwork on her desk, she spotted Colton Thorne's business card. He was the realtor who helped her find her townhouse. He had mentioned some in their brief talks about the clubs in the area, never specifying if any were BDSM clubs, but he seemed to know his shit. Picking up her cellphone, she dialed his number. When she got his voicemail, she left a message.

"Mr. Thorne, it's Ciara O'Malley. You helped with finding my townhouse. While you were here, you referred to the clubs in the area. Would you have any knowledge of any exclusive private adult clubs?" Ciara hoped he would understand the underlying meaning in her words. "If you have a free moment, please call me to discuss it. Thank you and goodbye."

Ciara dropped her phone on her desk and glanced up at

the clock on the wall. Seeing she still had another five hours to go on her shift had her groaning deep in her throat. Tonight, had been her slowest night since she had accepted the position. When the opportunity arose to move to another state and run her department, she couldn't refuse. Ciara had taken the increase in pay and a change of scenery as an added sign that she needed to make some changes in her life, thinking the night shift would be slow, peaceful, and less stressful. Yet, since she had arrived here, each night had been busier than the last. Now, tonight, when she had some time to herself, she couldn't find what she needed.

Ciara took a moment to think about the biggest reason she needed this change, the passing of her grandmother, her last link to the only family she had known. Her grandmother Ethel had been her biggest supporter. Anything Ciara had ever wanted to do, her grandmother had always been there cheering her on. She had been the one who taught Ciara to be kind, but not a pushover. She made Ciara take self-defense classes—so she wouldn't have to worry about her as much, her grandmother had told her. Ethel taught her how to cook, clean and bake. Gram would pull her piggy jar out for them to play poker, and on other nights, they'd play solitaire and cribbage. And as the two played, her grandmother would relay tales of her childhood. Gram told Ciara about the trouble she used to get into as a young girl and the lives she had saved in the Great Depression. The stories opened Ciara's eyes to the real world, prompting her choice of profession. Ciara believed everyone needed an ending to the story of their life. She wanted to make sure their families had all the answers to tell it. Ciara had listened as her grandmother weaved her tales of family members Ciara never knew, sucking each story in like a sponge so she could one day pass them on to her children and grandchildren, thus keeping her grandmother's memory alive.

The ringing of the phone pulled Ciara from her thoughts.

As she picked up the receiver, her gentle sounding voice filled the room. "Good evening, coroner's office. This is Ciara, how can I help you?"

"Hey, Ciara, it's Jacob. I'm really glad you're working tonight."

"What's up, Jacob?"

Jacob was the Patrol Captain in the area. Standing at six-foot-four, with sandy blond short hair and brilliant green eyes, he was an imposing figure, with linebacker shoulders, a barrel chest and a trim waist. He was the perfect specimen of a bodybuilder. Ciara had met him on her first day and had felt an instant connection with him. She felt like they had been friends forever.

"The van should arrive soon." There was a pause before he continued. "I really hate to do this to you, but the body arriving is top priority. As much as I'd like to think there was no foul play, in my heart I feel there's something not right."

"Why do you say that, Jacob?"

"Her age. She's too young to be on your table. If you could move her to the top of your list, I would owe you big time."

Her stomach had dropped with his words, but Ciara could hear the compassion and doubt in his voice. "Who is the deceased?" She wondered at the age of the female about to be a body on her table. Also, his request for special treatment told her that he knew the victim. Normally, high priority cases meant the department would be under scrutiny from the media, not to mention her superiors.

"Isabella Diaz."

Ciara heard a touch of disappointment in his voice. "Any special reason you believe she needs to be a priority?"

"You know how high-profile cases bring out the media and the crazies? Well, the twist in this case is that everyone in town knows her. Isabella is the daughter of Javier Diaz and sister to Diesel Diaz. She was also an advocate for the homeless."

Jacob left the names hanging as if she should know who they were.

"And?"

"And?" His voice rose in a questioning tone. "You don't know who they are?"

"I'm afraid I don't." She added, "I don't get many visitors in the medical examiner's office." She chuckled at the thought.

"Sorry, I forgot how new you are to the area. Javier Diaz is the leading defense attorney in the area, and his son Diesel is a member of the Celtic Demons Motorcycle Club. He recently received his patch, after healing from the torturing he went through a year ago for the club. Since then, they have revered him as a hero."

"So why does Diesel," she hesitated, mulling his name over in her mind and questioning who would name their son Diesel, then continued her question, "concern me?"

"He's going to want answers and being a member of the Celtic Demons makes her death club business. I'm just giving you the heads-up. Diesel's likely going to camp out in your lab until the results of your findings come back."

"Well, I'm glad it's a slow night. As soon as the body arrives, I'll get started on it right away. This way Mr. Diaz will be able to sleep in his own bed." She heard Jacob chuckle.

"That's why I like you, Ciara. You make life so much easi-er," Jacob commented.

"Let me get going so I'm prepared for the body when they arrive."

"Ciara?"

"Still here, Jacob."

"If at any time you feel uncomfortable, I'm just a phone call away."

"No worries, Jacob. I know how to take care of myself. But thank you just the same."

"Okay, Ciara. Call if you need anything."

"I will. Be safe out there, Jacob."

Ciara hung up the receiver and picked up her cellphone. She opened her search engine and entered Diesel Diaz. Jacob had piqued her curiosity while he was feeding her bits of information about the man. This would allow Ciara to fill in the blanks. The page came up, listing many stories, so she chose the one at the top. The first thing she noticed was that the article was written over a year ago. *'Motorcycle Club holds annual fund raiser in honor of their newly patched in member.'* She scanned the article quickly. She learned that although the fundraiser was in Diesel's honor, the money was donated to the children's burn/scar unit, in the same hospital where Diesel had been a patient. The article continued, *'In attendance were Diesel's father Javier and his younger sister Isabella.'* It went on to mention his father was a defense attorney and owned his own firm. His sister, a junior at Webster University, was pursuing a master's degree in counseling, with an emphasis on addiction and recovery. Ciara thought to herself, "His sister would have been graduating this year. What a tragic loss." She was finishing up the news clip, which revealed little information, when she heard the buzzer for the back entrance, letting her know the van had arrived. She shut down her cellphone and went to the wall panel to open the bay door, allowing the van to pull into the loading dock area.

She was standing on the loading dock by the time the van had parked. She watched as the two men exited the vehicle. Seeing it was Sam and Brian put a smile on her face. They were two of the most easy-going men she had ever met. In fact, if she didn't know them, she would never guess they transported dead bodies for a living. However, tonight when they emerged, they were not so jovial. Ciara knew immediately that they both either knew Isabella or knew of her. Having her own recent experience with losing someone she cared for, Ciara related to their feelings. They met her at the back of the van, their heads bowed in reverence. "I'm sorry for your loss. How did you know her?" she asked.

Sam raised his head. "We watched her grow up." He gestured toward Brian as he opened the doors of the vehicle. "My wife was one of her teachers, and Brian's wife taught her the piano." Sam turned teary brown eyes toward the van. "She was the prettiest, most carefree child, with the biggest heart."

Brian slid the tray out, preparing to transfer the body to the gurney Ciara had waiting. He quickly wiped the tears with the back of his hand. Brian's watery eyes met Sam's as they moved the black body bag to the gurney. When they were finished, Brian told Sam, "I'll bring her back. You grab the evidence bags and sign them over to Ciara's possession. I don't want any loopholes for the son of a bitch who did this." Brian then turned, placing two hands on the gurney, and walked the body through the sliding doors and into the morgue.

Ciara had also brought a cart to place any evidence bags on. She pulled it to the side door of the van and watched as Sam shifted the sealed brown bags to the cart.

When he finished, he pulled a clipboard holding the chain of command form from its resting place. Removing the pen from his pocket, he signed the document and then passed it over to Ciara, completing the conveyance of evidence per the CoC.

Ciara handed the clipboard back to Sam after removing the document. Glancing toward the door, she asked. "Sam, why does Brian think someone else was involved in Isabella's death?" Her attention turned back to Sam when he answered.

"Because Jacob said there was another set of footprints in the sand where they found her."

"Well, couldn't the footsteps belong to the person who called it in?"

"Maybe, but she was a tiny thing. These steps belonged to someone bigger." He looked into her whiskey brown eyes.

"Besides, Isabella wouldn't do anything to harm herself. She had everything going for her. An excellent family, a job waiting for her when she graduated and she was always happy. Suicide just wouldn't make sense, Ciara."

"Well, Sam, we will soon find out what happened to Isabella Diaz." She began pushing the cart toward the sliding door as Brian came walking back out, pushing the now empty gurney. "Take good care of her, Ciara, her family deserves answers," Brian told her in passing.

"I will, Brian," Ciara responded. Stopping just inside the doors, Ciara stood and watched the two men return to the van and get in. They both had their heads down, feeling their loss. As they drove away, Ciara gave a slight wave of her hand, saying, "Don't worry, gentlemen, I will find out what happened." Her voice echoed in the empty space.

Ciara locked the garage doors and pushed the cart back to the morgue. She moved it off to the side and prepared to start the autopsy. After changing into her scrubs and assembling all the instruments needed, she unzipped the black body bag. Shifting the body from the gurney to the table, she placed Isabella's head on the headrest, smoothing her jet-black hair away from the young woman's face saying, "Tell me what happened, Isabella." Ciara took a moment to look at the young woman lying before her. Picking up the remote on her cart of instruments, she hit the play button and soft music filled the morgue. Next, her fingers reached for the buttons on the fixture over the body on the table, to turn on the voice recorder. Finally, she picked up the camera to take additional photos of the body. Once she was ready, she began speaking. "Today is March tenth, two-thousand twenty, this is Doctor Ciara O'Malley, the medical examiner of Horry County and I will be performing the autopsy of Miss Isabella Diaz, age twenty-four."

"Hey, Doc, you starting without me?" 'Josie' Josephine Lopez burst through the swinging door.

Ciara, startled by Josie's appearance, jumped. Dropping the camera and placing one hand over her heart with the other one grabbing the table. Ciara rasped out, "What the hell, Josie? You were supposed to be off tonight." Reaching up, she paused the voice recorder. Josie was Ciara's intern. At five-foot-four, with multicolored hair and trim body, Josie was a ball of energy.

Josie began putting her gear on to prepare for joining Ciara. Snapping her glove into place, she approached Ciara and Isabella. Looking down at the beautiful woman, she whispered, "She was my friend. The minute I heard what happened, I knew they'd bring her here." She glared into Ciara's whiskey-colored eyes. "Ciara, this woman is the reason I am here today." Ciara gave her a puzzled look. Bowing her head, she continued, "If Isabella hadn't found me on the streets four years ago, I wouldn't be here today. She helped me get sober." Josie glanced up to see Ciara's reaction to her statement. When she said nothing, Josie went on to explain. "Isabella brought me into her home and helped me detox. She was by my side the entire time. When I needed help getting into this internship, she supported me with that. So, you see, if not for two very different circumstances, I literally would not be here." Josie pointed down to the ground with both hands.

Ciara was a little stunned by Josie's admission. The woman Josie exhibited was jovial, energetic, and confident. Not exactly how she pictured someone in recovery. *But everyone makes wrong assumptions about people*, Ciara thought to herself.

Before Ciara could say anything, Josie blurted out, "Please, Ciara? No one knows about my relationship with Isabella."

Ciara knew in her head that it was wrong to allow Josie to stay, but in her heart, she knew the girl had only the best intentions. "You may stay, but you cannot stay in this room. You can watch through the glass in the gallery."

Josie gave Ciara a quick hug. "Thank you, Ciara."

Ciara waited until she heard the door close and saw Josie perched in the gallery window before turning the voice recorder back on and picking up the camera. For the next five hours, Ciara shut out the rest of the world. Her focus was on finding out what happened to Isabella Diaz. She took samples of tissues, blood, and processed a rape kit. She set the last stitch on Isabella's chest and removed her gloves as the sun was rising to start a new day. She was removing the rest of her gear when she heard the buzzer for the front entrance. Ciara glanced at the clock, seeing it was six o'clock in the morning. She turned her gaze toward Josie with a questioning face.

Josie moved to the speaker, pressing the intercom button. "Do you want me to see who it is?"

Ciara placed a sheet over Isabella, then moved toward her office to check the camera at the entrance. Josie followed behind her, looking over Ciara's shoulder as she pulled up the screen.

"It's Diesel," was all Josie said.

Ciara felt a raw desire flood her body as she looked at the man on the screen. Her quick intake of breath had Josie looking her way.

"It's okay, his bark is bigger than his bite." Josie assumed that Ciara's reaction was to the size of the man standing outside.

However, it was quite the opposite. Ciara's eyes scanned Diesel's body, from his dark, trimmed hair and beard to the tips of his boots. She stood in silent wonder, and when his intense eyes glanced up at the camera, Ciara backed away from the screen.

"Seriously, Ciara. You have nothing to fear. I'm sure he's

just here to get answers. Do you want me to let him in?" Josie asked as Diesel rang the bell again.

Ciara needed to pull herself together before speaking to Mr. Diaz. "Yes, Josie. Please bring him into the gallery. I need him to I.D. the body. Then I'll talk to him in my office." Ciara watched on the screen as Josie granted Diesel entrance into the building. She followed their progress to the gallery. She waited a few minutes to allow Mr. Diaz time to adjust to the fact that when she opened the curtain and pulled back the cover from her body, his life would never be the same.

Chapter 2

R omeo 'Diesel' Diaz slapped the empty shot glass onto the clubhouse bar. His two drinking buddies, Allen 'Ace' Bentley, treasurer of the Celtic Demons, and road captain, Dominic 'Grave Digger' Santiago, followed his lead. Diesel swung his barstool around, glancing at the few members scattered about the clubhouse after Hunter and Willow's departure to the hospital. Most of the guests and members had either followed the couple or gone home after the two had wed. Diesel had no desire to return home yet. This had been the first night in a long time that he had felt like himself, after enduring the worst experience of his life at the hands of Vito Mancini, Don Santoro's right-hand man. It had taken him nearly two years to recover physically. With the help of Ace, Grave Digger, and the club, he was coming around. He was starting to feel like the fun loving, carefree man he used to be. Diesel glanced to the empty game room in the back of the club as he posed the question to his friends, "Anyone want to shoot a round of pool?"

Both Ace and Grave Digger looked to the backroom. Seeing no one was playing, they agreed. All three grabbed their beers off the bar and started making their way to the pool table.

Diesel had just racked the balls on the table, waiting for Ace to break, when Snake, the new prospect behind the bar, yelled to Diesel, "Hey, Diesel, the Patrol Captain is at the gate. Says he needs to talk to you."

Diesel had no idea what Jacob Stewart could want. Giving his brothers a quizzical look and shrugging his shoulders, he yelled back, "Snake, tell Chewy to let him in." Placing the pool cue on the table, Diesel headed for the door with Ace and Grave Digger following in his wake.

"What could Jacob want with you, Diesel? You forget to pay a fine for someone?" Ace teased him as the three left the clubhouse to meet the Patrol Captain in the driveway. They watched as the car's lights came into view. Once the car was parked, Jacob got out, placing his hat on his head as he approached them.

"What can we do for you, Officer Stewart?" Grave Digger requested.

"I need to talk to you, Diesel." Jacob's voice was filled with the empathy he felt.

"Sounds serious, Jacob, what's up? Everything all right at the dungeon?" Recently, Diesel, Saint, Yankee, and Ace had gotten together, along with Reed 'Judge' Brody as a silent partner, and opened Demons' Dungeon, a private BDSM club for an exclusive clientele. The club could charge an exorbitant membership fee for the security and anonymity. Every member signed a non-disclosure agreement as well as any guest they might bring into the club. Word had spread quickly through Hog Inlet and the surrounding areas as soon as construction began on the building. By the time the Demons opened the doors for business, they had filled their membership limit and had started a waiting list.

"The dungeon is fine. Could we speak alone?" Jacob glanced at Ace and Grave Digger.

Diesel turned his head to look at his brothers, then back at Jacob. "I'm going to tell them anyway, so you might as well just spit it out."

Jacob's watery eyes locked with Diesel's. "I'm sorry to have to inform you of this, but your sister Isabella has died." He gave Diesel a minute to digest what he had learned. Jacob then continued, "She was found a few hours ago on Hog Inlet Beach. A late-night jogger found her and called it in."

Diesel stood in stunned silence, trying to wrap his head around what Jacob had told him.

Before Jacob could continue, Grave Digger jumped down his throat. "What the fuck happened?"

The Patrol Captain trained his bright green eyes in Grave Digger's direction. "We are not sure yet. She's been taken to the medical examiner."

"You said this happened a few hours ago. Why are you just now telling me?" Diesel snapped at Jacob.

"I contacted your father. He told me he wanted to be the one to tell you, but you didn't answer your phone—"

Diesel interrupted Jacob, digging his hand into his pocket and retrieving his phone. Once Diesel had the phone in his hand, he realized he had shut it off for the wedding and had forgotten to turn it back on. Holding the button, he powered it on. He found ten text messages and five voicemails, all from his father.

Jacob looked at the intoxicated condition of the men before him and asked, "Would you like me to wait while you throw some water on your faces?"

Diesel's response was quick, "No need. We'll get one of the prospects to drive us." Jacob turned away, heading for his cruiser when Diesel yelled to him, "Thanks for letting me know, Jacob." With that, he dismissed the Patrol Captain and returned with his brothers back to the clubhouse.

"I'm going to my room to take the captain's advice. I suggest you do the same. If you want to join me." Diesel left the invitation open to them.

"If you think we're letting you go down to the morgue without us, think again. We'll wake up Bug and have him drive the cage. Meet back here in twenty." Ace took charge, making sure Diesel knew he wasn't alone. "You doing okay, brother?" Ace posed the question, expressing the concern both he and Grave Digger were feeling.

"I'm not sure, it just doesn't seem real. How could Izzy be dead? She is… was so full of life. She was going to save the world," Diesel stated, leaving them to stare at his back as he walked away. When he arrived at his room above the clubhouse, he removed his cut and tossed it on his bed. His fingers were shaking as he reached for the little buttons on his dress shirt. He tilted his head down to look at what his fingers could not do alone. A tear slid down the bridge of his nose, and then another. Frustration and anger tore through his body at an alarming rate. Gathering the material of his shirt tightly in his fingers, he ripped the garment from his body and howled an eerie cry of pain at the grief piercing his bleeding heart. Falling to his knees, he placed his face in his gathered hands and sobbed for the beautiful soul that was his sister Isabella.

When he had finally composed himself, he threw on a black Harley Davidson shirt that molded tightly across his chest and a pair of jeans that framed his hard ass. Tying his boots, he stood and retrieved his cut, and throwing it on, he left his room. Twenty minutes later the men were seated in a nineteen ninety-eight blue extended cab Silverado. The club owned a few cages for long runs, breakdowns, and for prospects to run errands. It didn't take long to get to the county morgue at this time of day. The sun was just starting to drive away the night as they pulled into the parking lot. Bug dropped the three men at the curb and then pulled the cage around to park, to wait in the vehicle for them.

Diesel stood in stunned silence trying to wrap his head around it. There weren't many windows around the structure or in the entrance door. When he was ready, he led the way to the door. Trying the handle and finding it locked, he hit the button on the intercom. He waited a moment and then looked up at the camera positioned off in the corner above the door. Becoming impatient with the wait, he rang the intercom again. This time the door opened almost immediately. A young woman with multicolored hair stood in the doorway. "I'm Diesel Diaz. I'm here to see my sister."

"You must not remember me, Diesel, but I'm Josie, the girl your sister took in," Josie remarked as she extended her hand in greeting and condolence.

Diesel shook her hand, vaguely remembering his sister bringing someone home from off the streets, but he had rarely been around much during that time.

Josie smiled to relieve the awkwardness then, saying, "It's been a while. If you'll follow me, I'll show you to the gallery." Josie led them through the narrow hallway to a room where several chairs were scattered about and a wall of curtain covered glass. Josie offered them coffee or water, but all three refused. Walking to the corner of the room, she pressed the button on the panel, informing Ciara that they were ready.

While Josie had escorted them to the gallery, Ciara had moved Isabella's body closer to the window for viewing. She had folded the sheet back away from Isabella's face, awaiting the time she would open the curtains. Upon hearing Josie's voice, Ciara pulled the cord, moving the curtains to the side. She then stood out of the way, giving Isabella's brother a moment to view her body. She watched as the two men on either side of Diesel placed their hands on his shoulders. She stepped up to the panel on her side of the glass. "Is this your sister, Mr. Diaz?"

Tears clouded Diesel's bright blue eyes as he stared at his beautiful sister's lifeless body lying on the cold metal table. Her hair had been pushed back from her flawless face. Diesel took a step forward, placing his hand on the glass, trying to touch her, his inner thoughts commenting on how peaceful she looked. He then turned his attention to the woman who had posed the question to him. She wasn't very tall, and the ugly lab coat that reached below her knees didn't help. Her auburn hair was pulled severely from her face, wrapped in a tight bun on her head. Thick black glasses framed her whiskey brown eyes. Diesel wiped the tears from his face. Looking her directly in the eyes and squaring his broad shoulders, he gave Ciara an affirmative head nod.

Ciara not only saw his pain; she also felt it. She bowed her head in sympathy and understanding. Stepping to the inter-com, she told him, "Take as much time as you need. I'll be in my office. Josie can escort you when you're ready." She then turned and left the room.

Diesel stood a few more minutes looking at Isabella. Ace was the first to speak to him. "Brother, you are not alone. Isabella was family, we all feel your pain."

Guilt flooded Diesel's next words, "I should have been there for her."

Grave Digger stepped up to him. "Diesel, she was a grown woman. You couldn't have done anything to change what happened tonight."

Before anyone said anything else, they heard the buzzer for the entrance. All three of the men's heads swung in Josie's direction with questioning faces.

Relieving their curiosity, Josie explained, "Someone is at the door." Josie twisted her face into a smirk at the men's reac-tion to the loud noise. "I'll be back in a moment."

She left the gallery and went to the front entrance. After receiving confirmation from Ciara, she pushed the handle, releasing the lock, allowing the door to swing open. Josie knew immediately who the older man on the doorstep was. "Hello, Mr. Diaz." She stepped aside to allow him entrance.

Javier Diaz stepped into the cold building. Standing at five-foot-eleven, Javier had a dominating aura about him. His suit was tailor made, and his shoes were made of a soft Italian leather. He had a full head of dark hair that enhanced his penetrating brown eyes. He wore a Rolex on his wrist and carried a Bottega Veneta briefcase. Everything about his outward appearance screamed power and money, yet his expression held only sadness. His eyes drifted over the woman standing before him, his eyes flicking with recognition. "I know you, don't I?"

"Yes, Sir. It's me, Josephine Lopez. I spent some time at your house a few years back."

"Yes, I remember now, the alcoholic living on the streets my daughter brought home. What are you doing here?" Javier looked the young woman over, suspicion clouding his question.

"I'm an intern here at the morgue, sir," Josie's quiet voice replied.

Javier looked closer, beneath the multicolored hair and makeup, and saw a sober person. At the time Isabella had brought her home, Javier would have bet money the girl in front of him would have relapsed. Yet, here she was, sober and working on a career. "Isabella would be very proud of you, as am I," Javier said humbly.

"Thank you, sir. I couldn't have done it without your daughter. She was my friend, and I will miss her very much."

Javier swung his body away from Josie, masking the raw pain her words brought to his heart. Composing himself, he croaked out, "Where is my daughter?"

Trying to save him the agony of viewing Isabella in this

sterile environment, Josie uttered, "Your son Diesel has already confirmed her identity, Mr. Diaz. You don't have to go in there if you don't want to." Josie swallowed back her tears, looking at the bewildered man before her, adding, "I'm so sorry for your loss, Mr. Diaz."

Diesel heard his father's deep voice from the gallery and stepped into the hall to meet him.

Javier's eyes locked with Diesel's and Josie's presence faded away as father and son shared their loss, and an overwhelming sadness filled the surrounding air.

Javier approached Diesel, asking him, "Is it really our Isabella?"

Diesel bowed his head slightly and nodded. Javier dropped the briefcase from his hand and reached for his son.

Josie, Ace, and Grave Digger stood to the side while the two shared the grief they all felt.

Diesel pulled back from his father, apologizing to him, "I'm sorry you couldn't reach me. I forgot to turn my phone on." Diesel's thoughts filled his head with another wave of dark guilt. "What if *she* tried to call me too?"

Before Diesel could blame himself further, his father stopped him. "You would have seen that when you turned your phone on," Javier stated. "Let it be for now, Romeo. I want to see my daughter." He glanced over Diesel's shoulder to where Ace and Grave Digger stood. "Is she in there?"

"Yes, sir," was all Ace replied.

Javier stepped around Diesel and walked to the doorway. Head down, he wrapped his fingers into tight fists, gathering his courage to look beyond the glass wall. He took several steps into the room, stopping a foot away from the gallery window. He had done this many times with clients in the past. Yet, he never imagined he would be here in the early morning hour, and certainly not to view his own daughter. There had been a time he imagined doing this very thing for Romeo. Those early days of Diesel's recovery had been touch-and-go for a while. But reality had shifted and totally blindsided Javier. He showed no outer emotion indicating he had viewed his daughter, except the slight tilt of his head and a quick intake of the stale air. However, coiled tightly in his wound fists, Javier's inner emotion had a raging desire to destroy everything around him.

Diesel stepped behind his father, placing his hand on his shoulder. "Let's go talk to the medical examiner and find out what the hell happened."

Javier released the tension in his hands, brushing them on his cheeks. "I think that is a good idea, my boy." Javier patted his son's hand. "Then we have some arrangements to make." He knew there was nothing he could do to bring Isabella back. But if anyone else were involved with his daughter's death, he would make sure they never saw the light of day again.

Diesel turned to his brothers. "I'll be a while. See if you can round up some coffee."

"You got it, Diesel, anything else?" Grave Digger asked.

"Yeah, let Judge know."

"I'll take care of that," Ace volunteered.

Josie stepped forward, inviting them to follow her. She escorted them to Ciara's office. Promising to bring back coffee, she closed the door after herself, sealing the three of them in the room together.

Ciara had stood from behind her desk when Isabella's family was led in. "Gentlemen, please have a seat." She waited for them to get comfortable. She sat back in her chair, introducing herself, "I'm Doctor Ciara O'Malley, and I performed the autopsy on Isabella Diaz."

"Javier Diaz and this is my son Romeo. Can you tell us what happened, Doctor?"

Diesel peered at Ciara. He knew she was the same woman he had seen behind the window by the way her hair was still pulled back. However, she had removed the lab coat and glasses. She sat in her chair with the posture of a queen, straight line back, shoulders pushed back, thrusting her generous chest forward. He took note of the way her whiskey-brown eyes flicked back and forth between his father and her desk, avoiding eye contact with him as much as possible. Diesel listened as she explained how she had taken samples that would take a minimum of two weeks for the results to come back and that the cause of Isabella's death would be left pending until then.

Javier waited until the doctor took a breath to interject his own question. "Dr. O'Malley, let's cut to the chase. What do you believe the cause of death to be?"

"Mr. Diaz, I prefer not to speculate. I would rather have the facts."

"But… you have a suspicion, don't you, Dr. O'Malley?" Diesel's piercing blue eyes bored into her as he asked her his question.

Ciara felt her panties get wet and her nipples harden as his deep baritone voice filled her ears. Her eyes snapped up to his, lost for words like a deer in headlights. She was about to stammer some incoherent words when there was a knock at the door. Grateful for the interruption, she paused to compose herself, while Josie served the men their coffee. Once she had collected herself, she thanked Josie and dismissed her. Realizing the men were both still waiting for her answer, she blurted out, "I do have some preliminary findings."

Javier placed his coffee on the table between the two chairs. He leaned forward, placing his elbows on his knees and clasping his hands together before he posed his next question. "Was she raped?" he asked, bracing himself for the answer.

"No, sir. I found no evidence of rape, but I did find semen."

The two men looked at each other for an answer to her

statement. "I had no idea she was seeing anyone, did you?" Javier swung the question to his son.

Diesel twisted his lip. "Not a clue."

Ciara watched as father and son interacted. She had a feeling that if both of them were unaware of Isabella's dating life, they were also ignorant of her medical condition. She cleared her throat, drawing their attention back to her. "From your reaction, I believe what I have to say might also come as a shock to you." She gave them a minute to brace themselves for some more unsettling news. "During my examination of the body, I found Isabella to be in the advanced stages of breast cancer. Through the autopsy I preformed, I would say she had about a month to live. I'm very sorry."

Javier and Diesel looked at each other with an unspoken compassion. Javier appeased her look of curiosity. "Isabella's mother Camilla died of breast cancer five years ago."

Diesel turned to look at the petite doctor behind the desk. He raised his eyebrows. "You said about a month. So, that's not what actually killed her, is it?"

Ciara held his gaze, knowing that no matter how she worded it, the results would be the same. "I found a needle mark in her arm. I assumed it was for her chemotherapy treatments until I found traces of phenobarbital. Like I said earlier, I will have the results in ten to fourteen days, at which time I will be able to give you the cause of death."

"You think she overdosed on purpose?" Javier's voice held an undertone of anger.

"I believe that is a possibility. If I had to speculate," she paused to look at Javier, "I believe Isabella took her own life." Ciara held her head high as she stated her conclusion.

"That's impossible," Javier protested. "First off, she would never do that because of her beliefs. Second, she was terrified of needles. There is no way she would have done this to herself."

"I know it's painful to hear, Mr. Diaz, but from a forensic point of view, it all points to suicide."

"I'm sorry as well." Javier said, standing from his chair. "I may not agree with your findings, but I know in my heart my daughter did not do this on her own."

Ciara stood as well, not wanting her authority diminished. She thought to herself, *he may have a theory, but I have facts.* She, however, would keep her words professional. "Mr. Diaz, again, I am sorry for your loss. When I receive the results, I will contact you." She walked around her desk to shake his hand. "After you have made arrangements, please contact our office to set up a time and date to pick up her body."

Javier shook her hand. "While you wait for your results, my son and I will find out what really happened to Isabella. Until then, we will make the arrangements for my daughter, and we will be in touch."

Mr. Diaz headed to the door as Diesel stepped up and took her hand in his. The static shock that burst along his hand didn't stop there, causing him to tighten his grip on her hand. "I look forward to our next meeting, Doc."

Ciara's reaction to this man could not be a coincidence. Her inner submissive had awakened the instant her hand made contact with his. "As do I, Mr. Diaz."

"Diesel," he corrected her. "As you can see, Mr. Diaz is my father." He graced her with a breathtaking smile.

She held on to his hand a second longer. "Again, I'm sorry for your loss, Diesel."

Diesel felt the loss of his sister, but it paled in comparison to the connection he felt for this woman. The change in his demeanor was evidence of that as he slowly released her hand. The smile left his face and a somber expression appeared. "I'll call you when we've made the arrangements." He reached for one of the business cards on her desk.

Ciara explained to him before he left, "You can talk to

anyone who answers. They will assist you if I'm unavailable." Replaying the words over in her head, she thought to herself, *what the hell are you doing? The man just lost his sister, and you're oh so subtly trying to give him your number. Way to go, Ciara. You need to get laid.* Realizing she needed to justify her response, she added, "As you can see, I work the night shift." Giving him her most innocent look, she raised her hands to her waist, palms up, and shifted her hips back and forth, bringing his awareness back to the room where they were standing.

Diesel, for the first time in a long time, was unsure how to respond to a woman. On the one hand, he was supposed to be grieving the death of his sister. But on the other hand, standing in front of him was the first woman to awaken more than lust deep inside him. Realizing the bad timing of their meeting deepened the frown on Diesel's face. He had sworn an oath when he received his patch, 'club first'. It was the first rule of being a member. Everything else in his life came second to the club. And in Diesel's life, after the club came family. So, as much as he would like to ask Doctor O'Malley for her personal number, he knew now wasn't the time. He flicked the card in his hand, then stuffed it into his cut. "Thank you for that bit of information." He then turned and followed his father back down the hallway, picking up Ace and Grave Digger as they left the morgue.

Stopping at the end of the curb, Javier turned to Diesel. "I'll go see what I can find out from Jacob. You head over to Deagan's Funeral Home. Talk to Frankie; he'll take care of transporting Isabella. Let him know we'll need an appointment with Claudine to make the rest of the arrangements." Javier's brain was going in a million directions.

Diesel looked at his father and saw his pale face showing bewilderment. His strong, calm father was showing his vulnerability, something he rarely displayed. "Pop, it will be all right."

Javier swung his son a glaring look full of the anger the

older man was feeling. "Nothing will ever be all right again, Romeo. Your mother is dead, now your sister. They aren't coming back." The reality overwhelmed Javier as he broke down in his son's arms.

Trying anything to console his grieving father, Diesel told him, "We'll make it right. You said it yourself. There's no way Isabella did this to herself. We will find the person responsible and make them pay for what they did."

That seemed to calm Javier. Pulling a handkerchief from his pocket, he cleaned his face. "But after what the medical examiner told us about Isabella's cancer, do you think it's possible?"

Diesel thought for a moment. "It's possible. She watched Mom suffer through chemo and radiation, only to die in the end. But my money is on someone else helping her."

"You have a point, and if someone else was involved," Javier's anger was now clear and set in a different direction, "I'm going to make sure the D.A. hands his balls over to me in a jar. That son of a bitch will never see the light of day again. That's a promise."

Once Diesel knew his father had gained control of his emotions, they parted ways, agreeing to talk later in the day. Each one would take care of business, before allowing themselves time to grasp the depths of Isabella's death.

Chapter 3

Ciara finished her shift and drove Josie home. Stripping out of her clothes, she jumped into a hot shower to relieve her aching muscles. She made herself a cup of tea and a plate of fruit then tucked her legs up underneath her body and got comfortable on the couch. Reaching for her remote, she turned on the local news for background noise. As she stuffed a grape in her mouth, she picked up her phone and retrieved Colton's reply to her.

Good evening, Doctor O'Malley. I just heard your message. I believe I understand what it is you desire. However, I would like some clarity, and not over the phone. If you're available tomorrow, meet me at Twenty-Nine-Nineteen Demons' Way, off SC-9, past Inlet Point Plantation. I'm there every day at three. See you then.

Ciara looked at the time on her phone, thinking, *if I sleep now, I'll have time to meet him before my next shift.* The problem would be actually falling asleep. Ever since she was a child, Ciara had not slept well. As an adult, she slept even less. However, if she and Colton were on the same page, she'd have a BDSM dungeon to help fill that time. Finishing her tea and fruit, she placed her dishes in the sink. Double-checking the locks on the door, she then shut off the television and went to her room. She set the alarm on her phone and closed the room's darkening shades, then climbed into bed. Rolling to her side, she thought about her day. No one liked death, but it was part of life. Ciara looked at death as a celebration of life. It was not only a time to recognize the person who died, but a time for their family and friends to wake up and realize life is uncertain, that tomorrow may not come and to take nothing for granted.

Ciara flopped onto her back, staring at the ceiling. She knew she was too keyed up to sleep. The possibility of finding a dungeon set her body on fire. It had been a few months since she had been physical with anyone. She had been so preoccupied with her grandmother dying and then moving. The anticipation of being dominated by a master had Ciara reaching into her nightstand. She removed her clit teaser and vibrator and then took off her shorts. Relaxing back on her pillow, she let go of the negativity of her night and focused on the positive. One definite positive was meeting Diesel Diaz. When a vision of him popped into her head, she released a deep moan as she inserted her vibrator.

Ciara pulled the midnight blue convertible mustang into one of the parking spots at precisely three. She spotted Colton getting out of his twenty-twenty black Range Rover. Hitting her horn to get his attention, then picking up her bag, she got out of the car. Her four-inch heels clicked along the pavement as she made her way over to him.

"You are punctual. I like that in a woman," Colton teased. He reached into the back seat and removed a suit bag, slinging it over his shoulder.

Ciara had felt a kindred spirit toward Colton when she

was introduced. Whenever she had met him at a new home showing, he had always worn a suit. Today, however, he was dressed casually. His black tee shirt cut across his well-built chest and was tucked into his khaki slacks. He stood six-foot-one, with black curly hair and brilliant hazel eyes. Admiring his tan, athletic body, Ciara saw what an exceptionally handsome man Colton was. She greeted him, then looked at the enormous building with a wrap-around porch. "What is this place?" Following the directions he had given her, she had turned off the highway and driven down a long, curvy, tree-covered road until she found Demons' Way, which led to a guard-gated entrance.

"This, my dear, I believe is the answer to your dilemma." He placed his free hand on the small of her back as he started guiding her to the door, explaining, "This is Demons' Dungeon, the most exclusive BDSM club on the Inlet. And... you just happen to be friends with its newest manager. Otherwise, your wait time would have been about a year." He opened the door, allowing her to precede him.

Ciara walked into the waiting area. In front of her, was a set of double doors. Next to them, was a reception area, and a door leading to the locker room was to her right.

Colton walked forward to the desk. "Hey, Parker, this is Doctor Ciara O'Malley. I'd like you to give her the necessary forms for membership. I'll be sponsoring her." He looked at Ciara. "Stay here, fill out the paperwork, and Parker will let me know when you're ready for the tour."

He left Ciara with Parker, to go check on the receipts from the night before and prepare for the doors to open tonight, while Ciara filled out her hard and soft limits, agreed to the bylaws, as well as the rules and regulations. When she returned the forms, Parker handed her a medical form. Ciara stopped her by handing her the medical clearance form from her doctor that the club needed.

Parker smiled at her. "You came prepared."

Ciara knew they would need medical clearance for her. "I don't want anything to delay my having access to the club."

"That's good thinking. Now, all I need is your membership fee, and you're all set."

By the time Ciara was finished, Colton was back to show her around the dungeon. Opening the double doors, he stood to the side and let her enter. Ciara stood in wide-eyed wonder, looking around the space. "This reminds me of the old speakeasies my grandmother used to describe."

"As you can see, this is the main area. They tried to keep it very casual. There is no playing in this area," Colton commented.

There were gatherings of four mismatched pieces of furniture circling a round table, scattered about in the free area. Arranged down the center of the room, couches faced each other, separated by long tables. The focal point of the room was the old-fashioned mahogany bar. Stocked mirrored glass shelves lit by LED lighting stretched the length of the bar area. Colton then led her past an enormous fireplace tucked into the corner of the room, through a curtain-covered entrance. "This is the public playroom, as well as the exhibition stage."

Ciara observed the staff cleaning and preparing for the night's activities. She saw the far wall contained a stage set in the center of two play areas. Each area contained spanking benches, stockades, sex swings, along with shackles and cuffs hanging from the wall. The back of the stage contained a wall of dark cabinets. "As you can see, we have a center stage. Members reserve time for exhibitions, and once a week we hold training classes if you're interested." Colton moved on with the tour.

"What are the cabinets for?"

"Brand new, never-used equipment. We keep it locked."

He went on to add, "We understand occasionally a Dom might want to introduce something new in a scene. We have taken the worry out of needing, but not having. If they need a flogger or crop, the member swipes their card and just like a refrigerator in a hotel, whatever is removed, we bill to the member. We have a cleaning staff that is on hand in all areas, taking that worry from members as well." He started guiding her out of the play area to the other end of the room. Walking through the curtain, he added, "These get pulled back at the request of members doing exhibitions, adding to their audience size." They entered the main area across from Delectable Desires, a five-star restaurant. Ciara noticed they passed another fireplace tucked in under the elegant staircase. "We also have butler service and a full wait staff for the fetish rooms upstairs." He pointed to the doors along the balcony railing above them on both sides. "There is a schoolroom, an office, and a medical office, among others. We even have one set up like the beach." He leaned closer to her. "The staff hates cleaning that one, sand everywhere." He guided her to the classic staircase. "Would you like to see them?"

Ciara smiled, glancing up the graceful staircase. "No, I think I'll wait until I'm actually going to use one if you don't mind."

"No worries here. If you change your mind, just let me know." Colton's eyes breezed over her attire before advancing toward Delectable Desires. "Do you have time for a bite to eat? I'd like to get your opinion on the new chef I hired."

Ciara looked down at her tank top, jeans, and sandals asking, "What? Am I underdressed for the restaurant?"

Colton chuckled before he answered. "No, not now. You might be overdressed if the club was open." He gave her a sly smile.

Ciara laughed at his joke and followed him into the nineteen twenties designed restaurant slash ballroom. She stood at the entrance, taking in the beauty and sophistication of the room. Crystal chandeliers hung over the polished dance floor. Round tables bordered the edge, with booths tucked into alcoves under the upper floor seating. The maître d' approached them. "Will you be dining in today, Mr. Thorne?"

"Yes, Cooper." He stepped to the side and went on. "Let me introduce you to my friend and our newest member, Ciara. Ciara, this is Cooper."

"Nice to meet you, Cooper."

"Any friend of Colton's is a friend of mine." He picked up two menus and escorted them to a table near the stage.

Ciara sat in the chair Colton held for her. She teased with him. "Okay, so no playing in the bar area, but you can get dinner and a show. Take-out is good." She took her napkin and laid it in her lap, chuckling.

"Absolutely, live every night." He paused and watched her wide-eyed expression before adding, "Yes, it's called a live band." He picked up his napkin as well and smiled at her.

Tossing her napkin at him, she chirped at him. "You're an ass."

Colton laughed and caught the napkin. "I know. The look on your face was priceless. Now, I take it you are pleased with what you saw?"

Ciara picked up her menu, gazing over the contents. "You nailed it on the head. This is exactly what I needed." She peeked over the menu at him. "Any suggestions?"

Colton handed back her napkin. "Anything on the menu. It's all delicious." He went on to explain, "Chef Declan has cooked all over the world. With several specialties, dishes to spice this place up, accredited to his twenty-eight years in the business, I couldn't believe I could snag him away from la Madia."

"That's exceptional news for you." Closing her menu and placing it to the side, she said, "I think I'll have the Chicken

Caesar salad." The bus boy came over and filled their glasses with sparkling water. Expressing her thanks, she picked up her glass to toast Colton. "To many nights of unadulterated pleasure." Colton raised his glass to hers, touching them together, and then taking a sip. "Now, tell me why we're really having lunch?" Ciara set her glass down.

Before Colton could say anything, Anika, the server, came over and took their order. Her eyes were fixated on Colton, only acknowledging Ciara briefly to take her order. Watching Colton and his interaction with the woman, she got the impression his attention was also drawn toward Anika. She smiled to herself, drinking more of her water until Anika left to put their order in.

"New love interest?" she inquired. Colton gave her a questioning look. "Oh, come on, Colton. You can't tell me you weren't just eye fucking each other?" She raised her eyebrows. "A word of advice. Don't mix business with pleasure. It never ends well." Changing the subject, she asked, "Now, why am I here?"

"I will take your suggestion under advisement." He placed his elbows on the table and leaned forward. "I'm thinking you might be the best person to advise me on a decision I need to make. I believe our situations are somewhat similar."

"Okay, what's the problem?" They paused their conversation as their lunch was served. After Anika left, they resumed.

"You recently uprooted your entire life to start over." He raised his hands, showing the room they were in. "I have an opportunity to run this place. But… in order to do that, I have to quit my real estate job. I believe your opinion will help me with my decision. You hardly know me, and your view of the situation isn't clouded by history."

Ciara sipped her water then wiped her mouth, "So, your dilemma is whether you should quit your secure paying job for the unknown?"

"Well, actually, I'll get a substantial raise."

"So, you're losing your benefits?"

"No. I'll have health insurance and a 401K."

"You don't like the hours?" Ciara was reaching for a reason he should not quit his day job.

"I prefer the nights," Colton confirmed.

"Then what's the problem? Seems like you only benefit from the move."

"Yes, but what do I tell my God-fearing, churchgoing mother?"

Ciara almost spit the water from her mouth, laughing. Once she swallowed and could talk, she asked. "That's your worry? Tell her you're the manager of a private club. So private, you can't tell her about it." She smiled at her smug response. She looked around the room, admiring the detail that went into the design. "It really is a lovely club. Who owns it? Or is that classified information?"

"I would think the name of the club would tell you all you need to know. But if you need specifics, my bosses would be Yankee, Saint, Ace, and Diesel."

"Diesel Diaz?" Ciara sat a little straighter in her chair.

"Yes. You know him?"

"I met him this morning."

"This morning?" Colton sounded confused.

"Yes, his sister died last night," Ciara enlightened him.

"Oh shit. I had no idea. What happened?"

Ciara did not want to say anything specific until she received all the test results back. "I'm not at liberty to say until I get the results back."

"You can't even tell me?" Colton tried to extract the details from her.

Ciara finished her meal and wiped her mouth with her napkin before dropping it on her plate. "No, not even you. Now, I must be on my way." She reached for her wallet.

"Put your money away; lunch is on me."

Ciara stood from her chair as Colton did the same. She met him halfway and hugged him. "Thank you for lunch and for sponsoring me. You are a good man, Colton."

Ciara was ready to leave when Chef Declan came out from the kitchen. "How was everything?"

"Superb as always, Chef," Colton complimented. "Chef Declan, this is Ciara. Ciara, meet Chef Declan."

"A pleasure to meet you. I am sure we will see more of each other." She picked up her bag, then turned to Chef Declan. "Everything was wonderful. Thank you, Chef."

"You are leaving?" Chef Declan asked, seeing Ciara gathering her belongings.

"Yes, I need to get to work."

"Next time I'll make you my special dessert."

"I look forward to it, Chef." Ciara leaned in and kissed Colton on the cheek, whispering, "You might want to let the staff know about Diesel's sister, so they are not blindsided."

"Good idea, Ciara, I'll do that. And thanks for the advice. It helped. Will I see you here this weekend?" His deep velvety voice flowed over her.

"Barring any unforeseen circumstances, you will see me Friday night." A smile formed on her face before she said, "I really need to leave now." She waved goodbye and headed for the exit. She was pushing the club door open when it was suddenly yanked from her hand, launching her into the arms of the man on the other side. Her hair flew forward, covering her face. A familiar sensation coursed through her body as the man's muscular arms wrapped around her, stopping her from falling. Ciara stood on her feet and flipped her hair away from her face. Whiskey brown eyes met with Diesel's clear blue ones, explaining the intense desire ramping up in her body. Jerking out of his arms, she felt the immediate loss. Quickly apologizing, she blurted out, "I'm so sorry. I didn't know anyone was on the other side when I pushed the door open."

Diesel had spent most of the morning with the funeral direc-tor, arranging his sister's final send off. He needed to get away and have a much-needed drink. He figured he would kill two birds by checking on the dungeon and having a drink or two. After all, he was part owner in this business. He put his kick-stand down on his cobalt blue, 2018 Harley Davidson Screamin' Eagle. It had a dreamcatcher, with the silhouette of an eagle centered in the netting, painted on the tank. The beak and eye of the eagle blazed with a bright yellow. Three white iridescent feathers stretched the length of the tank. On the rear fender, rested the head of another eagle. Looking at the side bags, the eagle's talons appeared to be ripping through the night sky. Diesel's finger gently grazed over the four-leaf clover with his mother's name on it. He had added this after she had died.

"Take good care of each other now," he remarked after he had gotten off his bike and headed for the front door. His mind was occupied with a list of things he had to do, and he wasn't paying attention as he whipped the entrance door open. His balance was thrown off by the body hurling its way toward him. He quickly caught himself as she landed in his arms. The first thing Diesel noticed was her intoxicating scent. Breathing in her exotic aroma, had his cock twitching. The second thing he noted was how perfectly she fit in his arms. His cock grew semi hard with her chest pressed up against him. He then finally realized why he had no control over his body. The woman pulled from his arms. Stepping back, she flipped her hair out of her face, revealing a very embarrassed Dr. O'Malley

"I'm so sorry. I lost my balance," she gasped.

Surprised by her appearance, he commented, "No, apologies necessary." Her eyes met his as he continued. "I didn't expect to see you again so soon. Were you looking for me? Have you found something else in my sister's case?"

Ciara was totally flustered by Diesel's appearance and stammered out, "Ah, no. I-I was here having lunch with a friend."

Diesel couldn't hide his disappointment that she wasn't there to see him. But he was curious as to who she was lunching with and why. "An unusual place to have lunch. Don't you think?" He knew the club wouldn't be opened for another few hours. So, whoever she had lunch with was part of the staff.

"I was invited to lunch; I had no say in where it took place. It did work to my advantage, though. You have an excellent chef, and I became a member." She slipped that little piece of information in. She then watched his eyes grow big with her statement. "You have a really nice place here," she commented, attempting to move the conversation in that direction.

"Wait a minute, did you say you are a member? Who sponsored you?" Diesel, on one hand, was thanking God above, but on the other hand, he knew that the membership wait list was extensive and there was no possible way she was even on it. "Who is your benefactor?"

"Your new manager, Colton. We've become friends." Her voice was shaky, and it took everything for Ciara to stand before him without squirming.

Diesel liked Colton. He thought back to how the two had first met. When they had been looking for a place to open the dungeon, Colton had brought them to this very spot. However, when the Demons had driven down the dirt road, both Yankee and Saint had given Diesel questioning looks.

Once they reached the clearing, there was nothing but a run-down shack. The Demons had gotten off their motorcycles and waited for Colton to walk back to them from his car.

"So, what do you think? It's perfect, right?" Colton flashed them a bright smile.

The three men looked at each other, then at the shack in front of them, and then at Colton.

"You didn't hear a fucking thing we said," Yankee stated. "We told you we were looking for a ten-thousand square foot building. I couldn't fit the bathroom in my house in that piece of shit." He pointed to the structure.

Diesel and Saint agreed with Yankee's statement. A grin grew on Colton's face. "You told me what you wanted, now let me tell you what you need. You need a secluded, out of the way location. You need ample space for parking. And… no matter what building I show you, it will need renovations. Here," he spread his arm toward the property, "with the budget you're working with, this place is perfect."

"But there's nothing here, Colton," Saint spoke up.

Diesel was the first to understand what Colton was trying to tell them. "I get it."

The other two men swung their heads in his direction. "Enlighten us," Saint expressed.

"With this property, we design everything our way, from the ground up. It includes how much of the land?"

"Fifty acres," Colton replied, a grin on his face. "Your budget allows you to purchase the land and put up anything you want."

"Is it zoned for a business? We don't need any shit getting the permits," Diesel asked.

"You'll have no problem with permits. And, yes, it's zoned for business."

In retrospect, Colton had done them a huge favor. Since then, Diesel had been trying to lure Colton away from real estate to run the dungeon for them. The man could definitely read people and knew how to please them.

Diesel's attention came back to the woman standing in front of him. "Yes, Colton is a good man." Ciara started to go down the steps of the front porch, but Diesel stopped her with his comment. "I have to say I'm captivated that you are now a member, Dr. O'Malley, yet surprised at the same time."

"You think because of my profession I wouldn't enjoy a relationship, sex, even fun?" Ciara's voice started to mount with annoyance. "It's because of my job that I crave a place like this." Her voice softened, realizing she was taking her frustration out on him. The butterflies that awoke when she was in his presence threw her off balance.

"That's not the reason at all. It surprised me that Colton used his one sponsorship on you. You see, each employee is entitled to sponsor one person. Why you?" he growled.

He almost sounded angry that Colton had been the one to get her into the club. "I can't answer your question. You'll have to ask him yourself, but I am grateful. If in the future, he needs my help, and I can assist him, I will. Right now, I need to go. I hope to see you again, Diesel."

"Oh, you will, Doc," he yelled at her back as she walked away. He intended to see a lot more of her, but first he needed to know where Colton stood. He pulled the door open and walked in.

Chapter 4

It had been a long three months and an even longer week, but Friday had finally come. *My first full weekend off,* Ciara thought. She shut off her alarm and lay back on her bed with a frustrated smile on her face, wanting so desperately to relieve the ache her dream had created. Yet, knowing if she held out until tonight, the possibility of her dream being played out in a scene would reap far greater rewards, she played it over in her mind.

She had taken the better part of the morning primping, waxing, and preparing to go to Demons' Dungeon.

"You are going to be late if you don't get your ass in gear," she said out loud, heading to the bathroom and stepping into the shower as her mind drifted to her dream once again.

She pulled up to the gate, flashing her membership card proudly. Parking her Mustang, she stepped out and adjusted her black leather corset under her dress. She had dashed across the parking lot, anxious to be inside. After storing her belongings and dress in a locker, she stopped to look in the full-view mirror. She made slight adjustments to her hair and applied some lipstick before leaving. Stopping at the front desk, she relinquished her membership card for a bracelet. It showed her status as an experienced submissive. It also allowed her to make purchases throughout the night. Finally, walking through the double doors to the common room area had the most alluring effect on her mind and body.

Ciara pulled her mind from the dream once more, back to the reality of the world. Standing before her closet, she needed to choose an outfit appropriate for a funeral. Colton had informed her they would lay Isabella Diaz to rest today. There would be a two-hour viewing at the funeral home, followed by a service at Our Lady Star of the Sea and then a forty-five-minute drive to Hillcrest cemetery. Isabella's final resting place, a spot next to her mother. Ciara felt a pull to attend the church service, not only to pay her respects to the family, but also to see how Diesel was doing. Ever since she had bumped into him at the club, he had not been far from her thoughts.

She believed her dream was so vivid because she knew she would see him at the service. And then the possibility of seeing him later at the club had her brain and body in overdrive. She grabbed a black Bolero jacket and a matching skirt from her closet, along with a lavender button-up shirt. She laid them on the bed for later. She threw on a pair of jeans and a gray tee shirt, returning to the bathroom to dry her hair and back to her dream.

After ordering a glass of cranberry juice, she sat at the bar, enjoying the ambiance, watching the distinct groups of people mingling with each other. She spotted Dominants and Mistresses, as well as submissives and slaves. Having no direct eye contact with any of the Dominants and Masters, she observed their exchanges with other submissives, some with established relationships, some collared, others negotiating terms for casual play. Ciara was about to leave the barstool when the curtains opened, indicating a scene was about to be shared in the playroom. Ciara ordered another drink and got comfortable. Both rooms got quiet as they pulled the curtains back, exposing the stage. She did not know who the couple on the stage was, but a few of the surrounding members apparently did. The hushed comments she could make out gave her the impression the sub strapped to the sex swing was there for a public punishment rather than a mind-blowing experience.

"As you can see, Nicolette is secured tightly in the swing she has nego-tiated to use," her Dom began to explain the scene. "Upon hearing that Nicolette had never used a sex swing before my mind began imagining all the deliciously wicked things we could do with it." He ran his hand down her thick brown braid, yanking her head back. Her blindfolded face was now beneath his. "However, Nicolette could not resist the pull of the internet after agreeing in our discussions to avoid any pictures or videos, showing all the stimulating uses this apparatus has to offer." He released her braid and sauntered around her, his hand spinning the swing as he moved. "So, tonight, instead of any one of those desirable positions, she will learn of its capabilities for punishment. Those of you who do not agree with my way of punishment, please, feel free to leave."

Ciara watched the crowd to see not one person leave. Apparently, the Dom on the stage was well-respected. She sat on the stool, her attention centered on the stage, but not even the scene being played out before her could diminish the effect Diesel was having on her.

She knew he was behind her before she saw him. She sat a little straighter in her chair as his intoxicating aroma surrounded her. His sultry voice whispered in her ear, "Do you approve of Master Caleb's punish-ment for Nicolette?" Ciara's entire body came to life as his warm breath feathered over her ear. "If my hand skimmed down your chest, would I find your nipple erect?" His hand slipped inside her leather corset, pinching down on her hard nub. A moan of need rumbled in her throat. As he leaned his hard chest against her back, his seductive voice floated over her. "One for one. Would my fingers also find you wet?" His fingers ventured down her stomach. Ciara started to close her legs but stopped on his command. "Open those legs and lock those five-inch heels on the stool." He slipped his hand inside her leather thong, stroking along her wet lips.

"Two for two, Dr. O'Malley," he told her, then kissed the side of her neck. She closed her eyes and rested her head back on his chest. She was giving him complete control of her body.'

Her thoughts were ripped from her dream as she turned off the blow dryer. Shifting her legs, she felt the moisture that had gathered in her panties. It was now time to file her dream away until after her Brazilian wax at the spa.

Diesel and his Celtic brothers escorted Isabella's hearse from the funeral home to the church on their motorcycles, an impressive yet sad sight. The church had filled quickly. It seemed like the entire town had come to pay their respects. Diesel and his father walked behind Isabella's casket to the altar and took their seats in the first pew. The minister moved forward and began the service. There were passages read from the Bible and music. Communion was offered for those who wanted to take part, and finally, the benediction to dismiss the somber crowd.

However, as the minister was about to give the final blessing, the church's doors burst open. A man was standing in the doorway, and in the vestibule behind him, were approximately fifty to a hundred homeless people. The man, about twenty-five or six, wearing a dark suit, led the procession down the aisle. His voice rang out loudly in the quiet church. "I apologize for our late appearance. It took longer to walk here than we thought."

The group was halfway to the altar before Yankee stood up and blocked their path. At the same time, other members of the Celtic Demons began standing. Yankee leaned into the man, speaking quietly, but his voice dripped venom. "What the fuck do you think you're doing, Patch? I told you the next time you came near Angel, I'd kill you. Do you remember that?"

Derek 'Patch' Mancini looked Yankee straight in the eyes when he replied, "I am not here to cause any trouble. We are here to say goodbye to the woman who actually cared about us. Now, if you would step to the side and allow us to do that, we will be on our way."

Yankee glanced Diesel's way, looking for confirmation. With a nod of his head, Yankee stepped aside.

Derek understood why they wouldn't want him here after what he had done. While he had been working for the Santoro organization, Derek had been prospecting for the Celtic Demons, looking to gain information on the club to send back to his brother Vito. But when Vito was killed, Derek had blamed Angel, Yankee's old lady. Derek knew he had made a mistake, when Angel allowed him to live after he tried to kill her on the Black Rose. The Demons had delivered Derek back to Don Santoro, along with a message from his daughter. 'Do what you must, but do not kill him.' That was the last time the Celtic Demons saw him.

He made his way forward, stopping beside the pew where Javier was seated. Extending his hand, he said, "Sir, we are all deeply sorry for your loss, and what I'm about to ask may seem a bit unorthodox. But I need to ask, would you allow the casket to be opened, so we may view Isabella one last time?"

Javier looked to Diesel for his input, knowing who the man was. "I don't see what it could hurt. We all viewed her at the funeral home." Diesel gave his approval.

Javier then glanced at the minister, who also nodded his approval. Getting the confirmation he needed, Javier walked over to the funeral director. Instructing him to open the casket, he returned to Derek. "I am immensely proud of the work my daughter did for the homeless and addicts she came in contact with. We intend to set up a charity in her honor to continue helping the people she loved being with. Please take as much time as you need." Javier then sat back down.

"Thank you, sir," was all he said as Derek moved to the side, and one by one, members of the group made their way forward, all of them respectfully kneeling to pray, then placing a white rose in the casket. When the last person had finished, Derek made his way to the side of the casket. He kissed his red rose before he placed it on Isabella. Leaning over, he kissed her forehead and whispered, "You will live on in my heart forever, my savior, friend, and lover. I miss you so much already. You were my rock; you were my reason to get up in the morning, you made every day special with your laughter, your silly jokes, and how passionate you were about helping others. You made me a better person, and for that, I will always be grateful. You gave my life purpose, and now you leave me with all the responsibility. I can only pray I live up to your expectations. You brought a light of hope to everything you did. And now that light has been extinguished. But I will do as I promised and carry on with your vision, to help and save the homeless and addicts living on the streets. I will always love you, my beautiful Bella." Kissing her one last time on her lips, he tucked a sealed white envelope under her hands, then he stepped back with tears streaming down his cheeks.

The group that halted the service had systematically left the church after viewing Isabella. Derek walked back to Javier and Diesel before following the group. Removing an envelope from his interior pocket, he handed it to Javier.

But before he could complete his task, through gritted teeth, Diesel hissed out, "Were you with my sister the night she died?" He didn't know how he was containing the rage he felt. His body swelled with anger, thinking this was possibly the man who had helped her die.

Derek knew what was coming and braced for the assault

he knew he deserved. He bowed his head and quietly said, "Yes." He waited a few seconds, and when he wasn't tackled to the ground, he looked up and saw why. Judge and Viking were restraining Diesel. He held the envelope out once again to Javier. "This will explain everything you need to know."

Javier took the envelope from him. "Now, get the hell out of here before I release my son on you."

"He's not walking out of here." Diesel spoke up. Glancing over the crowd, he spotted Jacob. "Jacob, I want to press charges against him."

Jacob walked forward. "For what, Diesel?"

"For murder, he killed my sister, you heard him. He was there."

"Diesel, there is no evidence to prove murder or that he was even there."

"There will be, and when the test comes back that Patch was with my sister that night, I'm going to ask for the death penalty." Diesel had spotted Ciara in the back of the church by Colton and Josie. He could have easily put her on the spot but thought better of getting her involved.

Derek interrupted Diesel before he could say anything else, "I'll be easy to find. I will be working on the same streets your sister did." His eyes flicked to Javier. "Read what's in the envelope. It will tell you everything you need to know." He turned on his heels and left the church.

"Are you going to let him walk out of here?" Diesel questioned his father.

"There's nothing we can do until we have proof. And now isn't the time; we should get back to the reason we are here."

The anger raging inside him began to dissipate, knowing his father was right on both accounts. But he didn't have to like it. If Patch had anything to do with his sister's death, Diesel would finish him.

The rest of the funeral went on as planned. When it was

over, Colton walked Ciara back to her car. "Do you think Diesel's right and that guy had something to do with Isabella's death?"

"You know I can't talk about an ongoing case, even to speculate. All I can say is we should have the test results back by Monday. Then we will know for sure."

"You coming to the club tonight?" Colton changed the subject, knowing he'd get no answers from her.

"I've been waiting a long time for tonight, and I intend to make every minute count. I'll see you later." She kissed him on the cheek and got into her car.

After she left, Diesel approached Colton. "Will she be at the club later?"

"I think Hell could freeze over, and that wouldn't stop her." Colton laughed at his comment.

"Good to know, I'll be there later. After all the shit that happened today, Ciara will be exactly what I need." He turned and got on his motorcycle for the ride to Isabella's gravesite.

Colton watched him leave and whispered, "And… she needs you too."

―――――

Ciara felt like she was retracing every step from her dream, right up to sitting on the barstool, but that's when the dream stopped, and reality began. She observed the different gatherings of people. The submissives kneeling quietly next to their Masters. The Mistress in the playroom who was stroking the cock of her submissive, while conversing with others. The couples who were stealing away up the grand staircase for a session in the private rooms above. The atmosphere was alive and invigorating. Her dream was coming to life before her eyes. She sat there, hoping that Diesel would come up behind her, but instead, it was Colton.

"Good evening Ciara, is it everything you wished for?"

"It's perfect, Colton. I knew you were the man to understand my needs." She spun the stool to face him. "Have you seen Diesel tonight?"

"Funny you should ask. Diesel instructed me to hunt you down the minute you were here and give you this card." He handed her what looked like a credit card. "This is the key to his private elevator. Follow me." Colton led her to the left side of the staircase and down a short hallway. When they arrived, there were four elevators. "This one is Diesel's." He pointed to one door. "He's waiting for you, and I believe you are exactly what he needs tonight." Colton kissed her on the cheek. "He is also what you need. Go be a good girl and have fun." Colton turned on his heels and left her alone.

Ciara looked at the card in her hand. She had a choice, go upstairs, and get lost in a few hours of divine pleasure, or worry about the whole ethic problem of getting involved with a family member of a pending case. She stood for a moment longer, then pushed the key card into the slot, opening the elevator door. Saying a silent prayer that she was doing the right thing, she stepped in. It was a brief ride up, and when the doors opened, she couldn't believe what she saw. In front of her, was a wall of glass leading out to a screened-in balcony. In front of the windows, was a gray L-shaped couch resting on a colorful throw rug. Sitting on the sofa, was an exhausted-looking Diesel. He had removed his jacket and tie, revealing the strained buttons on his white shirt. His composure was very relaxed, as he rose from his seat to greet her.

"Good evening, Ciara, I was so hoping I would see you tonight. Please come in. Can I get you something to drink?" He indicated she should join him on the couch.

He had been looking forward to spending time with her ever since Colton had informed him of her plans. The thought of her with another Dom, let alone another man, made his blood rage. He needed to know what this woman had infected him with. He hadn't been able to concentrate all week; he was smiling more. An image of her would pop in his head, and he'd spend twenty minutes wondering what she was doing. All these things because he knew she would be here in his dungeon tonight. The timing of their meeting couldn't have been worse as far as he was concerned. Yet, he felt in some small way, his sister had brought the two of them together, and he was not going to argue with his sister.

"Do you have cranberry juice?"

He tilted his head and smirked at her before teasing, "Doc, I have access to any kind of drink you'd like. I'm sure you noticed the bar and restaurant you passed by to get here?"

His comment broke the tension in the room. She laughed at her thoughtlessness. "Of course, I didn't even think of that. In my townhouse, it's whatever is in the fridge or water." She sat on the couch he had vacated.

"You're in luck, though, because I do have cranberry juice." While he got her drink, he spoke to her over his shoulder. "I have to be honest with you, Doc. I was more than hoping you would be here tonight." Walking back to her, gazing into her intoxicating whiskey-colored eyes, he handed her the glass. "I've imagined it since the first day I met you." He sat on the couch, relaxing, stretching his arm across the back. "But... nothing compares to reality."

Ciara's nipples got hard, and she could feel the wetness gather between her legs as a wave of desire coursed through her. "If I'm honest," she bowed her head in embarrassment, "I've also imagined it."

The apprehension Diesel had been feeling was released in his next breath. "Then please relax and let's get to know each other on a personal level." He moved his fingers to the buttons on his shirt. "Do you mind? It's very confining."

"It will be distracting, but you should be comfortable in

your own home. Which, if I may say, is extremely beautiful. Not what I was expecting." To the left of them, was the kitchen area, separated by a floor to ceiling wall of cubes. Some were filled with books, others with food. When she turned to the right where his bedroom was, the loft took on a masculine look, dark pine wood behind the king-sized bed. In front of the windows to the balcony, was what appeared to be a glass fireplace. What held Ciara's attention the most was his bathroom. "Is that an elevated glass bathroom?" Ciara had never been in such a unique living space. The amber lighting followed a path down the dark wood stairs to the large walk-in closet below, giving the room a soothing feeling.

"Yes, it is. The builder suggested it, and now I'm glad he did." He could see her excitement over something as simple as a bathroom. He wondered if she saw all things through such color-filled eyes. He stopped unbuttoning his shirt just before the large scar on his chest. Since leaving the hospital after his last skin graft, he had demanded every woman he was with wear a blindfold, and he instructed them not to touch him. The disgust he felt for his own body caused him to fuck just to satisfy his body's need. He didn't want that with Ciara. He wanted her to accept the real him. The magnetic pull he had toward her gave him hope that she would be the one to release him from his own prison. He also knew if he continued to obsess over his disfiguration, it would take him to a dark place, which was not what tonight was about. As much as he wanted to rip the band-aid off and show her, he knew he needed to build up to showing her his disfigured body. "Ciara." His voice deepened, getting her attention. "If I were to tell you we would not be playing tonight, would you want something stronger with your cranberry juice?"

Ciara had noticed his expression change and his body tense by what he was thinking. And as much as she would have liked to get lost in a night of pleasure, she sensed he needed her to just be with him tonight. Ciara felt she needed to put his needs before hers, so she told him, "Yes, Sir. A splash of vodka would liven it up." Diesel picked up her glass. "Would it be all right if I take off my shoes?"

"Go right ahead."

Ciara slipped off her shoes and wiggled her toes. "Oh, that's better. I haven't worn them for a few months. I need to get used to them again."

"How long has it been since you had a Dom?" He handed her the drink and sat beside her again.

"In all honesty, it's been a year and a half. I had been in the process of finding a new play partner when my grand-mother died. But…then the opportunity for my job here was offered, and I stopped looking altogether. Made no sense to look any further if I was going to move."

It surprised Diesel to hear how long it had been for her. "What happened with your last Dom?" He didn't want to make the same mistake if there was one.

"We grew apart. I wanted more; he was ready to move on. I was okay with it; we still talk occasionally."

Diesel wasn't sure how he felt about that, but she wasn't his yet. He would be sure to bring it up in negotiations. "I'm sorry about your grandmother. Were you close?" He wanted to know everything about her.

"Yes, she raised me when my mother died."

"Your dad?"

"He was never in the picture; he found out my mom was pregnant with me and bolted. I couldn't tell you if he's alive or dead."

He could hear the anger and disappointment in her tone. "Tell me about your grandmother." He watched her face brighten. This was the face he always wanted to see. He watched her curl her legs up underneath herself, take a sip of her drink, and then she started talking.

She told him about how when they cooked together, her grandmother would tell her stories of how she learned to cook at twelve, and how during the Great Depression, she would make stews and bake bread for her dozen or so cousins, while their parents looked for work.

She went on telling him about playing cards, and how her grandmother would tell her stories of her grandfather and the speakeasy he owned, and how he was the town bookie in a time when gambling went hand in hand with the mafia. About how many nights her grandmother wondered if he'd come home. She told him how her grandmother had been a maid at a hotel and how she had broken her arm at the age of seventy-five at work and drove herself to the hospital only to be sent home until the swelling went down.

"They actually let a seventy-five-year-old woman drive herself home with a broken arm?"

"Yup, they did. It was a different time back then. She didn't want to bother me; she knew I was studying." She took another sip of her drink and went on. "She taught me how to clean." She made the next statement in air quotes. "So, if a visitor pops up unexpectedly, you're not embarrassed by your own home." She laughed at her grandmother's explanation. "I remember one night I was coming home late from college. She would leave the front door unlocked for me. She told me she was lying in bed and she heard the door open. Thinking it was me, she waited for me to pop my head into her room. However, when the head popped around the corner, it wasn't me. It was an exceptionally large man. Now, what you need to know about my grandmother is she was all of five feet, but she knew how to protect her own. She grabbed the baseball bat she kept in the corner near her dresser and yelled at him, 'Who the hell do you think you are coming into my house in the middle of the night! Get the hell out of my house!' She then proceeded to chase him out of the house. When I got there, she was sitting at the kitchen table, a glass of whiskey in her hand, and the bat was resting close by." Ciara and Diesel both laughed at the picture she had described. "She was an incredibly special person. She taught me about right and wrong, loyalty, respect, and that lying was a sin. She instructed me not to be selfish, and to help someone without praise, to be grateful for what I have, but never stop reaching for more. She taught me the importance of commitment, compromise, laughter, and love. And... above all else. 'Never nag your husband about trivial shit when he walks in the door after working all day'." She wagged her finger at Diesel, mimicking her grandmother.

"She sounds like an amazing woman." Diesel felt Ciara's powerful love for this special person. "What was her name?"

"Ethel Casey, her name means, noble, vigilant, and watchful. Trust me, she lived up to the description of her name." Ciara noticed that Diesel had relaxed while listening to her. She pulled the chain holding a two-inch long locket resting around her neck. "She gave me this a week before she died. She told me it was a family keepsake and to never let it out of my sight," Ciara explained as she showed him the necklace. At the top of the locket, there was a thick metal cross that the chain slid through, and a two-carat diamond rested in the center. The face of the locket had another cross on top of it, edged with a ring of twelve more diamonds. A box clasp held the locket closed.

Diesel fingered the locket, commenting, "It's beautiful and antique. It must be worth a fortune. Why would she want you to always wear it?" He opened the locket. "Was there anything in it?"

"Yes, there was a key, but I didn't want to lose it, so I put it in a safe deposit box. Truth is I have no idea what the key is for. I figure one day it will come in handy for something."

Diesel turned it over in his hand, looking at the workmanship. "Did she tell you anything about the locket? Because, by the craftsmanship, it looks to me like they could have constructed it in Russia." Diesel looked at Ciara, taking special note of her auburn-colored hair and whiskey-colored eyes. "Are you sure you're all Irish, Dr. O'Malley?"

"Funny you should say that. As far as I know, I am, but I became curious about what nationality my father is." She pulled back the necklace, slipping it from his hand. "I recently did one of those DNA tests to find out. I'm still waiting on the results." His appraisal of her looks only added more doubt to her already wavering beliefs. Either way, she knew it was time to get going. She observed the clock on the wall. As much as she would have liked the night to continue, she knew he had had a long day. She started to put her shoes on, as she said. "I should get going. I'm sure I've talked your ear off enough tonight. Besides, I can only imagine how long today must have been for you."

Diesel had refilled their drinks while she had been talking. He had listened to Ciara talk about her grandmother, and he wasn't sure who he was more fascinated by. The remarkable woman she described, or the exceptional beauty before him. Desire unknown to him softened the heart in his chest. She was so animated and passionate about sharing her stories. The more she talked, the more he wanted to be a part of them. He reached out to stop her, taking her hand in his. "Please don't go. I was hoping you'd stay the night. You being here has taken my mind off what a shitty day it was."

Inside, Ciara melted at his request, remembering how she wished she had had someone to be with her when her grandmother died. She dropped her shoes to the floor. Smiling at him, she relaxed back onto the couch. "Okay, but if I'm staying, I need my bag from my locker. Because I am not sleeping in the confines of this corset." she teased him, adjusting the piece of leather.

He almost spit out his drink at her candidness. If he had his way, she wouldn't be wearing anything to bed tonight, but instead, he told her, "I will have Colton bring it up right away. We wouldn't want you to be confined." Picking up the phone, he made the call. Ten minutes later, Colton delivered her bag and membership card and retrieved her bracelet. After Colton left, Diesel told her, "I believe while you change, I will as well. You can use the bathroom."

She darted off the couch, picking up her bag. "Thank you; you have no idea how much I've wanted to check it out."

He laughed at her childlike excitement as she ran up the stairs. He was standing by the couch in his black tank and a pair of gray sweats when she came back down. She was a vision of beauty in her dark purple silk negligee, her chest barely contained, as the material enhanced her every curve. She, however, was oblivious to the stunning picture she presented.

"That room is heavenly. I love how the builders tucked the tub away, and how they positioned the mirrors, so you still get to enjoy the open view." She dropped her bag on the couch and stood in front of him. "What should we do now?"

His semi hard cock knew what it wanted to do, but his heart wanted more. "It's a beautiful night, would you like to sit outside for a while?"

"That's sounds nice. I love looking at the stars."

Diesel took her hand and led them to the balcony doors, opening them. He let her precede him thru the door. Standing behind her, he listened to her intake of breath when she looked up.

"Oh my God, Diesel. Did your builders think of this too?" She pointed up to the glass ceiling.

"Nope, that was all me," he responded proudly. "My mom and I used to stargaze. She would point out Ursa Major and Cassiopeia. It was our time together. She taught me to appreciate the beauty in a simple star." He came up behind her and wrapped his arms around her. "She never told me I'd be able to hold one in my arms, though."

Ciara snuggled against his warm body, her arms clutching his. "Your mother would be proud you are carrying on her love of the stars. But... I have to ask," she tilted her head up to look at him, "doesn't it get scorching hot in here during the day?"

He looked down at her. "Nope, I thought of that too. They are transitioning windows. When the sun blazes down on them, they darken like sunglasses."

"That's ingenious. Most people would have put up shades." She then smiled at him and turned her attention back to the stars.

"Yes, but then you wouldn't have seen such an open view."

"That's very true." Then, shifting the topic, she asked, "Tell me more about your family. What was it like growing up in a normal family?" She felt his body move from his laughter.

"What do you consider a normal family, Doc?"

"You know, a mom, dad, and a sibling. Possibly a dog?"

"Let's sit down. I need to be comfortable before I start." He moved to a lounge chair, and when she went to sit beside him, he asked, "Would you sit with me so I can hold you?" He flipped a switch, and soft lighting surrounded them. Finally, realizing the rest of the area, Ciara took in the bar area with a pool table in front of it, to the left. A hot tub was to the right and in between were lounges and tables with chairs. "I think I could fit my entire townhouse in here." She was teasing him again.

"Yeah, I've had some, hum," he paused, looking for the right word, "let's just say, lively parties with my Demon brothers."

He sat on the lounge, and she crawled up in between his legs, leaning her head back against his chest. The faint aroma of his cologne wrapped around her as his arms encircled her waist, pulling her close. Along with that came a feeling of serenity. It had been a while since she had felt truly safe and protected in a man's arms. And... she intended to savor every minute of it. "How long have you been a member of the Celtic Demons?"

"About three years. When you asked about a normal family, I had to stop and think, because these days the Demons are my family. After my mom died, I was kind of lost, started going down a very dark road. But my buddy Ace wouldn't let me. He told me about the Celtic Demons over and over for about two years before I finally gave in and started prospecting."

"What's prospecting?"

"Earning your right to become a member."

"So, tell me about both of them. I'm sure each one will have their own uniqueness." Ciara shifted her bottom against his semi-hard cock as she twisted to look at him.

Diesel adjusted himself. He usually had better control over his body. Yet, whenever Ciara was near him, his body betrayed him. She felt perfect against him, as if she were made for him. Now would be the ideal time to tell her about his disfiguration. But he wanted to hold on to this moment a little while longer. He began by telling her about his biological family, his strict childhood, his teen years, spent mostly on a baseball field, and how he had his pick of any college with a full scholarship. He chose LSU. He was close enough to home, but yet still thirteen hours away. He was in his second year, leading his teammates in every stat. Professional teams were scouting him, when he tore his labrum, a career-ending injury. The scouts disappeared, his scholarship went away, and so did his desire to attend college, although he did return eventually. The next few years, he did odd jobs. During that time, he met Allen 'Ace' Bentley. The two shared not only a passion for motorcycles, but the same taste in music as well. When his mom had gotten sick, Ace was there to help him deal with it. When she died, Ace was there whenever he needed him. Diesel touched lightly on the dark path. Looking for and finding an underground fight club. Each night he would go to the club hoping that his opponent would finally end his misery. Yet, with each fight, he only got stronger physically. His mental wellbeing, however, was still taking a beating. Ace told him about the Celtic Demons, explaining how being a part of the club had given him a purpose when he needed it.

Diesel had felt a kinship to almost every man he met at the club. Each was broken in their own way but had found camaraderie with the Demons. Diesel had now come to the part in his story where he would bare his soul to her and pray for acceptance. "As a prospect, it can take sometimes a year to become a patched member. And... trust me, there's a lot of shit the patched members put a prospect through. The sooner you earn your patch, the fewer shit jobs you have to do. While I was prospecting, an opportunity came up. If I volunteered for it, I would earn my patch faster. Plus, it was something I knew I could pull off." He took a sip of his whiskey. "I went to Judge, he's the club's president, and asked for the job. Judge wasn't too sure a prospect was right for the job, but the club took a vote, and I went. I was almost home free until one of Vito's henchmen overheard me talking with Judge." He took a big gulp of his drink, finishing it.

Ciara knew, from the article she had read, he had reached the time in his life where he had been tortured just short of death. She could hear his breathing change and saw how ashen his face had turned. "You don't have to relive it by telling me. We can skip that part."

He was grateful for her compassion. He skipped the details of his torture but told her of the excruciating surgeries and skin grafts. Like having to learn how to use his stomach muscles again and the therapy sessions on his hand so he could once again wrap his fingers around the grip of a motorcycle.

"Can I see your scars?" Ciara asked in a quiet voice.

"Showing you will make me vulnerable."

"Showing me releases you from any stigma you have. I promise my reaction will not be like any other from your past."

"I'm not sure what that reaction would be. No woman has seen or touched them. You would be the first and the only one whose opinion is important to me."

Ciara felt the pain of his words. The need to take away his suffering overwhelmed her. "Please show me your scars. Sir." She moved down to the end of the lounge, giving him room.

He spread his legs over the sides of the lounge and sat up. Following instinct rather than common sense, he gripped the hem of his tank and pulled it over his head, leaving himself exposed to her. He wanted her to see the hideous beast, but more so, he needed her to see the man inside. His eyes blazed into hers, looking for any sign of revulsion. But what he saw were pools of water welled in her whiskey-brown eyes.

Ciara couldn't help the tears that formed, knowing the agony he must have endured. It was amazing the man was still alive. Emotions flooded her system, anger, rage, resentment all for the people who had been so cruel. For Diesel, she had nothing but compassion, concern, and empathy. "May I touch you, Sir?" The pull she felt to heal him from the inside was so powerful. He had denied himself a basic human need, the physical touch of another person. She knew she had passed the first test by the way he reclined back on the lounge. Ciara then moved up between his legs. On her knees, she towered above him. Never taking her eyes off his, she placed her hands on his sturdy shoulders, grazing her fingers down his solid arms. Placing her palms on his ripped chest, she heard his slight intake of breath as if her touch inflicted discomfort. "Should I continue?"

With each body part Ciara touched, little pinpricks would follow in the wake. His body was coming to life with each gentle brush of her fingers. Her hands were above his repulsive scar. She was giving him the respect he would give to her as his submissive. A choice. "Please continue." He thought for sure she would reach for the scar, but instead, she grazed her nails down his obliques. Bringing her face close to his torso, leaning forward, she placed her soft lips on what he felt was his revolting body. Diesel's reaction was immediate. The unexpected kiss sent his senses into overload. The control he mastered over his body disintegrated. His body jerked as his cock got rock hard.

Her eyes watched his for any signs of unease, seeing only desire dilating in his clear blue ones. She continued her assault on his body, ripping down any doubt how she felt about his scar. She thought to herself, *they say nothing brings people together like a wedding or a funeral.* Ciara knew she needed to stop. She would have given anything to have continued, but she would not take advantage of him. She pulled back and sat on her haunches, looking at his confused face. "You said earlier that playing was off the table tonight. Plus, I'm sure you need to process the fact that I find your scar appealing. It tells me a lot about you."

Diesel sat a little straighter and said, "I'll come back to that comment about you reading my scar like a fortune teller." Getting up forced her to do the same. He stood in front of her, placing his hand on her hips. "Tonight, has turned into today, and we will not play; we are going to explore." He took her hand and led her back into the loft, straight to his bed. They lay down, facing each other. His fingers brushed her hair away from her eyes as he told her what he felt. "From the moment I set eyes on you, something shifted in me. It was like the universe was aligning, screaming, *'She will turn your life upside down, but she will do it in the most amazing way.'* Well, Doc, you have certainly done that already. I can't get you out of my mind, and I don't want to. Ciara, I want you as my sub, but more than that, I want you to be my old lady."

Ciara did not know what an old lady was, but it didn't sound very nice. Yet, she got the impression it was significant to him. She could absolutely agree to be his sub, but she needed clarification on what it was to be an old lady. "I can easily consent to be your sub. However, not to sound naïve, but what is an old lady?"

Diesel chuckled at her question. Forgetting she would have no knowledge of club terminology, he explained, "An old lady is a wife or steady girlfriend of a club member. It lets everyone know you're mine."

This time it was Ciara's turn to have a body trembling moment. She had never been a sub and girlfriend at the same time to the same man. "I'll be honest with you. It has been some time since I had a boyfriend. The last one was during my junior year in college. After I caught him cheating with my roommate, I swore off relationships."

"First off, I always want you to be truthful and honest with me. Second, I have no reason to cheat, and third, if you were my old lady, I could do this anytime I want." He slipped his hand behind her neck, pulling her soft lips to his. His fingers weaved their way through her long wavy hair. Palming the back of her head, he deepened the kiss.

Ciara's hand cupped the side of his face, returning the acceptance and passion his kiss was offering. She couldn't argue with his reasoning. She had also felt an immediate attraction, fascination, pull. She had no clue what it was. What she did know was this gorgeous man lying in bed next to her wanted the same thing she did.

Diesel pulled back from the kiss, gazing at her beautiful face. "I've wanted to do that all night."

The color rushed to her cheeks as a smile grew on her face. "I was thinking about it too, and it was so much better than I imagined." Yet, before they went any further, she needed to clarify something. "Diesel, if we do this, you understand I cannot talk to you about your sister's case. At least until they have made it public." She knew this was a matter that could complicate things for them.

"My sister's death may have brought us together, but it will not be the foundation of our relationship." He took a minute. "How's this, we can talk about my sister, yes. As far as the case goes, we will only discuss that if you bring it up. How does that sound?" He knew her loyalties would be torn, but he also knew if he disrupted the laws of justice, he would never forgive himself.

Ciara was grateful he understood she needed to be professional, as far as the case went. "I believe that could work." They had started their negotiations by getting a vital matter out of the way. Everything else could wait until later.

"Good, now I can continue my exploration of your incredible body."

Ciara's smile turned seductive as she slid the thin strap of her negligee off her shoulder. She tilted her head to the side; her long wavy hair cascaded to the bed. Moving up, removing the other strap, she let the silky material float down her body, leaving her chest exposed. "Let the exploration begin." She lay back on the bed, her hard nipples begging for his attention.

Diesel was eager to devour her, like a kid on Christmas day eager to dive right into his gift, but he knew if he savored the moment, it would be forever remembered. He rose up on his elbow, gazing at the magnificent gift before him. This woman accepted the beast he was. He wanted to burn the vision into his memory. Her hair arranged in a halo around her head, her eyes filled with need, and her majestic body waiting to come alive to his touch. He leaned his head down, kissing her, his tongue gently licking the seam of her lips. Teasing her, he slid his tongue to her chin, up her jawbone to her ear, whispering, "I intend on tasting every inch of this luscious body." He sucked her earlobe into his mouth, nibbling on it. She tilted her head, giving him better access to her neck. Taking her lead, he trailed a path to her delectable chest with a mixture of kissing, nibbling, and biting, circling his tongue around her dark areolas, hosting her hard nubs straining for his touch. He took one between his fingers, applying pressure, the other he sucked lovingly into his mouth.

She sifted her fingers through his hair as his tongue ravished her nipple, his other hand grasping and pinching. Ciara's nipples were so sensitive; she was using all her control not to come. He crept down her stomach, removing the silky material from her body as he went, unwrapping his present. He traveled farther downward, sweeping his tongue through her silky wet lips. A moan of unadulterated need escaped through her lips. Her hips pushed off the bed, as she offered herself to him. The sensation floating through her body was familiar, yet new. He worshipped her body. His mouth and tongue deliciously stimulated every nerve ending on her dripping wet pussy. His tongue licked slowly up to her clit. Ciara rose up on her elbows and stared into his mischievous blue eyes while he took her clit between his teeth and gently applied pressure, drawing a gasp from her parted lips when he gave her a quick nip, pushing his shoulders forward, pinning her legs open. In this position, she knew it wouldn't take long for her to come.

When he changed tactics, slipping two fingers into her narrow opening, drilling into her, then slowly withdrawing, his movements were deliberate and intensified her need to come. Ciara began using a battery of techniques she had practiced over the years to delay her orgasm until given permission. Although, she knew this wasn't technically a scene to play out. She also knew if Diesel continued with his seduction, she would disgrace herself as a trained sub. Needing to show him the respect he deserved, she begged, "Sir, I've held off as long as I can. May I please come?"

Diesel slowed his fingers down, maintaining a steady rhythm. Swiping his tongue off the tip of her clit, he gave his permission. "Ciara, there will be a time for rules, but not today. Come when you need to. We are exploring, remember? Now, let me get back to the sweetest nectar I've ever tasted." He wagged his tongue at her before raking it down to her entrance, then back up.

Ciara smiled at the way he taunted her. However, her expression quickly changed. Her head lolled to the side, leaning on her shoulder. Her eyelids covered a good portion of her whiskey- brown eyes, and her lips formed a perfect circle as Diesel went back to exploring. He added a third finger, stimulating her with quick, successive thrusts. At the same time, his tongue was driving her into a frenzy. Ciara tried to hold her position, but when her body erupted, her arms gave out, clawing at the bed sheets as wave after wave of pure heaven raced through her body. As she pushed her shoulders back to the bed, her hips pushed up and she shouted, "Oh my God, Diesel! Yes!" An overpowering euphoria coursed through her veins. Like an addict with their first taste, she never wanted the feeling to go away. She felt Diesel kiss her clit before he crawled off the end of the bed. Sitting up, she watched him remove his sweatpants, his thick cock springing free.

He stood before her, stripped of his clothes. He was exposing his vulnerability, his insecurities and self-doubts, yet he had no fear. From the moment he had met her, she had begun to open doors to feelings he had locked away a long time ago—sincerity, compassion, and understanding. She was so stunning, and his body was damaged like a monstrous beast yet she was blind to it. He had watched her eyes and body language when he had shown her his scars. She had not flinched or gasped in horror. She had shed tears for the broken body before her, not in pity but in empathy. Even now, he watched her eyes devour him as if he was Adonis. She took away any indecision, confirming what he had known when they met. She was meant for him. He inched his way up the bed, fitting his hips between her legs and hovering over her on extended arms. "I've been waiting a long time for someone like you. Someone who looks past the outside to see the man inside." He leaned down and kissed her neck, mumbling, "You are the only woman who has seen me or touched me since they tortured me. And… now you'll watch me while I slide my aching hard cock deep inside you." Inhaling her captivating scent, he went on. "I want to breathe in your unique fragrance. Feel your hard nipples graze along my chest. But most of all, I want to feast my eyes on your gorgeous face." He sucked her earlobe in, biting it, then releasing it. "And… when I make you come again. I will get to witness your captivating eyes fill with blinding passion." He stopped what he was doing and looked deep into her eyes. "I do have one command for today." She tilted her head in question. "Do not close your eyes. I want them on me at all times. Understood?"

Ciara didn't hesitate. "Yes, Sir." She understood this was a big moment for him, in addition to the life-changing day he had already experienced. She was not about to disappoint him. "May I touch you?" Not wanting to overstep, she caught a flash of uncertainty before he answered.

"Yes, I want you to touch me." The craving for a woman's touch when he was inside her had become an aberration. The need slowly slipping away with each woman who lay with their face on the bed, or on her knees wearing a blindfold.

Her warm hands reached up, her fingers locking together behind his neck, pulling him down to kiss her. Diesel shifted his arms to lean on his elbows. The most animalistic sound she had ever heard rumbled in his throat when his chest pressed down on hers, giving her pause. She watched as he closed his eyes and how his emotions started playing out on his face, as more flesh touched flesh. Ciara slipped her hand through his hair, gently pulling his face into the crook of her neck, hugging him tight against her body. Her hands then touched every piece of skin they could reach. At the same time, her lips nibbled and kissed his shoulder.

It took everything for Diesel not to enter Ciara's waiting body as he hovered over her. Then, when her hands gently slithered behind his neck, pulling him down, her chest pressed to his, a wave of emotions overpowered him. She instinctively knew what he needed, allowing him to set the pace, giving him time to adjust. Her actions only confirmed that she was the woman to free his soul from the despair it had been living under. With his head resting on her shoulder, he slowly lowered his body until it lightly rested on hers. The sensation was almost paralyzing when she hugged him, her hands caressing him. Moments in his life flashed through his thoughts like a movie as memories of when he had the world by the balls and couldn't appreciate a simple hug washed over him. He recalled the time when he was a cocky baseball star with his choice of women, avoiding anything to do with intimacy. In this moment he realized he might never get the chance to have that familiarity again. He started sucking in shallow breaths of air and his body jerked away, fearing her rejection. Yet, she held onto him, clasping her hands tighter into his skin, not allowing him to pull away.

Ciara felt the moment his thoughts had turned dark as his breath came in shallow gasps and then, by how he tried to wrench himself from her arms. It took everything she had to keep him locked in her arms until it passed. She wanted to take away his pain, but she knew she could only soothe it. She waited until Diesel settled back along her body. Her breath floated over his ear like a feather when she said, "I am here for you, Diesel. I don't care if we lie like this all night, I'm not going away." He pulled his head from her neck to look in her eyes. A grin formed on her face before she tried to lighten the mood by saying, "You see, I'm new to this old lady stuff." She started laughing when Diesel quickly sat up and began tickling her.

Her teasing brought his attention back to the devilish woman beneath him. Shifting his body quickly, he straddled her waist, tickling her until her laughter left her breathless. Diesel fell to the bed, taking her with him.

She sat across his waist, her knees tucked in along his legs. He was giving her free rein of his body. The laughter faded, but the smiles remained. She placed her hands on his chest and spread her fingers wide. She leaned her head and shoulders down, arching her back, so her nipples grazed his chest. Kissing his chin as she pushed back up, she watched his face as she reached behind her, scratching her nails along his hard cock. "I know you are ready for me here, are you ready for me here?" She leaned forward and kissed his temple.

He took advantage of her prone position and embraced her to his chest. "I may have moments when my insecurities might rear their ugly heads, but now is not one of those moments." He raised his head up from the bed, capturing her mouth, his tongue snaking along her lips, pushing its way in, kissing her passionately. She flattened her chest to his as they got lost in the kiss. His big hand roamed her back, sneaking down to grab a handful of her ass. "I love this ass," he mumbled out around their kiss, thrusting his hips up, rubbing his cock against it. "And... one day, he will get to enjoy it as well."

Ciara's sex-deprived body jumped to life, feeling his steely cock slide along her cheeks. Placing her hands on his chest, she pushed up from lying across his body, into a sitting position across his waist, straddling him. "I think you've waited long enough." She reached behind her, grasping his cock in her hand. Diesel moved his hands to her hips, raising them up. She hovered over the tip briefly before slowly lowering herself, joining their bodies together. There was no mistaking the groan of pleasure that erupted from Diesel's throat when she was fully seated. Ciara paused, floating on the sensation of him deep inside her. When she tilted her head back, her hair tumbled down her back, brushing his thighs.

Diesel watched her face transform as her tight channel devoured his cock inch by inch. It took everything in him to remain still, allowing her body time to adjust to his thick rod. Hypnotized by the intoxicating view before him, he placed his palms on her obliques and lovingly caressed them up to her firm breasts. Molding them into his hands, gracefully squeezing them, seducing each one, as he flicked each nipple, he passionately adored each mound, imprinting them to memory. Sitting up, he shifted one hand behind her for support and then sealed his lips around one hard nub and sucked it into his mouth.

Her hand sifted through his hair, palming the back of his head as her other hand reached to cover the back of the hand he still had wrapped around her other breast. Ciara moaned, arching her back at the unsurpassable desire coursing through her. When Diesel's teeth applied pressure on and off her tight nipple, her head jerked forward as a shock wave pulsed straight to her core. Her inner muscles began constricting around his cock. On any other night, Ciara would have prolonged the attention he was showering upon her. However, today was about Diesel's needs, wants, and desires. She kissed his forehead and gently dislodged his mouth. "Diesel, lie back." She waited until he was lying flat on the bed. She then placed her palms on his shoulders. At the same time, she raised her hips. When just the tip of his dick was left inside her, she rocked her hips back down. Slowly at first, wanting to draw this moment out for him.

But Diesel had something else in mind. He pushed off the bed. Wrapping his arm around her, he twisted their bodies around, changing their positions. "My turn now," he announced. He leaned over her, withdrawing his hips, then pushing back in. "Remember, Doc, eyes on me." She nodded her head, acknowledging his command. Diesel had thought the pinnacle of all his emotions united when their bodies joined together yet seeing the unbridled desire for him set off a kaleidoscope of blinding colors, causing him to use every ounce of his control not to come right then. Feeling like an untrained youth, but wanting to be the man she needed, he took control of his mind and body. He watched her beautiful face morph into one of pure passion, as he began moving faster, wanting to give her the release she coveted.

Ciara's body took over when her mind turned to mush. The overflow of adrenaline that rushed to her core caused her hips to buck off the bed, spreading her legs wider. Her heels dug into the bed, and she began meeting his body thrust for thrust, reaching her arms up, pulling him down to her, pressing her chest to his. Her hands roamed his back, and her nails left their mark, inducing Diesel to ramp up his pace, pumping his cock into her, igniting the fire simmering within her. Ciara's moan filled the quiet space before she admitted. "Mmm... Diesel, I can't hold back any longer."

Diesel felt her need, his thick cock fit snug within her tight channel, wanting to brand her as his. Any one of those things, could have made him come. Had he not been a trained domi-nant, he would have come the moment his chest touched hers. Her eyes locked on his as her hands spanned his back. This woman fueled every emotion he had buried long ago. His body reacted to hers like none other. He kissed her before he extended his arms up, positioning himself above her. He panted out, "I think we've denied ourselves long enough." Diesel began driving into her, pushing to bring them over the brink, into nirvana. Over and over, until he felt her walls begin to pulse around his cock, making him buck into her faster. Ciara grabbed onto his hips, encouraging him to go deeper and faster, something he had no problem complying with. Her eyes wanted to close so she could get lost in the feeling, but she had given her word. With her eyes locked with his, she gave her body over to him. The sensation that soared at lightning speed through her body, induced her to scream, "Holy shit, Diesel!" as the most blissful orgasm blazed through her. Ciara felt like she had died and gone to Heaven. The orgasm that erupted in her was so intense, she was looking at him through tear-filled eyes. She couldn't look away now if she wanted to because right in front of her whiskey-brown eyes, she watched Diesel's face transform. The tight jaw and strained face had changed into one of pure ecstasy. His head flipped up as his hips pushed one last time, staying in place. The growl that erupted from his throat was the sound she wanted to hear again and again. To Ciara, it was the sound of a man claiming his woman, a chord of satisfaction, and a tone of freedom.

When his head tilted back to hers, he wore a grin from ear to ear, as he struggled to get his breathing under control. When he looked down, he was staring into two tear-filled eyes, yet he saw the smile on her face. She blinked, and two rivulets slid from the corners of her eyes. Concern for her flooded his entire being. Wiping the wetness from her eyes, he asked, "Baby, what's wrong?" He pulled out of her and rolled onto his side, facing her.

"Nothing's wrong." He gave her a look of disbelief.

"Really, I'm okay," she reassured him.

But he wanted an answer. "Then why the tears?"

"It's hard to explain."

"Try me," he challenged her.

"Okay, well, a feeling so overwhelming surged through me. At one-point, flickering stars were surrounding your head. An abundance of endorphins ran rampant, and the tears were an uncontrollable result of that."

Diesel had a pretty good handle on women's emotions. He'd categorized this one as if they had been doing a scene and she had hit her sub space. Pulling her close in his arms, tucking her head into his chest, he held her.

Ciara wasn't surprised by his actions. She knew his instinct was to protect her, so she lay there for a few minutes, getting her body under control. She listened to his even breathing and the steady beat of his heart. She was using them to calm her own body. She picked up her head and kissed his chest. "Thank you, Diesel. I'm feeling better now." She pushed off him and got out of bed. "I'll be back shortly," she announced and headed to the bathroom upstairs.

He caught her hand before she slipped too far away. "Has this ever happened to you before?"

"No, first time, but wow, what a feeling. I'd like to experience it more often," she teased.

"What I believe happened is called sub-space. I'm sure you've heard the term, correct?"

"Yes, but honestly. I thought it was a myth," she taunted him, then added, "Until now." She gave him a smile before getting off the bed. "I'll be right, be right back."

"What did you say?" he asked her.

"What?"

"Did you say, 'You'd be right, be right back'. Most people say it only once."

Ciara smiled, realizing what she had done unconsciously.

"My grandmother used to say that to me. Sorry." Since she had been a child, her grandmother had always used that phrase with her. And until now, Ciara had only used it with her grandmother.

"Don't apologize. I think it's unique."

He didn't need to know how unique, Ciara thought, but replied, "I'll be back shortly." She gave him a sarcastic, yet playful smile.

He kissed the back of her hand and let her go, watching her and her luscious ass climb the stairs. Diesel took the time she was gone to grab two bottles of water and put the bed back together. He reclined on the pillows, a genuine smile on his face. He was watching the top of the stairs for her return. It had been a while since he had spent the entire night with a woman, and just thinking about her body curled up next to his, had his cock getting hard again. And then she was there, standing on the landing, her wavy hair cascading down her back, leaving him a perfect view of her exquisite body. As she gracefully descended, his gaze followed her down every step. He pulled the blankets back, inviting her to join him. "There is a bottle of water on the nightstand for you."

Ciara turned her head and spotted the bottle. Picking it up, she took a few sips, replaced it and got into bed next to him. He pulled her close, so she could rest her head on his shoulder. Her head tilted up at the high ceiling.

They lay there in comfortable silence for a little while. Ciara believed Diesel had fallen asleep until he said, "Thank you for coming to the church. For a brief moment I considered calling out to you. But I didn't want you involved in that mess."

"That's understandable. A strange man comes to your sister's funeral, then hands your father an envelope. It was all strange."

"To you, not to my brothers and me. 'Patch' or should I say

Derek, once tried to kill Angel. She's Yankee's old lady. That woman is considered a saint with me and the Celtic Demons."

"Now I understand the anger. What happened?"

"Derek blamed Angel for his brother Vito's death. So, he ambushed her on Yankee's boat. What he didn't realize was she didn't need a man to protect her. She kicked the crap out of him until he pulled a gun, but thankfully Yankee intervened, disarming him."

"Why do you say she's a saint?"

"Because without her, I would probably be dead. Until I got caught behind enemy lines, the Demons had the upper hand on getting their territory back. But once they discovered me, all that changed. They gave up their advantage to get me back. Be that as it may, Angel had a deal with her father. If she found her father's works of art, he would grant her anything she wanted if it was within his power. She was going to ask for her freedom. She wanted to retire from working for her father. But instead, she asked her father for the Celtic Demons territory."

"Wow, she sounds amazing."

"She is an intense woman yet kind and caring. You'll meet her soon."

Ciara got a warm feeling. Knowing that he wanted her to meet his friends, meant a lot. "I look forward to it."

Diesel rounded back to the funeral. "I didn't realize how hard today was going to be. My father has always been the rock of our family. When my mother died, I never saw him shed a tear. And today I watched him break down at Isabella's gravesite."

"Crying isn't a sign of weakness. It's a sign of strength," she interjected. "It's also a release, as I have just shown you."

"Maybe it was seeing my mother's headstone at the same time. I'm not sure, but it was a side I've never seen of him." He was quiet for a moment and then went on. "You know she was going to save the world, one addict at a time. I believe she would have figured out a way to do it too."

"Josie, my intern, is living proof of that."

"I never took the time to pay attention to what she was really doing. I was so entrenched in my own self wallowing. When I felt somewhat normal, I was again focused on trying to get my life on track. I wish she would have told us about the breast cancer. But I understand why she didn't. We would have tried to fix it by making her suffer through everything our mother went through, only to prolong her life a few more months, where she would have no quality of life and lose the battle in the end. I never thought she would take her own life, though." Ciara shifted in his arms so she could look at him. "I heard a song the other day, I don't know the name of it or who sings it, but there were two lyrics that have been running through my mind all day. It said something about finding peace in your decision, and that people don't always listen when someone is hurting." Diesel was quiet for a moment, then added, "There were days before she died when I would walk in and see her wiping her eyes. I'd ask if she was okay, and she'd say she had something in her eye. Or the time I heard her sniffling but kept on walking. Why didn't I stop, or push her for an actual answer when she said she was okay? Or actually take the time to sit and talk with her?"

"Because you thought you had more time. We all do. Plus, as you said, your mind was occupied with your own care. To be honest, Diesel, she had her mind made up. She wouldn't have told you, knowing you would try to stop her any way you could. By not telling you, she took the burden away from you. She was committed to her choice and not the choice you and your father would have made for her."

"I didn't get to say goodbye, though. Plus, did Isabella know I loved her? Because I can't remember the last time I said it to her."

Ciara reached up and placed her palm on his cheek. "Hey, Diesel," she said, drawing his focus back to her, "she knew. The words don't always have to be spoken for someone to feel their power."

Diesel reached up and removed her hand. Taking it in his, he brought it to his lips. "I believe you have a point there, Doc." Then, curling her hand in his, he laid it on his chest. "We have a few more hours before the sun comes up. Let's try to get some sleep until then." He was quiet for a moment, then added, "I'm really glad you were here today."

"I'm happy I could help." She kissed his chest. "And... falling asleep should be no problem. Since I'm lying pressed up against your warm body." She adjusted her head a bit and whispered, "Good night, Diesel."

He leaned down and kissed the top of her head. "Good night, Doc." He lay there for a while, listening to her even breathing. Stroking his fingers along her arm, he whispered, "You came into my life and brought me misery. You haunted my dreams and fueled my imagination. Then you gave me back the part of myself that makes me whole. You are every- thing I could ever want in a woman and more. I knew it from the moment I laid eyes on you. Sometimes fate has to stab you in the gut to wake you up. Well, I'm awake now, and I have no intention of entering that state again."

He then shifted into a more prone position, his eyes looking toward the ceiling. "I promise, Isabella. I'm going to pay attention to the people I care about. And never second guess myself again, to make sure they know they matter to me." He pulled Ciara closer to his body. "I'm putting Ciara O'Malley's name at the top of that list, Izzy. Because you've shown me just how temporary life can be. I love you, Isabella, and I miss you already; good night." He then closed his eyes and dozed off to sleep.

Chapter 5

Ciara woke to the most amazing aroma. Reaching for Diesel, she found his side of the bed empty. As she stretched her well-used body, she scanned the loft searching for Diesel and spotted him standing in a towel next to the dining room table laden with food. She sat up in bed, pulling the sheet up over her chest.

"I wanted to wake you earlier, but I couldn't bring myself to do it. I simply like seeing you in my bed." Ciara started to get out of the bed, but Diesel stopped her. "Stay where you are. I'll bring you anything you want."

"How can I tell you what I want if I don't see my choices?" Ciara stated, then gave him a sly smile.

Diesel realized she had a point. "All right, come over and show me what you would like, and I'll handle the rest."

Ciara slipped her legs over the side of the bed. Standing up, she found his tank and threw it on. She sauntered over to him. Standing in front of him, she placed her hands on his shoulders, then pushed up on her toes, and gave him a quick kiss. "Good morning, Diesel."

Before she could slip away, he wrapped his arms around her and gave her a good morning kiss, before commenting, "Good morning, Doc. How did you sleep?"

She laid her head on his chest as he hugged her to his body. "I slept like a baby," she mumbled, before stepping back to observe the feast before her. Then she looked up at him with wonder in her eyes, as she remarked, "How much do you think I eat?" She turned back toward the table and chuckled. "There is enough food here to feed my entire staff." She held up a peace sign with her fingers. "Twice."

Diesel knew he had gone a little overboard. "Yes, I was a bit indulgent, but that's because I don't know what you like yet." He waved his hand over the table. "Pick out what you like and get back into bed. And have no fear. Anything that is untouched, Chef Declan will make sure it gets to one of the shelters in the area."

It was like he had read her mind. Her eyes glanced over the table. She would have been happy with a cup of tea and a piece of toast, and maybe some fruit.

When she said nothing, Diesel asked, "If you prefer an omelet, I can prepare that as well."

Ciara stuttered out a few nos. "I'm sorry. I was trying to decide. I don't normally eat a big breakfast."

He commented offhandedly, "They say breakfast is the most important meal of the day."

"Yes, it is for a person with a normal workday schedule. Not for me. For me, dinner is the most important meal," she expressed to him.

Diesel paused a moment, mulling over what she had said. "It never dawned on me to consider your work hours." He turned her by the shoulders to look at her face. "If you would like something different, just say the word."

She smiled at his concern, then calmed him with her

words. "No, Diesel. I love breakfast foods. Sometimes I have breakfast for dinner." She glanced at the table over her shoulder. "If I eat a big meal before I lie down, I can't sleep."

"Well, since you are not going to sleep, have at it." He let go of her shoulders and explained what was under the covered dishes. "There are eggs, bacon, sausage, steak, French toast, plain toast, and hash browns." There were jellies and jams, fresh fruit, yogurt, and tarts. When he was finished, he waited for her to choose.

Ciara had only seen a spread like this at weddings. From lox and bagels to German crumb cake, to chilaquiles, plus a few things, she had no idea what they were. She picked up a plate and was about to fill it. Diesel tried to pry the dish from her hand, but she held fast. Yanking the plate back, she told him, "This is my taste plate." Diesel scrunched his face in confusion. "I'm going to fill it with a few things to snack on while I wait for you." She reached and took two miniature blueberry muffins and butter, some fruit and rounded it all out with a glass of orange juice.

A smile formed on his face as he watched her fill the plate. By the time she was finished, there was no room on the plate. "That's a snack?" His voice was filled with doubt.

Ciara innocently replied, "I am eating for two, you know." Diesel's face flipped from smiling to confusion so fast, she couldn't keep a straight face. She broke out laughing, almost dropping her plate. "You should see your face." Seeing more confusion, she interjected, "I was talking about you." She watched his face revert to smiling again. She giggled again, then commented, "You should have seen the panic on your face. Don't you want children, Diesel?"

"I think it's a bit early in our relationship to be talking about children yet. But to answer your question, yes, someday, not now, though. Now that you've almost stopped my heart, please tell me what you want."

"Good to know." She told him her choices then rounded back to her earlier comment. "Are you really going to stand there and tell me you're not going to pick something off my plate?"

"You have a point. Why is it that the same food tastes so much better off someone else's plate?"

Ciara had wondered the same thing repeatedly but had never come up with a reason. "I can't answer your question, because I haven't figured it out myself." She stepped back from the table with her plate. "I'm going to let you put our breakfast together, while I go back to bed."

Diesel watched her walk away, then began loading the plates and setting them on the prepared tray. He then brought it over to Ciara and set it down on the bed. "Coffee or tea?"

"Tea, please," Ciara requested, setting her napkin down on her crisscrossed legs.

Diesel retrieved their beverages and then stretched out on the opposite side, leaning on his elbow. After choosing a few items from the plates, Diesel asked her, "What are your plans for the day?"

"My townhouse needs to be cleaned, and I need to go food shopping. Why?" Both things could be easily set aside if it meant spending time with him.

"Good, so you're available. I need to meet up with my father at ten o'clock at his office to read whatever is in that envelope. After that, I'd like to take you to the clubhouse and then maybe go for a ride. What do you think?"

Ciara looked at him, then told him, "I could try to get the shopping done while you're at your meeting. But the cleaning, that will take longer."

"I had a feeling; that's why you're not going to do it." He watched her head tilt to the side, trying to understand where he was going with his statement. So, he enlightened her. "I'll get a few of the prospects to do the cleaning and the shopping. Then you will be free to spend the day with me."

"Diesel, that's very sweet, but I don't know how comfortable I feel about strangers alone in my home."

"It's all right, Doc. You make a list of everything you want cleaned today and they will do it. Nothing else, and you can trust them. I will hand pick the prospects and they will answer to me if anything is broken or damaged. I'll need the shopping list as well."

Ciara didn't quite know what to do. On one hand, it would be nice to spend the day with him. On the other hand, strangers would be in her home, her sanctuary. Would they riffle through her panties or find her private drawer? "Diesel, I'm not sure it's a good idea."

Diesel's eyes grew wide when he realized what it was she was worried about. "Have no fear, Doc, they will not go through your personal belongings. In fact, I can tell them your bedroom is off limits."

"Grandma taught me to keep my house neat. She said nothing about the bedroom. Diesel, it's probably the messiest room in the townhouse. Next to my bathroom." She gave him a sheepish grin.

"Trust me, the prospects won't do anything they're not supposed to. They follow orders without question, down to the last detail. This is how they earn their patch. If you think about it, you'd be helping them get closer to their goal." Diesel tried to persuade her. Then gave her a dazzling smile to emphasize his point.

Swayed by his undeniable charm, she gave in. "Fine, but I'm setting mouse traps in my drawers."

"Anything to make you feel comfortable. Plus, you will meet them before they go to your place. If you get a bad vibe or a weird feeling about any of them, I'll pull them from the detail. How's that?"

"Meeting them would definitely help. Better, thank you."

"Now, before you run away to get ready, you mentioned last night that my scar spoke to you. Can you explain that?"

Ciara shifted the tray to the floor, then moved closer to Diesel, so she could touch him while she told him. "Diesel, I see some very gruesome things in my profession." She traced her fingers along the puckered skin. "What it told me was that you're resilient. A man with a will to survive at all costs. Your body was broken and beaten, and yet it continued to pump blood through these veins. Because that bastard never touched your soul. It told me they never broke you and that your loyalty is beyond contestation." She leaned down and kissed his chest. She flipped her hair over so she could see his face. "Does that answer your question?"

"Yes," he whispered. At this moment he would have agreed to anything if it meant she would continue her downward descent. Then, as if she had read his mind, she kissed his stomach and wrapped her hand around his hard cock poking through the fold of his towel. Diesel could not contain the growl of anticipation.

Ciara slid farther down, her teeth biting into the towel, releasing it, then she watched it fall to the side. She positioned her body between his spread legs, on her knees. Her hand was still stroking his thick cock, and holding it still, she lowered her head. Her mouth hovered over his straining dick, the tip dripping with pre-cum. She shot her tongue out, grazing it against the head of his dick, barely touching it. With the next swipe of her tongue, she licked the rest of it. Savoring the taste of him, she moved to the base of his cock and lapped her tongue up the length of it, sucking the tip into her warm mouth.

Diesel had propped some pillows underneath his head, so he could observe her every move. Watching his cock disappear into her succulent mouth was a fantasy brought to life. She was making love to his cock. One hand caressing and gripping his balls while her other hand worked in unison with her mouth. Her head bobbed to meet her fingers, taking him deeper down her throat until she could take no more. Diesel started bucking his hips off the bed, loving the feeling of his cock hitting the back of her throat. *What is it about this woman that makes everything feel like the first time?* Diesel thought to himself. *And… if this feels incredible, I can only imagine what it will feel like when I have her strapped down to my spanking bench.* His imagination flashed a visual of how he pictured it, making his hips jerk up, kicking his brain into gear. Diesel pulled his cock from her mouth. He read the disappointment on her face. "Not to worry, Doc, we're not finished yet.

Ciara kneeled on her haunches between his legs, wondering if she had done something wrong by how abruptly he had put a halt to her worshipping his spectacular cock. But her thoughts quickly changed when Diesel moved behind her. He nuzzled her torso down to the bed, raising her ass up. When Diesel slid his fingers easily into her entrance, Ciara groaned with excitement.

"I like that your pleasing me gets you this wet," Diesel indicated. "Because now I can do this." He aligned his dick with her opening and pressed it into her until his hips touched her ass. Grabbing her hips in his hands, he held her steady as he began pounding into her from behind.

Ciara had been surprised by how turned on she had gotten. She had always enjoyed giving blow jobs, but she couldn't remember a time she had ever gotten so wet from it. So wet, that when Diesel entered her, there was no foreplay needed. She rose up on her elbows and dipped her back down to help anchor herself in place. At the pace Diesel had set, she knew this would be quick and hard. Ciara's body easily fell into the rhythm he was orchestrating.

She was drowning in the feeling of him filling her as he

was, pushing deeper and deeper and swiftly ramping up her body. Ciara tried to suppress her orgasm, but with the stimulation Diesel was inflicting on her, it made it virtually impossible. "Diesel, I'm going to come," she panted out.

Diesel knew he had set a maddening pace. After visualizing Ciara strapped down, there was no other gear but overdrive. His body was demanding what his brain had been withholding. Hearing those magical words released the hold on his brain from its responsibility and allowed his body free rein. His hips bucked into her a few more times before he barked out, "Now!"

Ciara heard his command and shattered into pieces. Her elbows collapsed and her head fell to the side on the bed. Her body melted, while her orgasm raced along his cock. "Oh God, Diesel, yes," she screamed.

Diesel drove into her one last time as his body erupted, and then stayed as still as a statue, letting her pulsing walls suck him dry. His groan of fulfillment filled the quiet room. When he pulled out of her, he rolled to the side, taking her with him.

Ciara snuggled her back against his chest. "I wish I could stay here all day," she whispered.

"I would agree with you on any other day. But not today." He gave her a quick kiss on her head, then rolled away and got out of bed. Glancing at the gigantic clock on the wall, he told her, "As it is, I will be a few minutes late to meet my father."

Ciara had not even thought about the time. She had been too preoccupied by their lavish breakfast and playtime. She immediately jumped out of bed. "I'm so sorry. I forgot all about your meeting." She grabbed her bag and was rummaging through it for her clothes, to throw on.

Diesel came around the bed and stopped her. "Baby, relax,

I'm not throwing you out. You can stay as long as you want. I just need to go." He moved to his closet, grabbing the clothes he needed. While he was dressing, he explained to her, "There are two things I want to show you before I go." He started walking toward the balcony. Ciara followed in his wake. He opened the sliding door and walked halfway into the room. "First, you see that door over there?" He pointed to the far-right corner of the room.

"Yes."

"That is the outside elevator. Instead of walking thru the club, you can use this entrance to come and go. Colton can show you where you can park, so the walk isn't so far. The key card he gave you will work with both elevators."

"Okay, and the other?" Ciara was surprised he wanted her to have a key to his home.

Diesel walked past her and took her hand, leading her to a door beyond the kitchen. He pulled a set of keys from his pocket. Opening the door, he stepped to the side and let her walk into the room. "This will be our playroom."

Ciara looked around the room. Anything one could need for a dungeon was in this room. The focal point was the king-sized bed in the middle of the space. The bed, with a royal purple and black velvet overlay patterned bedspread, rested on a black pedestal with four columns connected at the corners. To the left front corner of the room, was the door to a bathroom. Along the wall, there was an oversized black sofa, with varying shades of purple pillows on it. Along the same wall to the back, were the floggers, canes, whips, harnesses, paddles, dragon's tail, and so much more. She walked past the equipment, her fingers grazing against them. In the back right corner, was a dresser, which held vibrators, blindfolds, ball gags, nipple clamps and such. Behind the bed, on the back wall, was a St. Andrew's cross. There was a sex swing and spanking bench on the right. When she gently slid her fingers over the spanking bench, they collected the dust that had accumulated. She looked at him for clarification.

"I've never used the room. It's been here since they built my loft. I had no need for it." Seeing the dust on her fingers, he added, "I'll get someone from housekeeping to come in and clean everything."

Ciara walked over to him, feeling the pain from his soft tone. She tried to lighten the mood. "I think that's an excellent idea, because I hate to dust." Standing in front of him, she raised herself up to give him a quick kiss, then said, "It's a perfect room, and I can't wait to experience everything it has to offer."

The image of her strapped down to the spanking horse flashed in his mind, as a sly grin formed on his face, "And... I know the first piece of equipment we will use." His cock started to get hard, as his mind drifted again, but he filed the image away and took control of his body. "We will discuss all this later. Right now, I need to go." He waited for her to leave the room, then locked the door. Returning the keys to his pocket, he then grabbed his cut from the back of a chair. Throwing it on over his black Harley tee-shirt, he sat down in the chair to put on his boots.

When he stood up, Ciara couldn't help but notice the striking difference between the man standing before her and the grieving, suit-dressed Diesel. This man was the determined biker in jeans, work boots, and a leather vest with a patch of a skeleton leprechaun in the middle of the back. Above the patch, she read Celtic Demons, and underneath it, South Carolina. Two very different looks, but both sexy as hell. "You'd better go. I know how much I hate being kept waiting."

"I am." He took her face between his hands. "Go home, make the lists and if you wouldn't mind, some extra clothes to leave here. I have a strong premonition that you will be spending some time here." He leaned down, taking her lips in a passionate kiss. Breaking the kiss, he continued. "I'll pick you up at your place when I'm done with my father." He headed toward the elevator.

"Hey, wait a minute, how will I know when you're done with your father?"

"I'll call you."

"But I never gave you my personal number."

"I know. I got it from Colton. Your address too." He gave her a smirk, then turned and got into the elevator. "I'll see you soon. Enjoy my shower before you go."

"Oh, I intend to," she called back as the door closed. Ciara pinched her forearm, drawing a yelp from herself. "Yup, this is really happening," she said out loud to the empty room. Glancing at the clock, she figured she had at least an hour before Diesel would be finished. Her eyes flashed up at the open shower, then back at the clock. "Yeah, I have time, as long as I don't overindulge." Ciara made a mad dash up the stairs, stripped out of Diesel's shirt, and started the water. She opened the closest closet, looking for two towels then had to open two more before she found fluffy white ones. By the time she had found the towels, the water had reached her ideal temperature. She stepped in and let the water flow over her. Opening her eyes and looking down at the loft, was so surreal. She felt like she was on a pedestal. She found the shampoo and washed her hair, rinsing the soap away, and also washed away any doubts she might have had.

Diesel parked his blue 2018 Screaming Eagle next to his father's Mercedes. He sat and looked up at the sign above the door. "Law Office of Javier Diaz and Son." Diesel swung his leg over his bike and stood there. His curiosity was piqued, wondering what was in the envelope. At the same time, he had a bad feeling that whatever was in there, they were not going to like it. "Might as well get it over with," he said out loud to the parking lot and walked to the door. He took note of the empty waiting area. *Dad must have cleared his schedule.*

The receptionist greeted him, "Good morning, Mr. Diaz, you can go right back. He's waiting for you."

"Good morning, Carol. Yes, I know, I'm always keeping him waiting. It's good for his blood pressure." Diesel teased with her but continued on to his father's office. It wasn't normal that he was late, but he had gotten a little sidetracked this morning. A grin formed on his face as he knocked twice, then opened the door. Sticking his head in, he asked, "Are you ready to do this?"

"Yes, come in and shut the door. Why are you so late?" Javier barked at him, then thought better. "Never mind, you're here now."

Diesel walked in, closed the door, then took a seat in a chair across from his father. Getting comfortable, he told him, "Ready when you are."

Javier took the envelope opener from his desk and sliced open the letter. Straightening out the paper folds, he began reading aloud.

Dear Dad and Romeo,

If you're reading this, then I've gone to join Mom. I'm sorry I didn't say goodbye to you both in person. But I knew if I did, you would have tried to change my mind, and I couldn't have that.

When I learned of my diagnosis, it devastated me. I couldn't under-stand how it could have happened. I took all the precautions, went for all of my checkups, and yet this disease still ravaged my body. In a year's time, it invaded and spread at a faster rate than Mom's. I watched her try to be so brave going through radiation and chemo treatments. Seeing her crying on the bathroom floor as she pulled clumps of her beautiful long black hair out. Those days we sat with her as her body fought the poisonous drugs that were supposed to be helping her but caused her nothing but pain were so freaking difficult. I didn't want to put you and Romeo through that. Hell, Dad, I didn't want to go through that. I wanted to leave this world on my terms. This was my wish.

By now, you've met Derek. Romeo, I'm sure you will remember him as Patch. If I know both of you, you wanted to beat the shit out of him when he handed you the envelope. I suggested he give it to you in a public setting because I knew you would figure out he was the last person to see me alive.

Diesel interrupted sarcastically, "He sure picked a perfect public setting."

"You'll get no argument from me," Javier agreed and then went back to reading.

Dad, I knew you would rage internally, not wanting to make a scene, and I also wanted to keep Romeo's temper under control.

"Well, she got that right," Diesel chimed in.

"Would you please let me finish?" his father requested.

Diesel glared at him then gave a nod, and Javier went on.

I know I should have told you about Derek, but I knew of Romeo's history with his brother. Plus, I thought I had more time to tell you. We never take the time anymore to tell someone they are special or sweet or helpful. This world has become so cynical. When I found out I had even less time, I wanted to spend that time with him. I'm sorry if that sounds selfish, but I fell in love, Dad.

He was so broken when I found him beaten and living on the street. It took a few months for his body to heal, but I knew the emotional turmoil he went through would take longer. So, every chance I got, I would visit, and we'd sit for hours talking. He began to trust me and looked forward to my visits. And then I started making up excuses so that I could see him more. When he could function on his own, he started helping me. We would bring blankets to the homeless, as well as food. We'd stop and spend time talking with them, letting them know someone cared. While Derek healed, he detoxed at the same time. So, he tended to spend more time with the drug addicts. He would buy clean needles and alcohol swabs and hand them out. He had told me, "If they will not stop, I can at least make it, so they don't get any other diseases to add to their problems."

He even helped me study for my exams. Romeo, he told me everything you didn't. He told me of the torture his brother Vito put you through. He told me that until he took his last breath, he would have to live with the guilt of what happened to you. This was something he knew you would never forgive him for. Romeo, in his defense, Vito was feeding his addiction while playing mind games with his head. He had told me how the Celtic Demons had taken him in and for the first time in a long time he felt like he was part of a family. But he had 'fucked that up, like everything else in his life' (his words, not mine). He went on to say that, although he never got the chance to say it to her, he was grateful for the mercy Angel had shown him even after he threatened to kill her. Sending him back to her father Don Santoro for his punishment with the condition of not killing him brought him to me. Romeo, will you please tell Angel thank you from us? Without her kindness, I would not have found and helped Derek.

Spending so much time together, we developed feelings for each other. We fell in love. It started with small gestures at first. Coffee, then lunch, and he'd sit with me to make sure I ate. He would take my rounds working the streets so I could study. He brought me a flower each day. Then, he moved to massaging my shoulders and neck when the tension built up. He started very subtly taking care of me, but it differed from the care I received at home. At first I thought it was because he felt an obligation to repay me for the kindness I had shown him. But then, I started noticing how I felt when he smiled at me or how my heart would race when his hand would brush against mine. The momentary looks became long gazes. When we walked together, it changed from walking next to each other to him holding my hand or guiding me with his hand on my back. Our conversations, although still about helping as many people as we could, changed to include jokes and laughter.

He told me of his strict Italian upbringing. I told him about my loving Spanish one. He told me about his parents, and I told him about mine. Mom before cancer and Mom after cancer. So, when I had to go back for a follow-up appointment, only days after my mammogram, I asked him to come. I felt it in my bones that I was not going to receive good news. However, I didn't realize it was going to be devastating news. Having Derek there to hold and support me while I broke down reminded me of you and Mom. Right then, I knew I didn't have to tell you and Romeo. Because I knew he would take care of me like you did for Mom. I wanted you to remember me healthy and vivacious. The child who made you come to all of my concerts and dance recitals. The young girl you danced with at my sweet sixteen. I wanted you to remember the woman who stood beside you as they read the last rites to a beautiful wife and mother we had to watch wither away.

I didn't want to put either of you through that again. Hell, I didn't want to go through that at all. I was channel surfing one night and found a show called, 'Mary Kills People' and found the concept of the show fascinating. She helped people go to their eternal resting place on their terms, with dignity. That's what I wanted, and although Derek didn't like it, he supported my decision. We planned an entire day of activities for the day I had chosen. Then, if everything went as planned, we would make love on the beach. Finally, I would sit between his legs, sipping champagne, and watching the sunset as I drifted quietly away with no pain.

Romeo, you may hold old grudges toward Derek, but I'm asking you to resolve them or at the very least set them aside. Wear your scars as a badge of honor. Because believe me, brother, there is a woman out there who will look past them. But if you don't let go of the past, you will never find her, because you will be too focused on something you cannot *change. I say all this because Derek is going to need your help, just like he's going to need Dad's.*

Dad, I know you want him prosecuted to the fullest extent and locked away for the rest of his life for his part in ending mine. I'm sure you've already put the word out in the D.A.'s office that you want the bastard's balls fried. I hope you can beat the D.A. who takes the case because they are going to find the drug Pentobarbital in my system when they do the autopsy. They are also going to find Derek's semen. Once they learn Derek was the one with me, they are going to arrest him. So, Daddy, Romeo, my request from the both of you is make sure Derek does no jail time.'

"What the fuck?" Diesel burst out.

Javier wasn't happy with her request, either. His hand gripped the letter, wrinkling the paper. "There's more."

"What else could she possibly want? Isn't that enough?" Diesel was furious at his sister, Derek, hell, even his dad.

Javier continued to read.

Dad, I'm counting on you to be lead defense and, Romeo, you're second chair. I don't care what you have to do, but make sure you keep him out of jail. He didn't want me to die, either. He tried every day to talk me out of it. But I made my mind up. He helped me because I asked him to. Derek should not have to spend the rest of his life behind bars for doing something I asked for. I drew off his strength and love for me. Now, I'm asking you to save the man I love from going to jail. I know neither of you are happy with this request, but you'll see he's not the bastard you think he is, Dad. Romeo, given the chance, he'd step in front of a bullet for Angel. He's changed so much from the man you knew.

For my last request, Dad, I want you to set up a bank account for you and Derek. This way you can oversee the charity that Derek is going to run. Because if I know you, Dad, you're already working on one. I want Derek to run it. He will do the right thing, and I trust him to continue on with what I already started. You'll see, I love you both so much, and I know you love me and will eventually understand my decision. You could use this letter as exhibit one if you think it will help. Know that I will be safe with Mom, and you two take care of each other. Romeo, I'll see if I can get that woman I spoke about to show up in your life soon. Take care of Dad, Diesel (God I always hated that name, but it fits you).

With all my love,
Isabella

Javier set the letter down on his desk and sat back in his chair. He rubbed his hands over his bewildered face, looking up at the ceiling. "I understand now why she did what she did, and I don't blame her for that. She was much stronger than she gave herself credit for. If she had only told us..." His voice trailed off.

Diesel had gotten out of his chair as his father had finished her letter, pacing back and forth. "The outcome would probably have been the same. The only difference is we wouldn't have been blindsided." He placed his hands on the back of the chair he had vacated. "The elephant in the room now is do we defend a man we both despise and feel should be behind bars?" Diesel headed to the minibar in the back corner of the office. Pouring a shot of bourbon into a glass, he raised it to his father in silent question. With a nod of his head, Diesel poured another glass and continued. "She gave us no time to come to terms with her death before throwing this shit at us. What was she thinking?" He handed the glass to his father.

Both raising their glasses in a silent toast, they each downed the shot. "She was thinking about him."

"Well, that was obvious." Diesel sat back down in the chair, waving his hand at the letter. "Are we really going to do this?"

His father looked at him as if he had two heads. "Do we have a choice? I think Isabella made that decision for us. The proper question is can we win? We are going to have to find something that will at least raise a doubt."

"Maybe we'll be able to get the whole thing thrown out at the preliminary trial," Diesel raised the question.

"That would be an ideal scenario." Javier said in an offhanded manner. "Well, as of right now, he hasn't been arrested, so that gives us the edge on getting prepared for when he is."

Just then Diesel's cellphone rang. Pulling it out, he looked at the screen. After seeing who it was, he told his father, "I think our time just ran out." Answering the phone, he put it on speaker. "Good morning, Jacob, I'm with my father, and you're on speaker phone. What can I help you with? I haven't received any notice of a Celtic Demon being brought in." When Diesel became a patched in member, he also became the club's new defense attorney. Although his father's dream had been for them to work together when he passed the bar, Diesel had other plans in mind. However, now after years of his father trying to persuade him, his sister had done it with one letter.

"No, it's not about the club," Jacob started. "I couldn't stop thinking about what happened in the church. I went on your suspicion that he assisted her with the suicide. The DNA collected during the autopsy could prove he was there. I brought my idea to Judge Asher, and she agreed. I'm holding an arrest warrant for the DNA of one Derek Mancini. I thought you'd want to know," Jacob informed them.

Diesel's eyes locked with his father's. "Thanks for the courtesy call. I should also inform you that my father and I will be representing Derek from here on out. So, I'm putting you on notice you are not to question our client without one of us present." He waited for Jacob's reaction. He knew that what he had told him had thrown Jacob off his game.

"What's with the one eighty? I thought you wanted him arrested and fried for his crime. Now, you're telling me you're representing the asshole. I don't get it."

Diesel looked toward his father for confirmation, which he gave with a slight bob of his head. "The envelope Derek gave my father contained a letter, or should I say last will and testament. In it, Isabella bequeathed my father and me to represent him, should the need arise, going as far as to demand we make sure he doesn't go to jail."

"Oh, shit."

"Yes, oh shit is right," Diesel repeated his words. "All I want to do is beat the shit out of this asshole, and Isabella sidelined me from the grave."

"Man, that had to have sucker punched you and Javier."

"We're still trying to process her request." Javier chimed in. "We were hoping for more time to come to terms with it, but your warrant makes that impossible."

"I thought I was doing a good thing, Javier." Jacob's voice was filled with regret.

"You were, Jacob, and if circumstances were different, it would have been perfect. But with things such as they are, I think I know where we can find him," Diesel told him. "I'll meet you at the corner of Blossom and Main. If he's not there, we'll have to walk the rest of the way."

"I'll see you there." Jacob sighed and hung up.

Diesel put his phone back into his cut. "I'll go let the asshole know what's going on and meet you at the station. Try to find out which D.A.s are jockeying for the case." Then he headed for the door, but Javier's weak voice stopped him.

"We have to do whatever it takes to keep him out of prison. It's not going to be easy. I need to know that you're all in, Romeo."

Diesel stopped short of the door, his hand on the handle. He looked back at his father. "Isabella made sure we were both in. Do I like it? No, I don't, but I'll do whatever I need to. I just hope he can make bail. Otherwise, we only have fourteen days before the preliminary hearing."

"We'll deal with that. I can always transfer the money to Judge, and he can bail him out."

"We're not involving the club in this, Dad. This is our family matter, not the Demons'. And besides, half of the Celtic Demons would rather see him rot in jail. I'll see you in a little while." Diesel pulled the door open and strutted down the hallway, saying goodbye to Carol as he left the building. Getting on his bike, he pulled the phone from his pocket and dialed Ciara's number. Waiting for her to pick up, he glanced back at the sign over the door. "It took you less than ten minutes to unravel years of avoidance. Thanks a lot, Izzy." He finished his rant as Ciara picked up.

"Hey, you on your way?"

'No, I have something I need to deal with."

"Do you want to do it another day?" she asked.

"No, I'm not breaking our plans. I wanted to let you know I'd be longer than expected."

"Oh, okay." Ciara hid her disappointment. "Go do what you have to. I'll go shopping while I wait. If you get here before I get back, I'll leave a key under the flowerpot by the door."

"Thanks for understanding, Ciara, I'll fill you in later on what's happening."

"See you then." She hung up the phone.

Diesel looked at the phone in his hand, saying out loud, "Simple and easy, why can't all women be like that?" Placing the phone back in his pocket, he started his bike and headed over to meet Jacob.

Jacob was already there by the time Diesel pulled up. He stepped out of his cruiser and glanced at the sidewalks on either side of the two-way street. For as far as he could see, were tents, boxes, and make-shift shanties. He walked over to where Diesel parked. "Now, I understand why we need to walk," Jacob mentioned offhandedly. "This is where your sister came every day? I'm glad I don't work this part of town."

"Just because you don't see it, doesn't mean it doesn't exist." Diesel had been here a few times looking for his sister, but it had been a while since he had visited. "It always amazes me that not twenty minutes from my father's prestigious office, there are hundreds of homeless people trying to survive." Diesel got off his bike and shook Jacob's hand. "Unless he lied about carrying on my sister's work, we should find Derek in that tent. Otherwise, somewhere amongst these people." Diesel checked the tent and seeing no one inside, he told Jacob, "We'll have to walk."

"It's almost like trying to find a needle in a haystack." Jacob looked past Diesel's shoulder. "We should get going."

With the South Carolina sun beating down on them, they began their search. Most of the people they passed hung their heads in shame, others retreated in fear of being arrested. "I'll make sure I bring this up at the next town hall the mayor holds. He has to do something to help these people." Jacob spoke with an edge of disgust to his voice.

"It won't matter. Even if he could find housing for all these people, others would just fill the vacant spaces. Just like health insurance, this country has a problem fixing the homeless issue," Diesel expressed his views.

"No argument here."

They continued their search for three more blocks. Near the very end of all the makeshift housing, they found Derek and another woman handing out blankets and the few containers with food in them. Diesel watched Derek and his interactions with the people he talked with. Everyone seemed happy and pleased to see him. This was definitely not the Patch he had known. Jacob and Diesel waited for them to finish doing what they were doing, then walked over to him.

"Come down to help out?" Derek asked, knowing full well that was not the reason they were there.

"Derek Mancini, I have a warrant for your DNA. I need you to come with us." Jacob spoke loudly.

The woman Derek had been working with got all flustered. "What's happening, Derek? I can't do this on my own now that Izzy is gone. Now, you're getting arrested, for what? How am I going to get you out, or even afford an attorney?"

"It's okay, Doris, I believe I already have an attorney." Derek looked at Diesel, receiving an affirmative head nod. "It will be all right, Doris, let Oscar know when he arrives that I will be indisposed for a few days. Let him know he needs to handle anything that comes up until I return." Looking to Jacob, he asked, "Would it be okay if you cuff me before you put me in the car? Because I feel if you did it now, our return walk will be hindered with people trying to help me." Jacob and Diesel looked at each other. "I'm not going to run. I have nothing to fear."

"You're pretty cocky for a guy who could be arrested for murder if your DNA matches," Jacob informed him as they began their walk back to the car.

"True, but Isabella made sure I had the best defense attorneys in the county."

"You have a point there," Jacob conceded.

As they walked, Derek would wave and calm people from getting involved. Diesel was grateful they had left the cuffs off. With all the people willing to help Derek, they would have had a riot on their hands. By the time they reached the cruiser, they had collected a group of approximately twenty-five people. When Derek turned around for Jacob to put the cuffs on, he spoke to them. "Everything will be all right. This," he nodded his head in Diesel's direction and continued, "is Isabella's brother. He and his father will make sure I'm back with you in no time. Until then, Doris and Oscar will be here in my absence if you need anything." The crowd grumbled and voiced their disapproval, but Derek spoke to calm them. "This is just a formality. You'll see. I will be back before you know it." This statement seemed to quiet the crowd.

Before things got out of hand, Jacob put Derek in the back of the cruiser. Prior to closing the door, Diesel stuck his head in, informing Derek, "We are your attorneys, and as such, I'm instructing you not to say anything until we tell you to. Is that understood?"

"Yes, I understand." A little of Derek's confidence was shaken as the cuffs went on. "You will be at the station to meet us, correct?"

"My father should already be there when you arrive. Again, only speak to him."

Quietly, Derek conveyed to Diesel, "Thank you for doing this. I know we've had a rocky history, and you would have every right to walk away. But I'm grateful you chose to help me."

Diesel responded, his annoyance heard in every word, "I didn't have much of a choice now, did I?" Then he slammed the car door shut.

Jacob walked around to the driver's door, looking over the roof in Diesel's direction. "See you at the station."

'Yeah, I'll meet you there."

Jacob got into the cruiser and pulled away, leaving Diesel with the crowd.

The crowd which had followed Derek, pressed in around Diesel, asking questions. "Are you really going to get him off? How long will it take? Why is he being arrested? What did he do wrong?" The last question yelled at him, broke his silence. "He helped Isabella kill herself. There, are you happy? Your savior helped my sister leave all of you. You shouldn't be mad at us; you should be mad at him." He turned from the crowd and got on his motorcycle.

A woman wearing layers of clothing yelled back at him, "But only because she was sick. He would never have done anything to hurt her on purpose. He loved her too much."

Diesel had no response for the woman, so he started his motorcycle. The roar of the engine drowned out their voices. Yet, the woman's words reverberated through his mind the whole way to the station. When he arrived, he saw his father's Mercedes in the lot. He parked his motorcycle, then walked in, grateful his father was already there. Holding the door for two officers leaving the building, entering when they were clear of the door, he headed to the front desk and was greeted by the desk sergeant.

Holding his hand out to shake Diesel's, he said, "Hey, Diesel, sorry about your sister. She was a sweet kid."

"Thanks, Jim." Looking around the area, he asked, "I'm looking for my dad. Have you seen him?"

"Yeah, he's in interrogation room four. You want me to go get him?"

"No, I actually have to join him," Diesel said sheepishly.

Jim's eyes grew wide, with a shocked expression on his face. "What the fuck, Diesel? What happened to," he mimicked Diesel, "'there is no way in hell I'll ever work with my father. We have way too many dissimilar opinions to ever work together'. And yet, here you are." Jim got a sly look on his face.

"I know, I know. If it weren't for Isabella, I wouldn't be here now."

"What do you mean?" Jim inquired.

Not wanting to tell him the reason behind his statement, he snapped back, "Stop busting my balls, Jim, and get me an escort to room four."

The bite in Diesel's voice told Jim playtime was over. He looked over his shoulder and spotted Harper, sorting mail. "Hey, Jenson, escort Mr. Diaz to interrogation room four."

Turning back to Diesel, he told him, "I'll catch you at Demons' Dungeon. Really am sorry, Diesel."

"I know, Jim, sorry I snapped. It's been a rough few days. But yeah, see you at the dungeon, first round is on me." He shook Jim's hand and turned to see Harper waiting for him at the end of the counter.

"You can follow me, sir," her soft voice announced.

Walking toward her, he let her know, "You know this is a formality. I've been here more than enough times to know exactly where each interrogation room is."

"I know, sir. I like to keep things formal," she responded as she held the door open for him, a big smile plastered on her face. As he passed her, she whispered, "Will you be at the club tonight?"

His simple answer of, "No," quickly erased the smile from her face. Her face dropped further when he closed the door on her, turning his attention to his father. "Where are they?"

"I'm assuming Jacob stopped at the hospital before coming back here."

"Then what are you doing here?" Diesel railed at his father.

"Relax, I had a feeling that's what Jacob would do. I sent Benjamin to meet Derek there."

"Oh," Diesel hesitated. "Well, that was a smart move on your part."

"It's been a while since you've worked a genuine case, hasn't it?" Javier looked up at his son from the chair he sat in at the table. His briefcase was resting by his feet, while a folder and papers were spread before him. "They should be here soon. Benjamin sent me a text when they left."

Diesel walked to the other side of the room, grabbing the empty chair against the wall, and joined his father. He glanced at the folder that read *Evidence Collected*. He knew when he opened it, there would be pictures of his sister's lifeless body. It was one thing to see her in her casket; it was an entirely different thing to see her at the crime scene. The rawness of her death had not dissipated yet, and here he was about to rip apart any mending that had started.

He reached for the file, but his father stopped him. "You don't have to look at them. I already have."

"I will have to see them, eventually," he quietly responded. His father removed his hand and Diesel flipped the file open. The first photo he saw was one of the footprints in the sand and a champagne glass lying next to it. The following three pictures were of the surrounding area. The fourth and so on were all of Isabella. He thanked God she had not been shot or stabbed. Because these photos were similar to her lying in her casket. In fact, they did not look like crime photos at all. She was propped up on a log, facing the ocean. Her eyes were closed as if she had fallen to sleep. What consoled Diesel was the fact that she had gone peacefully, without suffering. The photos confirmed that. "She looks so serene."

"I felt the same way when I looked at them," his father agreed.

Still gazing at the photos, Diesel commented, "I always saw her as my little sister, but she grew up and I missed it."

"I thought the same thing about you when I saw you lying in that hospital bed. I resented your club for taking you away from me and for putting you in that bed. Yet, I went every day to check your progress, and there was always another Demon sitting in your room. That's when I understood my perception of a motorcycle club was very wrong."

"Dad, can we not do this here?" Diesel and his father had argued nearly every time they had seen each other when he had become a prospect. And... here he was geared up for another one.

"You don't even know what I was going to say," Javier pointed out. "All I was going to say was that after the interactions I had with your president and some of your brothers, I comprehended how wrong I had been."

Diesel looked at Javier's face, seeing no condemnation. His father's confession surprised him, but before he could respond, Jacob walked in with Derek. Benjamin trailed behind. "Jacob, if you don't mind, we'd like some time with our client before you question him."

"No problem, Diesel. I'll check with the clerk and see if he can get him on the docket this afternoon with Judge Asher."

"Thanks, Jacob. Appreciate it," Diesel called back as Jacob closed the door and left them.

As soon as the door shut, Javier asked, "Did everything go okay at the hospital?"

"Yes, they are putting a rush on the results. We should have them Monday," Benjamin answered. Joining father and son in the interrogation room, Benjamin took a seat in the corner, while Derek took a seat in the last chair opposite the lawyers.

Javier then turned to Derek. "I'm not happy about defending you, but I will do it because my daughter requested it." He flipped open a file. "Now, I want to know everything that transpired that night. Leave nothing out. Understand?" An underlying growl was present in his voice.

Derek began explaining and answering questions thrown at him in between, recalling the events of the night to the men in the room. When he finished, Benjamin was asked to find Jacob for his interrogation of Derek. By the time it was over, it was nearing three o'clock. Jacob had received confirmation that the clerk had been able to get Derek on the docket list. Derek would be standing before Judge Asher within the hour.

Diesel looked at the clock on the wall. "Dad, you got this arraignment?"

"Yes, I can handle it. You have something more important to do?"

"In fact, I do. This was not how I intended to spend my day at all." For the past hour, all Diesel had been thinking about was Ciara and how she must be thinking he had blown her off. "If you must know, I am going to pick up Ciara O'Malley and bring her to the clubhouse. Initially, it was to introduce her, but now I need to inform Judge about all this."

"Ciara O'Malley, isn't she the medical examiner who did Isabella's autopsy?" Javier inquired.

"Yes, she is, and before you say anything, we've already set boundaries pertaining Isabella's case."

"That's good, but I'm sure that was before you found out you would be representing the defendant in the case?" Javier pointed out.

"Well, yes, but that changes nothing." Diesel knew it did, but he wasn't going to let it stop him from pursuing the fine doctor.

"It kind of does." Benjamin spoke up timidly. "If Doctor O'Malley is called to the stand, anything she says can be thrown out because of your involvement with her."

Diesel's eyes threw daggers at Benjamin, knowing that what he said was absolutely true. "We will make sure no one finds out about us," he asserted through gritted teeth.

"You're willing to take a chance we could have a mistrial or even lose totally for a woman?" Javier's voice had an edge of doubt to it. "Besides, you hardly know her."

"I know she's the first woman I've felt comfortable with in a really long time. And I'm not going to miss the opportunity to see where this can go."

"You should go and be with her, Diesel," Derek chimed in. "If I learned anything from being with Izzy, it's that you should never waste the time you have. Because in the blink of an eye, it can be taken away."

Diesel eyes flipped to his father's when he said, "Even he gets it."

"Go, Benjamin and I will take care of the arraignment. But I'm warning you, Romeo, tread lightly where Doctor O'Malley is concerned, for Isabella's sake." His father added just a touch of guilt with his last words.

"I hear you, Father, and I will be careful. Call me later tonight and fill me in on the hearing." He got up from the table and walked to the door, where, turning, he looked at Derek. "I'm still on the fence with you, but we'll do everything we can to keep you out of jail, per Isabella's request." He turned and left the room, walking past the front desk and straight to his motorcycle. Seated on his cobalt blue Screaming Eagle, he pulled out his phone and dialed Judge.

"What's up, Diesel?" Judge asked.

"Where are you?"

"At the clubhouse. Everything all right?" Judge's voice was laced with concern.

"Yeah, I want to give you an update on everything that's going on. I need to pick up Ciara and then I'll be over." Judge heard the dejected sound in Diesel's voice.

"Who's Ciara?"

"She's part of what's going on. I'll fill you in when I get there."

"I'll be here." Judge hung up and looked at his phone, thinking, *whenever a woman is involved, there could be several things wrong.*

Diesel hung up and quickly dialed Ciara, letting her know he was on his way. He could only pray he had read her right and that she wouldn't fly off the handle in public.

Ciara had been getting ready to sit down in front of the television with a salad to watch a movie when she received Diesel's call informing her he'd be there in twenty minutes. She threw a cover over the salad and shoved it into the now packed refrigerator. She turned the television off and ran to her room to change. She knew she'd be riding on his motorcycle, so she chose a short sleeve green shirt, a pair of jeans, and her boots. She'd grab her leather jacket from the closet before they left. She was in the process of pulling her hair up when she heard the doorbell. She finished what she was doing and answered the door.

Before she could utter a word, Diesel took her face in his hands and kissed her. Her body melted against him. She snaked her arms around his neck and held onto him when he deepened the kiss. Diesel pulled back from the kiss, resting his hands on her hips. His forehead touching hers, he asked. "It's been a hell of a morning, Doc. You ready to ride?"

"You want to talk about it first?" She pulled back to look at him, concern on her face.

"Nope, that's what riding is for, but I will let you know what's going on soon." He wasn't happy about keeping her in the dark. He would tell her, just not by himself. "You have everything you need?" He released his grip on her.

"Come in. I need to grab my jacket, backpack, and phone, then I'll be ready to leave."

He closed the door and followed her down the hallway, past a bathroom and the staircase. She stopped by the counter in the kitchen. He continued past her into the living room area and walked over to the windows on the far wall. Looking out, he commented, "Nice place, nicer view." He saw an in-ground pool, and beyond that, a walkway leading straight down to the beach.

Ciara yelled over her shoulder, "That and the fireplace were what sold me on the place." Turning from the counter, she threw her backpack over her shoulder. "Ready when you are." Reaching for her leather jacket in the closet, she added,

"I've never been on a motorcycle before; I'm so excited to try it."

Diesel loved the innocence of her excitement. "It will only take one ride to determine if you like it or not. My opinion," he paused for dramatic purpose, "you're going to love it." He walked back to her, wrapping his arm around her waist as he guided her out the front door, locking it behind them.

Walking through the parking lot, Diesel had the distinct feeling they were being watched. Once they were at his motorcycle, he relieved her of her backpack and placed it in the left side bag as he inconspicuously looked around the area. "You have a choice, wear a lid or don't wear a lid?" Diesel informed her. Standing up, he glanced over her shoulder back at the building, holding a lid.

"What's a lid?" Ciara asked, a confused look on her face.

Diesel chuckled at her question, forgetting his terminology. Her question pulled his focus back to Ciara. "It's a helmet. In South Carolina, you don't have to wear a *helmet*." He stressed the word. "But I always carry one for out-of-state runs." He took another look around. He saw nothing out of place, yet the uneasiness remained.

"Ohh," Ciara drew out the word. "No, I think I'd like to ride my first time without a helmet. Er, lid," she quickly countered.

Once he returned the helmet back in the side bag, he got on the motorcycle and pushed aside his feeling of unease. He told her, "The most important thing to remember is to lean with the motorcycle when I turn. Got it?"

"Got it. Your motorcycle is beautiful. I love the artwork on it."

"My mom always hated me riding, but she understood." He touched the tribute to her on his tank. "As soon as I have time, I'll have something for Isabella put on the other side." He got a faraway look before snapping out of it. "Ready

when you are. Put your foot on the footrest and climb on."
Diesel pointed to the flat piece of metal her foot would
rest on.

As she did, the roar of the engine came to life. Once she
was settled behind him, he yelled over his shoulder, "Hang on
and enjoy the ride. If you need something, tap my shoulder to
get my attention. Ready?"

"Ready."

He backed the motorcycle out of the space and slowly
made his way to the intersection leading to the highway.

As soon as they pulled away, a tall man rounded the corner
watching the two leave. He wore a dark sweatshirt with the
hood pulled up, covering his facial features. He fished a phone
from his pocket, dialed and waited for a response. "Yes, they
just left." He listened for instructions. "You got it, boss; she'll
never know I was in the house." The heavy Russian accent
hung in the air. "I'll call when I have news." The stranger
hung up the phone and made his way to Ciara's front door.
Picking the entrance lock, he slipped inside, and closed the
door behind himself.

When the light changed, Diesel put more throttle into the
bike, and as he did, he felt her two hands latch onto his waist.
The closer they got to the highway, the more her nails dug in.
"Relax, Doc, it's like driving a car. Once you're on the highway, you cruise. Just remember, people do this every day." He
had second guessed himself about taking her on the highway
for her first ride, but he knew once she settled in, she'd relax.
Besides, the highway was the fastest way to the clubhouse. He

knew Judge would wait on him, but he didn't want him to wait longer than was necessary.

By the time they had driven two exits, Ciara eased into riding. She released her death grip on his waist to her hands resting on his hips. When she was finally comfortable, she leaned back on the backrest. That's when she started noticing how free she felt. She looked to the blue sky above, seeing for miles. She noted the different fragrances and odors. The first was the smell of diesel fuel, then cut grass. They exited the highway and rode through town where the aroma from the bakery and assorted restaurants filled her senses. The road turned more rustic as they drove out of the town. A few miles later, they turned off the main road, past a guard shack, and down a paved, tree-lined driveway. As they rode closer, Ciara could make out an extensive building at the end. Diesel parked his motorcycle near the door and waited for her to get off.

Ciara stood in place, getting her legs under her, and looked around. Beside a crap load of motorcycles in the parking lot, there was a five-bay garage, and growing houses beyond the clubhouse as far as the eyes could see. "Wow, I had no idea how big of a motorcycle club the Demons were," Ciara announced.

"We have chapters up and down the east coast and surrounding states." He got off his bike and stood before her. "How was the ride?" he asked, a grin forming on his face.

She slapped his chest playfully. "You know exactly how it was," she stated, but went on to explain. "First, it terrified me, but once you said that people do this every day, it took my fear away and replaced it with trust. Trust that you knew what you were doing and would never put me in harm's way."

He gave her a quick kiss, then moved his hand to her waist, leading her up the stairs into the clubhouse. He opened the door, letting her precede him as he remarked, "I knew you'd love it."

Once they were inside, they were greeted by a bunch of his brothers. He breezed her to the bar, finding an open spot near the end to order drinks before going upstairs. He looked at her with a questioning look for what she wanted.

"Cranberry juice is fine. I haven't eaten much today."

He leaned in close to her ear. "Have no fear. After our ride, I will make sure I feed you."

He waited for Scar to look his way, but before Scar walked to the end of the bar, the prospect retrieved a beer from the refrigerator. Carrying the bottle and setting it down in front of Diesel, he asked, "What can I get your lady?"

"Scar, this is Doc. Doc, this is Scar," he introduced, then ordered for her.

"Nice to meet you, Doc, be right back with your drink."

While they waited, Diesel introduced Ciara to a few more people who approached them, never using her actual name. He also pointed out the different areas of the clubhouse, the sitting area with television lined walls opposite the bar. In the back, was a game room with pool tables, darts, and video games. Next to there, was the stage area where members played live music on certain nights. He pointed out the kitchen behind the bar area and the stairs leading to Judge's office. Scar returned with her drink and Diesel led the way. "Come on, Judge is already waiting."

Ciara had been a little intimidated walking into the clubhouse. She knew absolutely nothing about motorcycle clubs, except for the typical stereotype bullshit. She could see daggers being thrown her way by some of the women scattered about. Yet, every man Diesel introduced her to made her feel welcome.

"Follow me." He spoke next to her ear, so she heard him over the noise in the crowded area. He led her to the staircase and followed her up. When they arrived at the landing, Diesel led the way to Judge's office. He held the door open for her to walk in, but she took two steps in and stopped dead in her tracks. Diesel stutter-stepped around to avoid bumping into her.

Ciara stood frozen like a deer in headlights. Seated, but now standing, were five of the biggest men she had ever seen, and one giant. They all wore the same 'cut' that Diesel had on. After she had called it a vest, he had quickly corrected her terminology. She took a step back, bumping into Diesel as the one behind the desk approached them.

"Doctor O'Malley, we haven't met yet, which in my business is a good thing." Judge walked forward timidly, extending his hand. "I'm Reed or Judge, whichever you prefer. It's nice to meet you. Please come in, you have nothing to fear here." He tried to ease her apprehension.

Ciara reached out to accept his hand. "You have to excuse me, I was unprepared for all of you to be here, and you're all so big." She released his hand and took a deep, calming breath.

Judge looked past her to Diesel. "Sorry, dude, but you got me worried on the phone, so I called a few friends. Hope you don't mind?"

Diesel moved forward, taking Judge's hand, fisting them together, bumping their chests and patting each other's back. "It's been a rough couple of days, but today, the shit really hit the fan."

"Well, you already have a beer, so introduce Ciara and let's get to it." Judge stepped aside and closed the door once they were in the room.

Diesel took her to Yankee first. "Ciara this is Killian, or Yankee, he's the club's vice president. Next, is Hunter, or Saint, he's the club's secretary." As she was introduced to the men, they each shook her hand and greeted her accordingly. "Over there is Eric, or Viking, he's the sergeant of arms."

"Indeed, he is," Ciara teased.

"This is Dominic, or Grave Digger, he's our ride captain, and finally this is Allen, or Ace, he's our treasurer." Diesel had greeted his brothers the same way he had greeted Judge.

"It's nice to meet you all." She looked closer at Ace. "You were with Diesel at the morgue, correct?"

"Yes, I was. Excellent memory, Doc. Here, take my seat," Ace volunteered, moving out of the way for her to sit.

When she was seated, everyone except Diesel took theirs. He stood behind her chair with his hands resting on her shoulders. "You all remember the envelope that Patch handed my father?" They all mumbled their agreement. "Dad and I read it this morning. Apparently, we are to be his attorneys." Ciara turned in the chair, but he held her in place. "In the letter, Isabella explained everything, basically requesting Dad and me to keep him out of jail." He went on to explain what the rest of the letter said, the warrant, the hospital, and finally the interrogation room. "As you can see, I will have my hands full for the next couple of weeks. Let everyone know if they are busted for anything, they'll be in the tank until I can get to them."

Ciara had sat quietly, listening to everything Diesel had said. Her professional self told her it was time to separate from him. However, the woman in her screamed there had to be a way. She understood why Isabella did what she did; she was looking out for her boyfriend by trusting her father and brother to protect him from her decision. Isabella could never have known how her death would steer Diesel onto Ciara's path in life. Or how the couple would connect on so many levels.

Yet if she and Diesel stayed together, it would be a conflict of interest, and she could lose her job. A little piece of her cringed at the thought of not being with him. She glanced around at the men looking at her. She knew they were thinking the same thing. She brushed his hands off his shoulders and stood, turning to face him. "We are all thinking it, but I'll be the one to ask it. Why did you bring me here to hear this? You know that during a preliminary trial, the prosecution will certainly call me to the stand. If they ask if I had prior knowledge of that letter, I will have to tell the truth. Why would you do that?" Ciara was on the verge of tears.

"Because I don't want any secrets between us. Most of what I told you is already public knowledge. I informed you of the letter to explain why I'm taking the case. Plus, it was easier to tell this one time instead of many."

"That's great, you probably also thought by telling me here, I wouldn't make a scene, correct?" The other men all looked at Diesel with a touch of pity on their faces. Ciara took a calming breath. "You were right. I'm not going to make a scene, but I am going to speak my piece." The tension fueling the air dissipated in the room with her answer. "This whatever is going on with us is brand new." Her voice held a touch of sadness when she said, "We can put this on hold," she waved her hand between herself and Diesel, "until everything is settled with the case." She lowered her head and started to move around him toward the door.

Diesel blocked her way when she tried to pass by him. "Now, it's my turn. Yes, this thing between us is new. That's why I don't want to waste a minute. If there is one thing I learned from my sister's death, it's that we do not know if we'll see tomorrow. As far as the case goes, we will have to amend our agreement to neither one of us talking about the case, period."

"Diesel, it's more complicated than that. We can't be seen together."

"And… yet, here you are." He waved his hand around the room.

"Exactly my point."

"If I may, Diesel?" Judge interrupted.

Ciara turned to face Judge. "Ciara, you are standing in a room with men you can trust. Each one of us would put our lives on the line for him. You have nothing to fear from us."

"And the room downstairs?"

"Also trustworthy, or they wouldn't be here. Plus, they have no knowledge of what is taking place here." Judge looked over her to Diesel. "But I wouldn't push the envelope by bringing her to the clubhouse for the next few weeks." Looking back at Ciara, he said, "Yes, he may have been a chicken shit for telling you this information in a room full of strangers. However, the reason goes further. He came to us for help, and you, my dear, is why he needs our help. Do I have that straight, Diesel?"

"You nailed it, Judge. Dad and I can get the bastard off, but I can't have Ciara getting hurt in the process. At the same time, I don't want her out of my sight. What the hell do we do?"

"Well, the obvious thing to do is put your feelings on hold until everything is said and done," Ace butted in. "But... I know you, and that's not an option."

"Then if that's not an option, you'll just have to sneak around. I've heard that it can add to the adventure," Grave Digger chimed in.

Judge spoke to Diesel. "Who all knows about the two of you besides us?"

"Colton, my dad and Benjamin."

"All trustworthy. I agree with Grave Digger, if you want to continue seeing each other, you'll have to do it undercover. But you're taking one hell of a chance," Judge countered. "If the prosecutor in the case gets wind of the two of you in a personal relationship, it could blow the case up. Not to mention both of your careers."

"I've already given her the key to the private entrance at the club. Any other ideas?" Diesel asked the group.

Ciara sat and listened as these men were deciding her life for her. "Um, do I have a say in any of this?" she cut in. "Because this is the first time I've ever discussed my personal life with a group of men."

"Of course, you have a say," Diesel told her. "That's why we're here."

"Then I want to go riding." All the men turned and looked at her, their mouths dropping open at her request. "What? I want to clear my head before I make a decision that could possibly cost me my job and credibility. The ride over eased my stress about coming here. I'm hoping it will give me some clarity about all this." She turned back to Diesel with anger in her tone. "And… in the future, I would appreciate a heads up instead of being ambushed." This time when she pushed past him, he let her go. After she opened the door, she turned to the room, saying, "It was nice meeting you all. I wish the introductions had been under different circumstances." Then to Diesel, "I'll be by your motorcycle. I'm sure you have a few more things to discuss." She then turned and left the room, closing the door behind herself.

The room of men looked at him, Viking speaking up first. "She has a point, dude."

"I know she does. I just couldn't think of another way," Diesel confirmed.

"You could have at least warned her we'd all be here," Yankee voiced his opinion.

"I didn't know you'd all be here." He threw a hard stare at Judge.

Judge raised his hands, palms up, and shrugged his shoulders. "I knew you needed help; I just didn't know what kind of help." He blew the accusation off. "You know me. I like to be prepared. So, how can we help?"

Diesel glanced at Yankee. "We're going to need character witnesses. You think your father-in-law would be helpful?"

"I think Anthony could be persuaded to put in a good word for him. I'll ask Angel to talk to him. I think he'd do anything for his only daughter carrying his grandchild. But if you can avoid putting him on the stand, I would. Don Santoro was not very pleased with the boy the last time they met."

"I'll keep that in mind," Diesel tossed back. "There is one other thing I need. Before we left Ciara's townhouse, I got the distinct feeling that we were being watched. You think you could spare a prospect to monitor her place. She'll be with me the rest of the weekend, at the dungeon."

"I'll send Dancer, Bong, and Rider to look around the area, then leave Rider to scout around the next few days to be on the safe side. You have any idea why someone would be following you or the good doctor?" Judge questioned.

"Thanks, Judge, I appreciate it. There could be any number of people who would follow me, but I couldn't imagine anyone wanting to hurt Ciara." Diesel looked at the doubtful looks on each of their faces. "Let's not make something out of this until we have something concrete. I'd better go before she thinks I abandoned her. I'll keep in touch with updates."

"Mind if I join you two?" Ace asked sheepishly. "I could use a mind-clearing ride."

"I think we all could, Diesel," Judge agreed. "We can also show Ciara the unity and protection the club can offer. It'd be a step in the right direction to let her know she can trust us. What do you think?"

"I'm good with that. If I get my way, she'll be riding with us for a long time." Diesel's entire persona relaxed.

"A piece of advice," Saint ventured to say. "When you ride, have her wear a lid. You get my drift?"

"Point taken, Saint."

They all rose from their seats. "Any idea where you're going?" Judge questioned.

"I was going to take her to the safe house, but things took longer than expected. Plus, I know she's hungry, just like I am."

"How's this? We'll take the long ride to Demons' Dungeon? Besides food, you two need to talk," Grave Digger laid out the route and added his advice.

"I get it. We will talk. Can you all get off my back now?" Diesel had taken enough of their busting on him for his poor decision. "Can we just go, *now*?" he emphasized.

The other men followed behind him. Ace mumbled to them, "Don't think I've ever seen Diesel this unsettled over a woman. He always has his shit together."

"Where women are concerned, no man ever really has his shit together. There are too many variables to try to figure out," Yankee commented. "Especially pregnant ones."

Saint high-fived Yankee, saying, "Amen, brother. I've been there."

Diesel stopped short, addressing Judge, "If you could, Doris is working Blossom Street by herself. She could use some help while Derek is out of commission."

"I'll send Bug, Chewy, and Crow. Let her know they will be at her disposal until further notice. Gentlemen, we've dropped the ball in this area. I want the club doing its part to help with the homeless. Pass it around. I want ideas brought to the table next church."

The men all agreed in unison with Judge. "I need to find those three and then we'll be out. Viking, you get in touch with Dancer and Bong, fill them in on their new assignment," Judge announced, affording Diesel a head start.

Ciara was standing at the end of the building, looking around the grounds. The large patio area was set up with a fire pit and barbeque grill, and seating was everywhere she looked. She turned to face the five-bay garage and in her peripheral vision she caught sight of Diesel approaching her.

Over his shoulder, she watched as the door to the clubhouse opened. Judge, as well as the other men from the room, followed him, along with three new men she had not met.

"I hope you don't mind, but my brothers would like to join us on our ride. You okay with that?" Diesel asked, trying to feel out her mood.

"That's fine, Diesel, and stop worrying about me. We both knew last night that the death of your sister could be an issue for us. To say I enjoyed finding out how much of an issue in a room full of unknown men, would be an understatement. But I think I get it, and after I realized what it was, it felt kind of nice."

Diesel wasn't exactly sure he understood her meaning. "What do you mean?"

"I mean, it felt nice to be part of a family again. You said it last night, the Demons are your family. You had a problem, and you went to your family for help. And you brought me, like I was part of the family."

He walked to her and kissed her then pulled back. "I'm going to make sure you always feel that way." He stepped back and watched a smile form on her face. "Saint made a suggestion after you left. He thinks you should wear a lid anytime we're on the bike." She gave him a confused look. "It will help with hiding your identity."

"That does make sense." She moved closer to the motorcycle while Diesel retrieved the helmet from the side bag. He handed it to her and then swung his leg over his motorcycle and settled onto the seat before starting it. While she strapped on the helmet, she yelled over the roar of all the motorcycles coming to life. "Where are we going?" When she had the helmet in place, she stepped on the footrest and pushed her leg through until she sat down behind him.

"You'll see, just sit back and enjoy the ride." Diesel pulled his bike in behind Hunter's as the group lined up behind

Judge. When everyone was ready, Judge led them off the compound and out onto the open road. "Hold on, Doc. Judge likes to blow out of the compound, then throttle down to cruising." He felt her arms wrap around his waist, pressing her chest against his back as they hit the pavement and Diesel hit the gas.

Chapter 6

hey rode for about an hour before Yankee, Ace, and
Saint pulled off with them at Demons' Dungeon,
while the rest of the riders went back to the club.
They followed Diesel around to the private parking area. The
surrounding area was lined with hedges, making it virtually
impossible to see anything beyond the thick brush-covered
branches. For added privacy, there was a solar panel-lined
roof that supplied the entire building with electricity. Diesel
parked his motorcycle and Ciara got off and handed him the
helmet. Separated from the other riders, Diesel led her to the
elevator. They stepped in when the door opened and rode up
the one floor in silence. When the door opened, Ciara moved
to leave, but Diesel stopped her. "I'm sorry for putting you in
that position earlier."

"I accept your apology." Releasing his grip on her arm yet
still holding his hand, she dragged him through the balcony
area. Her tone had a dramatic edge to it. "Right now, I need a
bathroom, a drink, and food, in that order." She pulled him to
the loft sliding door, dancing around, waiting for him to
open it.

He released the lock on the door and stepped to the side, as Ciara pushed her way past him and flew up the stairs. Diesel laughed at the sight of her. "You should have told me. We could have stopped," he yelled, closing the door and dropping the keys in the bowl on the stand. While she was upstairs, he went to the kitchen, pulled two beers from the refrigerator, then walked back into the living room.

He was seated on the couch when she stepped out onto the landing. "Whew, I didn't think I was going to make it." She descended the stairs and joined him on the couch. Removing her boots, she tucked her legs up underneath herself and accepted the beer he handed her. Tapping the long necks together, they each took long draws on their beers. "Ah, that's good." Ciara drew out, then took another sip. She relaxed back onto the couch. "You know this will not be easy."

"Maybe, maybe not." He paused, tipping his bottle back as he finished his beer and placed it on the table, then continued. "Nothing in this world is easy if it's worth having." He was about to elaborate but was interrupted by his phone. He pulled it out, looked at the screen, and saw it was his father. "I need to take this. It's my father." She nodded and Diesel got up from the couch and walked out onto the balcony.

Closing the door behind himself, he picked up the call and asked, "What's up, Dad?"

"The judge remanded him into custody while we wait for the DNA results. Preliminary trial Friday after next. I suggest you clear your schedule; we have some work to do."

"I've already informed Judge I'll be unavailable to the club until this case is over."

"And… Ciara?" his father asked.

"Is none of your concern."

"Romeo."

"No, Dad. You have no say in my personal affairs."

"I hope you know what you're doing," Javier expressed.

"What time tomorrow?" Diesel steered the conversation away from Ciara.

"How's ten?"

"See you then. Night, Dad." Diesel hung up the phone. Walking back into the living room, he tossed it on the table. "Well, the judge denied bail, and the preliminary trial begins in two weeks."

"Diesel, I'm at a loss here. There is so much at stake. Do you honestly think we can pull this off, without either of us getting screwed in the process?"

Diesel pulled her onto his lap. "My mother always told me, *'Life is full of opportunities, and with each one, there will be a degree of risk. The ones that have the most impact on your life will rely on your strength to overcome your fear because they are the ones that will matter the most.'* I think what we've started here matters. That's why I believe we will get through this and come out stronger on the other side." She started to interrupt, but he stopped her. "Hear me out. You work the night shift, correct?"

"Yes, you know that already."

"I'll be working with my dad during the day. I also have my responsibilities with the club. Technically, anytime we have in between all that will be our time. We've already agreed talking about the case is off limits. Besides, if I'm only going to have you for a few hours to myself, I intend to use them wisely." He pressed his palm to the back of her head, holding her in place as he kissed her.

When he pulled back from the kiss, a shy smile formed on Ciara's face before she teased him, "Well, when you put it like that, who am I to argue with you?" She pecked his nose with a kiss and was going to climb off his lap, but he held firm. "I need to go back down to your motorcycle. I left my backpack; I was in too much of a hurry earlier." This time when she moved, he let her get up.

"You stay here. I'll go get it." Diesel got up and moved

toward the door. "When I come back, I'd like you to join me in my playroom. After the day I've had, I need my sub tonight."

"Is the door open, Sir?" It was like a switch flipped; that fast, she was there to serve him. Reaching into the bowl next to the door, he pulled out the one she needed. Taking the key from his hand, she told him, "I'll be waiting for you, Sir." She dipped her head down and waited for him to leave. As soon as the elevator door closed, Ciara bolted to the playroom. For as much as Diesel needed her, she also needed him. Leaving the door to the playroom open, she moved into the room. Quickly removing her clothes and setting them off to the side, she positioned herself at the foot of the bed. Her back was to the door, kneeling, with her palms on her thighs, her back straight, and her head lowered, as she waited for him.

When Diesel returned, he set her bag down on the couch. He moved to his closet, hanging up his cut and removing his boots. Closing the closet door, he thought about removing his shirt, but his insecurities kept his hands at bay. He padded his way across the loft and stood observing her from the doorway. Being an owner of Demons' Dungeon had its advantages. It afforded him accessibility to Ciara's hard and soft limits. So, he knew her likes and dislikes, terms normally discussed before engaging in a Dom/sub relationship.

Ciara knew he was near because she heard his sharp intake of breath. Knowing he was watching her, sent a wave of pleasure to her core. It had been a while since she had been in this position. She could only pray he was pleased. He walked into the room, past her, to the dresser in the far corner. She heard him opening a drawer and closing it.

Diesel had gotten a brush and hair band. Coming up behind her, he grabbed her hair, brushing the knots free. He then braided it, telling her, "When you come into the playroom, I want your hair braided. Is that understood?" Diesel's voice lowered with his command.

"I will be better prepared next time, Sir." Ciara knew better than to leave her hair down, but she hadn't been sure how long he would be. She also knew he wouldn't want to hear her excuse.

Diesel finished the braid. Wrapping it in his fist, he yanked her head up, so she could see his above hers. "That's my good girl. Your safe word, Ciara, what is it?"

"It's orchid, Sir."

"Now we can begin. I want you in the middle of the bed, arms above your head, legs spread wide." He helped her up from her kneeling position and watched as she positioned herself the way he requested. Diesel walked to the left side of the bed, taking her wrist in his hand. He snapped the cuff on it. Moving to the other side, he repeated the same process. When both cuffs were secure, he walked to the head of the bed. Pulling the cable connecting them, he yanked Ciara's arms farther up and apart. Once that was set, he moved to the wall by the door, selecting one of the spreaders. Returning to the bed, he placed it in between her legs, fastening the cuffs to her ankles. He then adjusted her legs to the widest position and locked it in. Finally, he attached the spreader to the cable tethered to a pulley on the ceiling, pulling her legs up, leaving a beautiful view of her ass. He stood admiring the vision before him. Her head rested on the pillows, her mouth slightly ajar. Her breasts were pulled high, pushing her erect nubs up, begging for nipple clamps. But he would save those for another day. His eyes roamed to her apex, wide and wet, waiting for him to devour.

His cock had been hard since he had entered the room but feasting his eyes on her had made it painfully aware his jeans needed to go. He considered leaving his shirt on until he saw her head nod ever so slightly. He reached for the hem and pulled it over his head, tossing it to the floor. Again, looking to Ciara, seeing her smile of approval, blocked out his demons of doubt. Releasing the button on his jeans, he carefully lowered the zipper, freeing his hard, thick cock. After stepping out of his jeans, he went to the nightstand, removing a blindfold. Placing it over her eyes, he saw her disappointed frown. "Have no fear, I will remove it. But for now, I want you to give me your trust."

"You have my trust, Sir." Ciara's voice was soft. She relaxed on the bed, letting her other senses take over. She listened as he moved around the room. She could only guess that he was collecting various toys to use. Letting her head clear, she took a deep breath and exhaled slowly, freeing her mind from the day, the clubhouse, the ride, including trying to figure out what Diesel was doing. She allowed herself the freedom to simply feel and experience, when the light touch of a feather floated along her stomach, tickling her. A smile touched her lips as her body jerked in reaction, trying to move away from the sensation.

Diesel leaned close to her ear. "I will allow your movement this time, but next time I will not be so lenient."

A chill ran through her body as his sultry voice drifted to her ear. Ciara was better prepared as the feather drifted over her hard nipple ever so gently. She restrained her shoulder from pushing back on the bed, forcing her chest up to feel more. He then duplicated the same sensation on her other breast. Still, she held firm until she felt his mouth close over her areola, pulling a moan of desire from her and a slight shift of her hips, which might have gone unnoticed except for the jingle of the metal rings on the spreader, alerting him.

He removed his mouth from her chest, and before she could apologize, she felt the sting of a crop hitting her right ass cheek first, followed by four more alternating swats. Ciara knew she should apologize for disobeying him, but it had been some time since she had felt the sting of a crop, or anything else for that matter, on her skin. She was so wet, she felt moisture drip through the cheeks of her ass as she basked in the arousal she had been missing.

"Ah, my lovely doctor. Does the sting of my crop excite you?" Diesel collected the honey seeping from her body with his finger. Bringing it to his mouth, he allowed his tongue to lick it clean. "No need to say anything. I have my answer." He continued to use his mouth to nibble and lick her soft skin from her shoulders to her stomach and every piece of flesh in between. Each time his touch caused Ciara to flinch, his crop landed on her ass until it was a lovely shade of pink. Diesel then removed the blindfold, watching as her desire-filled eyes fluttered open, a radiant smile gracing her face. "My God, you're beautiful."

"I was just thinking the same thing," Ciara's passion-filled voice returned.

He leaned down, sealing his lips on hers. His tongue swept across hers, begging for entrance. Her response was immediate, allowing his tongue to dance passionately with hers. Diesel molded his hand around her breast, gently squeezing and releasing while he was finger flicking her nipple. His mouth left hers, but he continued to kiss her cheek, her chin, her neck, trailing a path to her chest. Stopping briefly to pay attention to her straining hard nubs, he resumed his trek down her body, tickling her again as his tongue rimmed her naval, once again making her body move, yet this time he allowed her to react without punishment.

Ciara reveled in the feel of him moving down her body. But when he moved away again, she raised her head. Watching him through the tiny slits her eyelids allowed, she followed him as he went to the end of the bed. He placed both hands on her ankles that were still locked in the spreader, grazing his fingers down toward her dripping pussy. His mouth was following in their wake, the whiskers of his beard creating goosebumps along her skin. He took his time, inch by agonizing inch, closer and closer, until he finally swiped his tongue through her wet lips. Her head flew back as a cry of relief escaped her mouth. The sensation was so raw! He had worked her body into a frenzy. Ciara knew she would not be able to hold back her orgasm if he continued to tease her. "Sir, may I have your permission to come?" Ciara panted the words out as she pulled her head up to look at him.

"No, my sweet Ciara, you will come when I give the command," Diesel murmured. Lowering his head, his hands on her thighs, his tongue licked along her hard clit. She was quick to react, and her hips pushed up for more. He knew it wouldn't take much to make her come, but he wanted to draw it out as long as he could. He removed his right hand from her thigh and slipped two fingers into her tight entrance. The tip of his tongue continued torturing her clit, his fingers working in unison, bringing her to the brink of the cliff, then pulling back before she careened over the edge. Finally, Diesel removed his fingers and stood up, his cock seeping pre-cum from the tip. He kneeled on the end of the bed, dipping his head below the bar. He pulled her hips forward, driving his hard cock deep inside her, pausing briefly to allow her body to adjust. Diesel's lust-craved eyes met the burning need of Ciara's.

"Can I touch you, Sir?" Ciara pleaded.

Without answering her, he put his hand on the bed. Using his other, he released the Velcro cuffs on her wrists. Before he could move away, Ciara stretched her neck up to kiss his chest. She then rested back on the bed. Her shoulders burned from her arms being restrained above her head. They needed the blood to circulate and flow before she could move them. First, she made fists and rolled her wrists. Diesel pulled out of her, then gently pushed back in. Next, she folded her elbows down, while Diesel replicated his movement. Finally, she stretched out one hand to his cheek and the other to his oblique. This time Diesel pulled out and plunged quickly back in.

Still new to her touch, he had not expected the electric shock that rocked his body. When she had kissed his chest, the current went straight to his dick, further surging him when her hands connected with his skin. He began rocking his hips faster, ramping both their bodies on, striving for that incredible release. Diesel's voice boomed out in the quiet room, "Come now!"

Ciara latched both hands onto his shoulders, her nails digging into his flesh, holding on fast as Diesel bucked his hips, stroking the smoldering embers into a blazing fury. He set a demanding pace, tunneling into her.

After all the prepping and edging, Ciara was more than ready. Feeling him inside her and being one with him, was unlike anything she could have dreamed. They moved in perfect unison, both straining to reach the plateau that would send them over the brink. She cried out as the pleasure overwhelmed her. Blinding, sparkling lights burst behind her eyelids as she surrendered her body to his command, yelling, "Oh my God, Diesel," as her orgasm spiraled out of control.

Diesel pumped into her a few more times, trying to hold off as long as he could, savoring her trembling body pulsating around his cock. That was until she called out his name, triggering an uncontrollable switch, driving his body to erupt. He pushed deep into her, followed rapidly by his hips banging into her with short, hard thrusts.

Ciara heard his throaty growl when he came. He then changed his thrusting pattern, coaxing her body into another maddening orgasm. Her arms dropped from his shoulders, spreading her arms wide as she clawed at the bedcovers, her chin tilted up toward the ceiling.

Diesel loved the look of ecstasy on her face. He wanted to always see that dreamy, satisfied expression. Her body glistened in the dim lighting, stray pieces of her long hair stuck to her body and her bewitching eyes glazed with bliss. She was a beautiful mess, but she was his beautiful mess, and he'd do anything short of going against his club to protect her. He pumped one more time into her and stayed there.

When she opened her eyes, she was looking up into his crystal blue eyes. Their breathing was erratic, but smiles touched both their faces. "Thank you, Sir," Ciara purred.

For as much as Diesel wanted to stay exactly where he was, he knew he needed to care for Ciara. He leaned down and kissed her, and when he moved away from her lips, he declared, "Thank you, my extraordinary sub." He pulled out of her and got off the bed. Then he went to the mini fridge in the corner of the room and withdrew a bottle of water. He cracked it open and took a long swig. Next, from the shelf above the fridge, he picked up a bottle of ibuprofen, shaking two pills out onto his hand. He walked back to the bed and held the pills out to her. After she accepted them, he handed her the bottle of water. He then moved to the end of the bed and reached for the line, lowering the spreader to the bed, easing it down gently. A slight moan of pain escaped Ciara's mouth. He held the bar in his hand, allowing the blood to flow slowly back into her legs. With the bar resting on the bed, he unclasped her ankles. Taking first the right ankle in his warm hands, he gently rubbed the area where the cuff had been. Then, he repeated the same process with the left ankle.

Ciara pulled her body up on her elbows to watch him. He had used caution when he released her legs. She hadn't felt the pins and needles until he lowered the spreader bar. With each section he lowered, more blood flooded her veins, causing her to moan slightly. Once he had the spreader lowered onto the bed, he immediately removed the cuffs, allowing the rest of the blood to reach her feet. Ciara was thankful for his warm hands rubbing the feeling back into her feet.

"Does that feel better?" He had watched her every expression, making sure he didn't miss a wince as he rubbed her legs.

"Yes, Sir, much better."

"Good, now flip over, I have some ointment I'd like to rub on that scrumptious ass."

Ciara grinned at him before she turned over. "Yes, Sir."

Diesel had picked up the bottle of lotion and squeezed some onto his hand. He tossed the bottle on the bed, then rubbed his hands together before laying them on each cheek and holding them in place after he felt her wince. "Lie still, Ciara, this will help." He then began applying it to her bruised ass.

Ciara wasn't prepared for the cool cream on his hands, making her flinch. However, Diesel didn't linger and began massaging her crop-marked derriere. She lay there silently as he administered her after care. But when he was finished, she swung her legs over the side of the bed, never expecting the tingling sensation that assailed her feet again.

"Where are you going?"

"I was going to get cleaned up," Ciara answered.

Before she could move any farther, Diesel was by her side, scooping her up in his arms. "I know we haven't spoken of your responsibilities in the playroom. So, I will give you a pass today, but in the future," he started walking out of the room with her in his arms, "you will wait for me, and I will carry you as I am now. First, because I will have put your body through a rigorous workout, and second, because I want to pamper my sub." Nothing pleased Diesel more than having her pressed up against his body. This was something he had always wanted to do, but since he had never brought a woman to his playroom or his loft, he never dreamed it would ever be possible.

Ciara smiled at him and wrapped her arms around his

neck, relaxing her head against his chest as she said, "I could get used to this."

"That's what I'm aiming for." He kissed her temple and laid her in their bed. "I need to take care of the playroom," Diesel let her know, before he walked away.

"While you do that, I will clean up."

"You sure your legs will hold you?" he asked with concern in his voice.

"Yes, Sir, I have the feeling back in my legs again. Don't worry, Diesel." Ciara took hold of his wrist. "I'll be right, be right back." She released his hand and made her way to the bathroom.

He smiled as she went up the stairs. When she was out of view, he went to his closet and picked out a pair of sweat shorts and a tee shirt, throwing them on. He picked up his phone as he made his way back to the playroom. Calling Colton, he ordered dinner and fruit to be sent up.

The food arrived just before Ciara came back down, wearing one of his tee shirts. She found him in the dining room, setting two beers down at their place settings. "Did you hear my stomach rumbling?" A lovely shade of red covered her face, embarrassed he might have heard it.

"No, but I heard your list when we arrived." Diesel held the back of the chair for her to sit down. Leaning over, he kissed her neck and mumbled, "Besides, it was my fault we were detoured." He stood and moved to the chair at the head of the table, removing one of the silver domes to expose a porterhouse steak and a loaded baked potato, with butter and sour cream. Under the other dome, was a cheeseburger platter with French fries and all the fixings, including onion rings and a pickle. "You choose."

Ciara looked at both, her mouth salivating. "They both look so good. Could we share?" Her eyes tilted up to his.

"I don't see why not, but I prefer to eat off my own plate."

He took his knife and sliced through the hamburger and then the steak. Once he did that, he switched one piece of each to his plate and did the same with the baked potato.

While Diesel cut the meat, Ciara also helped by picking up a handful of French fries and placing them on his plate. After they separated their dinner, they each chowed down. Once they had devoured their food, Diesel removed the dome of the third platter, revealing a bowl of fruit, with whipped cream and sauces in dipping bowls. Diesel placed the platter between them, took a strawberry and dipped it in the whipped cream, and held it out for her to bite.

Ciara leaned over, biting the section with the cream on it and moaning with delight, "Oh my, that is so good."

Diesel popped what remained of the strawberry in his mouth and agreed with her.

"Diesel, do you honestly think we can pull off this trial without either of us losing our job?"

"I can't answer that." He took her hand and pulled her from her chair onto his lap. "All I can tell you is I will do whatever I have to in order to keep Derek from a life in prison and you by my side."

Ciara took a piece of pineapple, dipped it in caramel and then through the whipped cream. She held it for him to bite, then popped the remaining piece in her mouth. "My grandmother used to say, *'If something is worth having, it's worth fighting for.'* I think you are definitely worth fighting for." She leaned forward, pecking the tip of his nose as she wrapped her arms around his neck, hugging him.

"We will have to be careful after this weekend. You know what would make everything much easier?"

"What?"

"If you stayed here for the next two weeks."

"That's a delightful idea, but I think this is too new for us to be living together. Besides, I just bought my townhouse."

Diesel was about to argue his point of view when his cell phone rang. Sitting her in his chair at the table, he went to retrieve his phone. Looking at the screen, he told her. "It's Judge, I need to answer this." She nodded her head in understanding as he picked up the call. "What's up, Judge?"

"Is Ciara still with you?"

"Yeah, why?" His eyes glanced her way.

"Rider just called. You were right about your feeling. When he arrived at the townhouse, he saw a person dressed all in black leaving. He tried to follow, but the guy lost him. I would suggest you let her know and don't let her go back until we find out what's going on."

Diesel turned away from her. "We were just discussing her staying here until after the preliminary hearing. Now, I have grounds to keep her here. Did Rider have any further information on the mystery person?"

"He believes he's a pro, by the way he snuck away and got into a nondescript car. I've told Rider to continue watching the townhouse in case they come back. But... Diesel, I think the good doctor has a stalker, not you."

"Shit, Judge, this is the last thing we need right now. Thanks for letting me know. I'll make sure Ciara stays here until we figure things out."

"Weren't you already planning on doing that?" Judge had a touch of amusement in his voice.

"Yes, but she has made her opinion known. She's not too keen on the idea." Diesel's eyes met Ciara's. "Now, she has no choice. I'll talk with you later, Judge." He hung up and tossed the cellphone back on the coffee table and walked back to Ciara.

"What was that all about?" Ciara knew they had been talking about her.

"Earlier, when we left your place, I thought someone was

watching us. Judge just confirmed that I was right. Why would someone be following you?"

Ciara gave him a blank look. "I have no idea. Could you give me a few more clues? Like, what did the person look like? Maybe it was just a colleague seeing if I was home."

"No, Ciara, they were walking out of your locked front door when Rider arrived. He tried to follow him, but whoever it was caught on and lost him." He looked at her bewildered face. "You seriously do not know who it could be?"

Ciara got up from the chair, telling him, "No, not a clue, but I'd like to go check on my place. Would you take me?" She walked past him toward her clothing.

Diesel stood in her path, gaining her attention. "Hey, it will be okay." He wrapped his arms around her, securing her body to his. "I'll take you home, on one condition." She raised her head off his chest to look at him. "You pack a bigger bag, throw it in your car, and stay with me until we know why someone would want to break into your home."

A slight chill ran through her body when he mentioned the part about a stranger in her home, her sanctuary. *Would it feel like home after this invasion of her privacy?* she thought before asking, "Can I answer you after I've seen my townhouse?"

"Doc, I was being polite by giving you an option." He changed his tactics, "Answer me this, do you honestly believe you will feel comfortable there tonight, or any other night, for that matter, not knowing what really happened? Alone!" His voice rose to make his point.

Ciara knew in her heart she would be on edge were she to remain there tonight for sure. She also knew if she stayed with Diesel, she might never want to leave. She stepped out of his arms and stood at arms' length, "I will agree to this week. After that, we renegotiate."

"Deal." Diesel knew she wasn't ready yet for the living

arrangement he had already envisioned. But... he would be patient until she was.

They then both threw on clothes and headed for her townhouse. Once they arrived and pulled into the parking space in front of her home, Rider walked over to talk to them before they could walk in. "Except for the chase, it's been pretty quiet." He looked toward Ciara. "I didn't go inside," he confessed, respecting her privacy. "Which means someone could still be in there."

Ciara stood a little taller, even though inside, her stomach was doing flip-flops at the thought of some stranger ransacking her house. And yet, on the outside, she kept her crap together. "Thank you for the report, Rider, and for keeping an eye on my place." She held her hand out to him. "I'm Ciara by the way."

Rider waited. Being a prospect, he needed to wait until Diesel had given his approval that would allow him to shake her hand. Rider then accepted her hand and introduced himself to her. "Nice to meet you, ma'am. They call me Rider."

"Ciara will be fine. Nice to meet you as well, Rider." She grinned at the tall, handsome man before her then shifted her attention to Diesel. "We should go see what the damage is." She removed her keys from her bag and started walking up the brick path to her front door. Diesel and Rider followed in her wake. When they arrived at the door, Ciara moved forward to put the key in the lock, yet her hands were shaking so much, she couldn't make the connection.

Diesel stepped around her, taking the keys from her hand, and opened the door. After the lock clicked, he handed her back her keys and then whispered to her, "Stay here with Rider until I tell you it's all clear. Understand?"

Ciara snapped out of the terrifying feeling that had gripped her. She focused her eyes on Diesel as she sternly whispered back, "I understand." She saw the slight cock of his eyebrow right before he disappeared down the dark hallway. While she and Rider waited outside, they watched as his shadow moved from downstairs to upstairs.

As he descended the stairs, he commented, "Honestly, I see nothing different from when I was here earlier." He flipped on the light switch as they walked inside. "But you would know better than I if something is out of place." He stood to the side and allowed her to pass, while he waited with Rider.

Ciara walked cautiously into her home, through all the downstairs rooms. She saw nothing out of place and made her way back toward them to climb the stairs to her bedroom. As she walked past, Diesel followed behind her. She arrived on the landing and flipped the light switch, illuminating the room. Her bed sat to the right of her, loaded with cream, gold, and light blue assorted pillows. Beyond that was a cream-colored lounge couch. Directly across from her, were the French doors that led out to her balcony. Across from the lounge to the left of them, was a fireplace with a large television mounted above it. Ciara glanced to the left at her vanity set. Two large towers with mirror doors framed a table, with a mirror above it, a chair below it, and a drawer for stationary in between. Resting on the table, was her jewelry box. Ciara's eyes had scanned the entire room and still could not see anything out of place. She left the landing and turned to the right. She walked down a short hallway, flipping on the light switch of her bathroom. After giving it a quick once over, she moved to her closet. She walked to the door at the end of the hallway and turned on the light. Straight in front of her, was a bench seat with a cushion on it and shoe cubbies below it, set in the wall below a double window. On either side of the window, were more shoe cubbies holding an assortment of women's footwear. The walls to the right and left, held drawers and racks holding her uniforms and the rest of her clothing.

Diesel let out a low whistle before commenting, "Damn, woman, you have more shoes than clothes."

As if she didn't hear his comment, she blurted out, "I don't get it. Nothing appears to have been touched." She pushed past him, turning off the light in her wake. She stood in the middle of the room and spun slowly in a circle, stopping when her gaze landed on the jewelry box. Her feet propelled her forward to stand in front of the vanity.

"What is it, Ciara?" Diesel asked as he came up behind her.

She needed to make sure before she answered him, "If I wasn't so anal about the placement of things, I would have never noticed it." She glanced over her shoulder and announced, "He was in my jewelry box. See this?" She waited for him to join her. "See this scratch." She pointed down to the vanity table. "The jewelry box is supposed to be covering it."

Diesel saw the mark she was talking about. "Well, it's not covering it now. Check and see what's missing."

Ciara lifted the lid and pulled out the tray. She then opened all the drawers, scanning each item. "I don't under-stand; everything is here. My grandmother's earrings, the emerald ring I bought in Jamaica, even my ruby necklace is still here."

"He had to have been looking for something more specif-ic." Ciara turned to look at him, and Diesel reached out, fingering the necklace around her neck. "Maybe he was looking for something with more meaning behind it."

Ciara's fingers slid down the chain, taking the locket from his hand and into her palm, turning it to see every side, looking for anything distinctive that would tell them he was right. "You honestly think this is what they were looking for?" She held it up to gaze at the diamonds that encircled the cross. "I always thought these were cubic zirconia. Do you think they could be real?"

"I'm not sure, but didn't you tell me your grandmother warned you to keep it safe?" Diesel probed. "You also told me there was a key in it that was in a safe deposit box. Maybe the key is what they were searching for," he pointed out.

"But... why? Who would even know about the keepsake, let alone the key?"

"I don't know, but we're going to find out. Will you now pack a bigger bag and stay with me at the club? At least until we know what's going on," Diesel calmly expressed, yet inside, he wanted to demand she stay.

Ciara knew it was the sensible thing to do, so she didn't hesitate with her reply. "I'll need a few minutes to pack." Diesel stood and watched as she flew around her room, picking out the items she would need to bring with her—skirts, jeans, shirts, and her uniforms for work. She selected five different pairs of shoes and all her toiletries. She then threw them into her suitcase. "If I forgot anything, I'll stop back tomorrow before work to pick it up," Ciara commented as she zipped the suitcase closed.

Before she could lift the suitcase off the bed, Diesel was at her side, relieving her. "I'll take care of this. Where are your keys?"

"I left them on the counter in the kitchen."

"And... which car is yours?"

"The blue convertible Mustang, it's in slip number forty."

"Okay, you ready to leave?" She looked around the area, shaking her head yes. He then guided her downstairs to where Rider was waiting for them. "Rider, I want you to drive Ciara's car back to Demons' Dungeon. I'll get Bug to pick you up and bring you back for your bike." Ciara started to protest, but he cut her off. "If they know where you live, they know what you drive. Rider will drive your car; you will ride with me."

Ciara was too exhausted and worn out to argue. "Fine, I

just want to get out of here," she voiced as she walked past him, out of her house.

Diesel closed and locked the door as the men followed behind her. "Ciara, wait for me by my motorcycle." He waited until she was out of earshot. "Rider, pay attention. Make sure you're not followed. If you feel someone is following, bring her car to the clubhouse, and I want a call when you get there. Understand?"

"No problem, Diesel, I'll keep an eye out. I'll make sure no one knows where Ciara is." He took her bag from Diesel's hand and added. "By the way, Diesel, she's a keeper."

"And... that's what I intend to do, Rider. I want you to become the good doctor's shadow, and I mean shadow. I don't want her to know you are keeping watch over her."

"You got it, Diesel. Text me her schedule, and I'll be a ghost in the wind," Rider reassured him.

"As soon as I have it, so will you."

"Catch you later." Rider took her bag and made his way to her car. He threw the suitcase into the trunk, then got in and left.

Diesel joined Ciara by his motorcycle and handed her a helmet. "I told Rider if someone is following him to bring your car to the clubhouse. That will throw your stalker off as to where you really are staying." She started to interject, but he stopped her. "Ciara, I will not play with your safety. Rider will borrow a cage and bring your bag over to the club."

Ciara gave him a confused look. "What the hell is a cage?"

Diesel chuckled. Lightening the atmosphere, he explained, "A cage is a vehicle or truck. Let's head back to my loft. It's been a long day for both of us." He got on his motorcycle. Turning the key, he ignited the roar of the engine. Ciara got on behind him, and they made their way back to Demons' Dungeon.

Chapter 7

"I swear I'm going to put a bounty out on the head of that little shit Boris," Konstantin Stepanov pronounced as he slammed the phone down on the receiver. Konstantin was next in line to become Pakhan of the Stepanov Gang when he could prove it.

"Have you heard from Alexsy?" Sasha asked.

Konstantin leveled his whiskey-colored eyes on Sasha. "Who do you think I was just talking to?" The snip in his voice was minor compared to the volatile outrage he normally used on someone who asked him a stupid question. Konstantin had grown up under the strict guidance of his father. He stood at six-foot-three, with severe cheekbones on his oval face and a goatee of dark auburn hair that was trimmed under his straight nose and around his chin. At sixty, he was still a handsome man and an opposing figure.

Konstantin was raised to be a strong but also a just leader. He was schooled in everything from English to blowing up cars. The biggest mistake of his life was leaving Russia to build his empire in America. His father had been less than pleased with his decision but said he understood. The day Konstantin was leaving, his father handed him a jewelry box. Inside it, was his late mother's jewelry. His father told him, "In case times get tough." And... then Konstantin had left his life in Russia behind.

When he had arrived in the United States, Konstantin established his residency in New York, found a job, and began studying to become an American citizen. He joined a study group, where he met Joslyn, his teacher. He had been fascinated with her; she was beautiful, single, and his passport to passing his test. They had started dating at the same time he was learning everything about America. That was until the day he attended the ceremony to take the Oath of Allegiance to the United States. Joslyn had attended with him, and they celebrated with dinner when Joslyn told him she had taken a pregnancy test, and the results were positive. He had almost choked on his food. He wasn't ready to be a father. He had so much he wanted to do that didn't include a wife and a child. Konstantin had told her all of this at dinner, including he wasn't ready to be a father. She had sat opposite him with tears trickling down her face, asking him what she was supposed to do. He had regrettably told her he didn't care if she kept it or had an abortion because, either way, he wouldn't be there. He had gotten up from his seat, threw some cash on the table and walked out. It had been the last time he had seen her. Konstantin had moved on to build his empire, amassing a small fortune, along with the notoriety and respect as the largest Russian gang in New York. His success mirrored the likes of his father's control in Russia. Konstantin knew one day he would run both the Russian and American gangs. He had lived in America, never looking back, until a few months ago when he had been called home by his ailing father.

Konstantin had sat with his father and listened while the older man had apprised him of the Russian Stepanov Gang's business. As the next Russian Pakhan, he needed this information. His father had unexpectedly turned his life upside down the night he had asked Konstantin to produce the locket from his mother's jewelry case. Konstantin regrettably told him he no longer had it in his possession and asked of its importance.

His father explained, "For generations, we have handed the locket down to the next Pakhan. In recent years, we began inserting a key inside the piece of jewelry. The key opens the safe deposit box holding the last will and testament of the present leader, along with the Stepanov family ring, a rare two-carat alexandrite octagon-cut stone, surrounded with two rows of baguette diamonds, in a band of rose gold. Without it, anyone can challenge your right to run the gang."

Konstantin had felt the weight of his father's words every moment of every day until his father died. He knew who had taken the locket, yet he had no idea where she was. He then began searching for Joslyn, only to find no information on the woman from the time they had separated. It was like the woman had simply never existed.

And then like a beacon of light in the middle of the night, they found a match to his DNA sample. Sending his errand boy, Alexsy, was the first step in his plan to recover what was his. Konstantin believed he had finally found Joslyn, only to be told that Alexsy had found, instead, a woman in her thirties and no locket, on top of being seen and followed when he tried to search her townhouse.

"I should have sent you, Sasha. Sometimes the incompetence of Alexsy is mind-blowing."

"What do you want to do now, boss?" Sasha inquired. Sasha was Konstantin's second and bodyguard as well. He stood at six-foot-seven, with blue eyes and light brown hair, and the body of a brick house.

"I think it's time we take a trip back to the States. I need to check on things in New York. While we're there, we'll check in on this woman in South Carolina. I need to find out for sure what Alexsy was talking about."

"I'll make the arrangements, boss. When do you want to leave?"

"As soon as possible. I need that locket, and this woman is my means to retrieving it."

"You got it, boss. I'll take care of everything," Sasha promised.

Konstantin sat behind his desk. "Let me know when it's time to leave. I have some loose ends to tie up before we depart." Once Sasha had left, Konstantin moved to the bar and poured a drink. He took a sip from the glass, pondering his time with Joslyn. He couldn't blame her for taking the locket. He had left her with nothing but a baby in her belly. Konstantin had thought for sure Joslyn would have sold it to have an abortion. Now, this other woman held his DNA. Could she possibly be his daughter and if so, could he merely ask for the locket and leave? And that was if she even had it.

He couldn't help but wonder if this woman was possibly his child. He wondered what she was like. Who she looked like? If she took after her beautiful mother? Did she look anything like him? He finished his drink, leaving the glass on the bar. Picking his jacket up from the chair, he walked across the room, opened the door, and switched the light off. "Well, I'm going to find out, one way or the other," Konstantin said out loud to the empty room as he closed the door.

The two weeks before the trial had flown by for Ciara, between working at night and her days with Diesel. Due to the fact that she had been subpoenaed to appear for the prosecution, she had been given the night off from work to prepare. The two had managed to keep the court case separate from their relationship and under wraps from any prying eyes. And as much as she wanted to spend the night with Diesel, he needed to be in attendance at Demons' Dungeon. Ciara decided she would spend the night at her townhouse. She sent Diesel a text letting him know what she was doing and then packed her things. When she was ready, she stood by the elevator looking around his loft. She had enjoyed staying here and could see herself living here. Yet Diesel had made no mention of making this a permanent arrangement after the trial.

Rider had watched after her home every night that she had been at Diesel's and reported back to them each day that everything had been quiet. This gave her the confidence to move back home. She picked up her bag and stepped into the elevator as two tears slid down her face.

Diesel had received her text. He didn't like the idea but understood her reasoning behind it. He knew Rider would watch over her and protect her with his life if necessary. He texted her back that he wanted a call from her when she got home and resumed what he was doing as he waited to hear from her. Diesel had gotten involved with a problem at the club and lost track of time when he next looked at his phone for her text and found none. According to his watch, it was nearing one o'clock in the morning. He then dialed her phone, but it just rang and then went to voicemail. He assumed she had forgotten and gone to sleep. He dialed Rider's phone for an update and received his voicemail as well. At that moment, Diesel knew something wasn't right, so he called Judge.

"Have you heard from Rider today?" Diesel asked when Judge picked up.

"Well, hello to you too, Diesel," Judge sarcastically commented.

"Stop fucking around, Judge, have you heard from him or not?"

"No, Diesel, I haven't heard from him. What's up?" Judge's tone quickly changed.

"I can't get a hold of Ciara or Rider."

"Rider probably didn't hear his phone, and Ciara should be at work. Correct?" Judge questioned.

"No, she's not at work. They gave her the night off. She sent me a message earlier that she was going home for the night. She was supposed to text me when she got there, but I lost track of time with shit at the club, and I haven't been able to contact her," Diesel explained.

Judge's commanding voice came thru the receiver, "What the hell were you thinking, letting her leave tonight? You knew things weren't right at her house! Get your shit together and meet us at Ciara's."

"I never wanted her to leave in the first place, but it wasn't my choice," Diesel threw back at him. "But… that's not the issue right now. We have to find her."

"Don't jump to any conclusions yet. We still don't know if there is anything really wrong. She could be sound asleep in bed." Judge tried to sound optimistic.

"Sorry, my mind has already moved to the worst possible outcome," Diesel confided in him. "I'll meet you at Ciara's." He hung up and found Colton. "I need to leave; I can't get in touch with Ciara or Rider."

"No worries, boss, we have everything under control here now. Go take care of what you need to." Colton started walking with Diesel to the door. "I'll keep trying to reach her." When they reached the front door, Colton pulled his phone from his pocket and added, "Don't worry. Ciara will be fine. She's a smart and strong woman, Diesel."

"Thanks for the pep talk, Colton. I'll let you know what's going on as soon as I know." Diesel flew out the door and got on his motorcycle.

He made it to Ciara's in record time. When he arrived, Judge, Yankee, Viking, and Ace were already there and were standing around a dazed Rider. Diesel didn't stop by them, but headed straight for her door, which he found was still locked. He glanced back at his brothers before kicking the front door open. He walked into Ciara's house yelling her name. He climbed the stairs two at a time. Then, standing on the landing, he surveyed the destruction of her bedroom.

As he stood there, the others entered the house. Diesel turned from the bedroom and met them in the disastrous kitchen. Doors to the cabinets were open, food, dishes, and glassware were scattered everywhere. The doors to the refrigerator and stove were open as well. Diesel picked up a knife from the floor and, seeing blood on it, shot his anger toward Rider. "What the fuck happened, and where the hell were you?" Diesel's voice thundered.

"I'm sorry, Diesel. One minute I was watching the lights go off in her place, and the next thing I knew Judge was kicking me awake. I swear to God I didn't fall asleep," Rider pleaded, holding his head.

"It's true, Diesel. We found him on the ground. They left a huge rock next to him with blood on it," Judge defended Rider. "Try to calm down, so we can figure out what happened."

"Isn't it obvious? Someone came in and took her, and by the way this place looks, she put up one hell of a fight." Holding the bloody knife up, Diesel's voice filled with anguish. "Or is this her blood?" A flash back to when he had been held captive ran through his mind. A cold sweat began to take over his body, and he started to hyperventilate.

Ace pushed his way past everyone, grabbing Diesel by the

shoulders, and began quietly talking to him. "Diesel, it's me, Ace. I need you to calm your breathing down for me, brother. Ready? Breathe with me." When Diesel's blank blue eyes focused on Ace's face, he continued talking, "That's it, Diesel. You're not with Vito. You're in Ciara's house." Ace waited until he knew Diesel was himself again before removing his hands. "Better?" he asked.

Diesel looked around the room at his brothers. It had been a while since he had allowed what had happened to him to take control over his thinking. However, the similar circumstances with Ciara had triggered it. He bowed his head with embarrassment, then spoke up. "I'm sorry, guys. I really thought I had my PTSD under control."

"Diesel, if this is going to dredge up old memories, maybe it's better if you sit this one out. We'll find out what the hell happened to Ciara," Judge suggested.

If looks could kill, Judge would have been a pile of ash. "There is no fucking way I'm sitting this one out. I can keep my shit together. Now, let's move on. How are we going to find her?"

"I'm thinking one of her neighbors might have a way to help in that area." Saint spoke up. "I noticed a few cameras by some of their doors."

"Well, what are we waiting for? Go wake them up and see." Diesel jumped on the idea.

"Diesel, you know what time it is?" Saint politely asked.

"Do you really think I give a shit what time it is? The sooner we look at whatever the cameras might have caught, the sooner we can find her," Diesel railed back at him.

"He's got a point, Saint. I want all of you to go door to door and see what you can find out. Diesel and I will sift through the rubble and see if she left any clues," Judge ordered.

Diesel watched as his brothers left to do as Judge

commanded, then he turned to face Judge. "I told you what I went through. I don't want her to suffer the same outcome. We need to find her."

The torment in his voice tore at Judge's heart. If Skylar had been taken, Judge knew he wouldn't be as leveled-headed. "We'll get her back. Now, start looking for anything that might help."

Diesel looked at the mess. "You take down here. I'll head back to her bedroom." He climbed the stairs and stood, looking. Using the flashlight on his phone, he began searching for anything that would tell him where she might be. He started with her dresser, seeing her jewelry box ripped apart. He then moved over to her bed, finding the charger for her phone, but no phone. Turning his phone over, he dialed her number, then waited. He heard the ringtone from her phone in the room and followed the sound. He moved to the opposite side of the bed and kneeled down. Pulling the bedding out of the way, he found her ringing phone and despair drenched his senses. He picked up the phone and examined it to see if she had made any calls after she had gotten home. What he found was a voice recording. He took the phone and ran back downstairs, yelling for Judge, who met him in the hallway. "Listen to this."

Ciara woke to the sound of muffled voices. From what she could hear, it sounded like they were speaking Russian, like they did at her house. She listened closely and, at the same time, tried to figure out where she was. She opened her eyes cautiously, not wanting them to know she was awake yet. The room was dimly lit, allowing her to move her eyes back and forth, avoiding detection as she searched for her captors. She tried moving her hands and feet but found them bound. When she looked in the direction of the doorway, she could make out the silhouettes of two men sitting at a table playing a card game. Ciara tested the bindings on her hands to see if she could slip out of them, but they were too tight. Saving her energy, she gave up trying for the moment and relaxed on the bed. Through the door, she could see a living room and kitchen. She turned her head and looked around the large room she was in. An open plan bathroom was to the right of her, and a balcony to her left. A television was positioned above the fireplace in front of the bed. Ciara then stared at the ceiling, trying to remember what had happened.

She had just shut her light off and was settling into bed to watch the news when she heard a thud in her living room. She had thought about calling Diesel, but she knew he was working and didn't want to disturb him for what was probably nothing. So, she had gotten out of bed with her cellphone in her hand and went to investigate the noise herself. But as she stood on the landing, she caught a glimpse of a large man headed her way. Taking a deep breath to calm her nerves, she ran back to her bed. She knew she had no time to call anyone, so she set her phone to record and hid it by her bed, praying Diesel would find it. She then lay back and waited for her opportunity to strike. Ciara turned her head toward her dresser and waited for his arrival. She had watched as the large man went to her dresser and opened her jewelry box, taking everything out then and tossing it on the surface of the dresser. When he didn't find what he was looking for, he slammed the box down, making Ciara jump. He then turned toward the bed where she was, and through slitted eyes, she watched his approach. When he was within her reach, she sprang up on her bed, kicking him in the sternum and knocking him back on his ass, gasping for breath. She jumped off the bed and started running for the stairs, but he grabbed her ankle, causing her to fall to the floor.

While he still had hold of her ankle, she yelled at him, "I

don't know who you are, but believe me, I will not make this easy on you." The man started mumbling something in what had sounded Russian to her. Ciara then flipped over and kicked him square in the face with her other foot. He let go of her and she scrambled to her feet and dashed downstairs, where she encountered another man in her living room. This man was larger than the other one. He caught sight of her and moved in her direction. She ran to the kitchen and grabbed a knife from the wooden block then stood her ground, waiting for him to approach.

She held back, biding her time to strike at the precise moment. They circled one another for a few steps and then the man reached for her wrist. Ciara didn't hesitate as she brought the knife down and sliced it across his palm, leaving a gaping gash.

"You fucking bitch. If you weren't so important to my boss, I'd kill you right here!" the man shouted with the same accent as the other one.

"Who the hell are you, and what the fuck do you want?" Ciara held the knife out, warding him off from getting any closer.

The intruder grabbed one of her kitchen towels, opening the oven door as he did, and wrapped it around his hand. "We were sent to bring you back with us," he told her, as the other intruder joined them, one of his eyes nearly swollen shut.

"Bring me back to where? Who the hell are you?" Ciara screamed at them. Her hands began to tremble as her adrenaline started to wane. She tried looking for an opening. *If I can only get to the back door, I can lose them in the brush by the beach.* She saw an opportunity when the man she'd cut began speaking Russian to the other one. She bolted over the extended counter.

That was when the man she cut blurted out, "You have

something that doesn't belong to you. We are here to collect it, and you. Your father wants to meet you."

The words reverberated in her head, *My father, my father, how? After all these years.* The shock of his statement caused her to stumble. Ciara fell to the floor, the knife sliding out of her reach. As she tried to get to her feet, the other man roared forward, tackling her down to the ground, and that was the last thing she remembered.

Ciara began thinking of what the man had said and wondered how they could possibly know who her father was when she didn't even know? Her thoughts then flipped to questioning where she was and when this meeting would take place. She quickly closed her eyes when she heard the outer door open and close.

"Why hasn't she woken up yet? The boss is getting impatient," the voice growled in broken Russian.

"I don't know. Alexsy is the one who tackled her. I was just the driver," another voice boomed out in perfect English.

Ciara heard someone approaching the room and twisted her head in that direction. She slit her eyes open enough to try to see what the man looked like. He was tall, with light hair, a square jaw, and a straight nose. Her eyes ran down to his hands and saw a fresh bandage on one. This was the man who had been in her house last night. A man who seemed to have a lot of power. Ciara knew if she stayed quiet, she would never find out what the hell was going on, so, she made a mewling sound, catching his attention. She moved her hands and feet, groaning as pins and needles assailed her body parts.

"I see you're waking up." His voice pierced the quiet room as he entered and turned on the lights.

Ciara opened her eyes, quickly closing them, fluttering her eyelids against the bright light. Once her eyes adjusted, she focused them on the man standing in the doorway. "You were at my house last night. Where have you taken me?"

The man held up his hand as he responded, "Yes, I was, and I have a little reminder of it."

"Can you remove the ropes? They are cutting off my circulation." Ciara held up her hands.

"After the damage you did last night, I don't think so."

She let her arms fall to her body. "You also mentioned knowing my father. How is this possible? You're apparently Russian by the sound of your accent, or were you lying?"

"Very observant, and as far as your father is concerned, I will let him explain."

"And is this how I'm supposed to meet him?" She held her hands up again. "Tied and bound."

"If I had my way, that is exactly how you'd meet him. However, when you go before my Pakhan, your ties will be removed. But... if you try to hurt him in any way, daughter or not, I will kill you. Do you understand?"

Ciara heard the menacing edge in his voice and knew he wasn't lying. "I will be on my best behavior," she answered sarcastically. "When will the meeting take place? I have a trial I need to get to and have no time for this." She knew she was pushing his buttons because she saw the anger appear on his face.

"Why, you insolent, stupid woman! You are about to meet one of the most important men in Russia. You will show him the respect he deserves, or I will..." His voice trailed off when she cut in.

"You'll what? Beat me, starve me, kill me? I think after I speak with my father, none of that will be an option."

"You foolish girl, you have no idea what kind of man your father is."

"But I will, as soon as you take these fucking ropes off and bring me to him." Ciara was tired of the head game this man was playing with her.

"Watch your tone, Doctor." He watched her eyes get

round. "You will show your father respect when you are in his presence. Do you hear me?"

Ciara was a little unsettled that he knew she was a doctor, but hell, why not? They knew where she lived. She kept her tone even and casual. "Respect? Respect is earned, not given. It's the same as trust. However, I will mind my manners as my *grandmother*," she stressed and drew the word grandmother out, "taught me."

He moved to the end of the bed and removed the bindings so she could walk. When she held her hands out, he told her, "Those, we will keep in place until I know you will not attack my boss." He moved away from the bed, allowing her to sit up and swing her feet to the floor. She sat there for a moment while the blood rushed back to her feet. The dull throb drumming in her head felt like a full-on college band playing when she sat upright. Ciara took a minute as she talked herself out of getting sick. As soon as her stomach settled, she slowly stood. She looked down, finally realizing they had dressed her in a pair of sweatpants and thrown a sweatshirt on over her pajamas. "Well, I'll give you some credit, at least you thought to throw some clothes on me," Ciara snipped at him.

"I would not present you to your father in your nightwear, dressed like a streetwalker." He moved forward to take her by the arm and guide her from the room.

Ciara looked at the table where the two men were playing cards. She spotted the other man who had taken her from her home. His eye was now open but had changed to a rainbow of colors. "How's the eye feeling, asshole?" she taunted as they walked past to the door. The man shot up from his chair, knocking it over.

"Sit down, Alexsy," the man walking with her shouted.

Alexsy said gruffly, "That bitch deserves a good beating."

In the blink of an eye, the man escorting her flew across the room, taking Alexsy by the throat and pinning him to the table. "Threaten the daughter of Konstantin again, and they will never find your body."

"Come on, Sasha," Alexsy choked out. "You know she deserves one for what she did to us."

Sasha banged Alexsy's head on the table again. "Shut your fucking mouth, Alexsy. I'm done warning you." Sasha shoved the man's head to the table one more time, then let go of him and returned to Ciara. Grabbing her elbow and guiding her out the door, he barked at her, "Let's go before you start any more trouble."

Ciara jolted forward as he tugged her out the door. She looked around, seeing they weren't at a hotel as she had thought. He dragged her along a paved path lined by beautiful flowers and bushes. When they were coming to the end, Ciara began to make out the main house, which was anything but a house. This was an enormous mansion. A lawn of green grass drew her eyes to the massive private house. They approached the stone stairs, guiding them up to the outdoor patio and pool area. If Ciara hadn't been scared out of her mind at the moment, she would say the place was absolutely gorgeous. But in a few minutes, she was going to meet a man claiming to be her father, and she couldn't control the butterflies that were fluttering in her stomach. Seeing the kind of company he kept, Ciara could only surmise that he wasn't a good man. Yet, she struggled with the little girl inside her who still wanted to believe he had a place for her in his life. Why else would he go through all this trouble finding her?

Sasha guided her through a set of French doors and into a large, open den area. Adjusting her eyes again, she scanned the elegant interior. On the right-hand side, was a bar that took up the entire wall. To her left, were tables set before a large sitting area built into the wall. Straight ahead of her, was a fireplace with a television above it and a long black couch before it, as well as one other attached at the end, making an L-shape.

Ciara saw the back of a lone head sitting on the couch with his arms spread out across the top of it. His hair was dark with auburn highlights mixed in. As they walked closer, she could see his profile and noticed his relaxed posture. She could also see his goatee that brought out his severe cheekbones. When she was finally standing in front of him, their eyes met, and Ciara had found the one obvious thing they had in common, whiskey-brown colored eyes.

"Sasha, remove the bindings; I'm sure Ciara will be a good girl."

Ciara held her hands out once again, and this time Sasha took a knife and cut the rope. Once he removed the remnants of her ties, she rubbed her wrists.

"Come sit by me, Ciara." He spread his right hand toward the couch. "Would you like something to drink?"

Ciara hesitantly sat down near him. "Anything in a sealed container." She wasn't taking any chances of being drugged.

"You can relax, Ciara. I have no intention of hurting you. I'd like the chance to get to know you. I'm Konstantin Stepanov, and according to the DNA results I received, you are a ninety-nine percent match to be my daughter. I've been searching for you for years."

Sasha handed her a bottle of water. She opened it and took a long sip before answering him. "You've been searching for me? Really? Why? Because you couldn't be bothered with me when I was born?" Ciara noticed that this man, who claimed to be her father, spoke perfect English, with only a touch of a Russian accent. "How do I even know if you really are my father? You may have received some kind of notification, but I haven't."

"If you're questioning the results, we could always take

another test. Or you could just tell me where the locket is." He observed her face carefully for a reaction.

Ciara resisted the urge running through her to touch the necklace around her neck, grateful they had not found it. Now, she knew what he really wanted. "Why is a locket so important to you?" she asked, needing to know the relevance of it. "Describe it to me."

"So, you know what I'm talking about, eh?" When she didn't answer, he went on to portray it in great detail. "The locket is made of Tungsten. At the top, there is a metal cross that a chain can slide through, and a two-carat diamond rests in the center of it. The locket itself has another cross on top of it, edged by a ring of twelve more diamonds. A box clasp holds the locket closed." Konstantin could tell by her expression, she knew exactly what he was talking about. "Where is it, my darling daughter?"

Ciara couldn't believe the accuracy of his description. "I may know where such a necklace can be found. But first, I want to know why you want it. What does it mean to you?"

Konstantin could feel his daughter was as cautious as he was, and until she heard the answer she wanted, he could sense that she wouldn't budge on its location. Her response to the question made him realize he couldn't help but feel a connection with her. "I understand, Ciara. You want to confirm the reliability of my words. Unlike anyone I have ever met, I will give you my trust, because you are my daughter. I will explain myself. The locket holds a key," he heard her slight gasp, but continued on, "it opens a safe deposit box with my father's last will and testament and the Stepanov Gang ring. I need what's in the safe deposit box more than I need the necklace—a necklace that was stolen from me." Konstantin could see her anger building; he knew if he poked her hard enough, she'd tell him everything he needed to know. "It was never supposed to be in your mother's possession in the first place. She stole the necklace, like she stole you."

Ciara immediately snapped back, "That's not the story I was told."

Konstantin had poked at her loyalty to her mother and had won, prompting her anger. He liked his daughter's spunk, but he wasn't fond of her stubbornness. "And... what was the story you were told?"

Ciara knew she had just confirmed her knowledge of the necklace, but she didn't care. She would not let him slander her mother. "My mother told me that the minute you found out she was pregnant with me, you left her."

"That's true. I had an empire to build, and I wasn't ready to be a father," Konstantin admitted. "But that didn't mean I didn't want you. And although I left, I realized it was a mistake. Yet, when I returned to find the both of you, you were gone. It was as if neither of you had existed. Now, I know your mother changed her name to hide you from me and that's why she disappeared." He paused for a moment. "I tried for years to find you." He leaned forward, placing his forearms on his knees.

Ciara watched Konstantin as he explained his view of how things went. She had no way of knowing if what he said was true, so she tested her theory. "Or were you simply looking for this?" Ciara reached for the chain around her neck, pulling the locket free from her shirt.

Konstantin's eyes grew big, and he sat straighter in his chair. He wanted to snatch the necklace off her neck but knew he needed to gain her trust. At least enough trust for her to give him the locket. "I will not lie to you. When I found the locket missing, it was my motivation to search for your mother."

Ciara took note of how the man had practically drooled when she had shown him the locket. "But... why is it so important to you?" She tucked the piece of jewelry back in her shirt.

"I told you, it's not the locket itself, but the key inside it. There was a key inside it, correct?"

"There was, but I had no idea what it was for, so I put it in a safe place," Ciara answered him. "Why do you need it now, after all this time?"

"My father, your grandfather, recently passed away. Before he died, he informed me that the key to the safe deposit box holding his will and the ring was in that locket." He pointed to her chest. "You see, my father had given it to me in my mother's jewelry box. I knew how precious the necklace was to my mother, and he knew I'd never sell it. He knew I'd keep it for its sentimental value, and I did. To my naivety, I never looked inside the locket, so I had no knowledge of the key's existence. When I told my father your mother had removed the locket from the jewelry box, he almost killed me. Since then, I expanded my search. I did a DNA search just in case Joslyn didn't abort the child."

"Don't you mean since you rejected my mother?" Ciara would not allow him to slander the woman who gave up everything for her, including her life.

"You have your version, I have mine, and I hope to change your opinion of me if you will give me the chance. Anyway, I need the key to get the ring and prove to all that I am Pakhan, of the Stepanov Gang, along with my father's will."

Ciara had no idea if he was telling the truth, but the desperation he displayed left her with little doubt. Had her mother really changed their names to keep Konstantin away from them? That was going to the extreme unless a person was in witness protection. Yet, the way he had gone about acquiring the key was causing Ciara to have tremendous doubts. "And you believe that sending your lackeys to my house was the way to go about this? Breaking into my house and scaring the shit out of me? Not to mention the disaster they left behind in their wake. I think a phone call would have sufficed. Hell, even coming to my house and knocking on the door would have been better. You can't sit there and tell me that if they had found the necklace, we would be sitting here having this conversation?" Ciara's emotional side was starting to show. "You would have gotten what you had come for and disappeared without a word. Do I have that correct?"

Konstantin looked at his beautiful daughter. When Alexsy had returned empty-handed, he knew this meeting would be unavoidable. He had formed an opinion before meeting her, and this woman was not what he had expected. At first, the key was all that was important to him. But the more he sat with her, the more he wanted to get to know her. Still, he knew she had no place in his life. She would become a weakness, or worse, a target if the other bosses found out about her. "Yes, you are correct, but let me explain." Explaining himself was a foreign concept to Konstantin. "By us meeting, in my line of business, it now puts you on the radar for anyone wanting to take my place or hurt me. Something that would have never happened if my men had simply found the locket, yet here we are."

"So, rationalize for me, what kind of business puts targets on people's backs?" She wanted to hear him say it.

Konstantin's eyes flashed to Sasha, who was sitting at the bar, his head already shaking in a negative manner. Although Sasha had been a trusted friend and confidant for years, Konstantin didn't always take his advice. "My business is a part of a complicated world. It would be too much to explain right now. However, if I don't have possession of the Stepanov ring, I may not have a business."

Ciara had a feeling he was going to dodge the question and rose from her seat. "Then I believe we are done here," she expressed as she started walking toward the exit.

Konstantin stood up quickly, blurting out, "You get a quarter of your grandfather's estate, which is quite substantial." He dropped that bomb, hoping it would get her to stay.

"Seriously," she shouted. "You honestly believe I care about some inheritance from a man I never knew. Listen up, Konstantin," she used his given name, "I've had enough of this crap." Ciara had no idea where all her courage was coming from, but she was going to use every ounce of it. "This has been nice," she fluttered her hands between the two of them, "but I have a trial I need to get to, where a man's life is at stake. So, tell your man here to drive me home now, or I'll call someone I know who will have no problem coming to pick me up."

"Yes, I know all about your biker friend and his club, the Celtic Demons. They have a very successful rate for running businesses. Yet, it would take an army to get past my security."

"Fine, then your man here can take me." She directed her command Sasha's way. "Let's get going. I hope they haven't yet requested a continuance for the trial." Neither man moved from their spots. Ciara stood in the doorway to the room and placed her hands on her hips as she berated both of them, "Look, I don't give a shit what you need right now. If you're smart, you will tell Sasha," she said his name with a sneer, "to get his ass moving because if I don't make this trial, you don't get that key." She announced it loudly, bribing him with what he wanted most. "Your choice, gentlemen."

"You have no right to demand anything." Sasha yelled, defending his Pakhan.

"Sasha," Konstantin shouted, "you will not raise your voice to my daughter. Besides, she has a point. She has some place to be, and we have interrupted her plans." Sasha looked at Konstantin as if he had two heads. No one spoke to the boss like that without ramifications. "Give me a minute to change, and I'll be right with you." Konstantin walked past her and out the door as he headed for the staircase.

"Are you serious? There's no reason for you to come with me to court. It has nothing to do with you," Ciara shouted to him, with a touch of panic in her voice. She was trying to get away from him with the only excuse she had. Once she was at court, Diesel would be there to help, but right now the odds weren't in her favor.

"Yes, I'm being serious. I would love to see my daughter in action." Konstantin's voice was filled with pride.

"The only thing I'm doing in court today is testifying to doing an autopsy."

"Yes, I understand this is not your actual profession, but like you said, your testimony could put that man in jail for the rest of his life," Konstantin yelled over his shoulder as he left her standing in the hallway. "I'd like to watch that." This time he almost sounded jovial.

Ciara stood with her mouth dropped open to the floor. Konstantin's determination to accompany her to the hearing left her totally confused about this man.

"I will warn you once, Doctor, don't disrespect that man again. You don't understand the pressure he is under to retrieve that ring."

Before Sasha could continue with his threat, Konstantin came down the stairs in a black Valentino suit. A black and gray tie ran precisely over the buttons on his pressed gray shirt. Ciara had to blink from the shine on his Armani shoes. Add a Fedora, and he'd look like a character from the Godfather. "Sasha, could you pull the car around? We need to get Ciara to the courthouse."

Sasha gave Ciara a look, telling her that their conversation wasn't over. "Yes, sir, right away." Then he turned and left them alone.

Konstantin walked over to Ciara, asking, "Are you ready to leave?"

Ciara looked him up and down. "Is this your court attire? Because you look like you're going to walk the red carpet at the Emmy's."

"I have a reputation to uphold. Now, should we go? I believe we should swing by your loft and let you change as well. We wouldn't want you showing up to court looking like that." He put his arm out to escort her to the car, but she left him standing there. As she approached the main door by herself, a housemaid opened the door for her. They walked to the black Bentley, and another person opened the door. They entered the car and sat back on plush leather. "Sasha, take us to Ciara's townhouse."

"Yes, sir." Sasha put the car in drive and pulled down the long stone driveway and out the private gate. They hadn't turned out the driveway before they drove up to a wall of motorcycles in front of them, slowing them down to a stop. As they sat in the car staring down this face-off, another group of motorcycles came up behind, blocking them in.

"It seems your boyfriend has come looking for you. Shall we go see what it is they want?"

Diesel, Judge, and Rider, along with any other Celtic Demon available, had scoured Ciara's neighborhood, looking for any neighbor who had a security camera that captured what had happened after they took her out of the house. They then went back to the clubhouse to piece it all together. They found one camera that showed two men carrying her to a waiting vehicle, where they threw her in and drove away.

Saint then checked the feed from his gym on Main Street in town and saw them taking her out of town. He hacked into the city's cameras, finding the car driving toward Myrtle Beach. Once the car was on the highway, he lost them. Saint then searched for houses in the Myrtle Beach area that had been purchased or rented recently. He had found several, however, only one had been purchased, and the new owner had a Russian name. Diesel had filled Saint in on his belief that Ciara could be of Russian descent. Saint found that Konstantin Stepanov was listed on the deed, prompting him to do an extensive search on the name, and he informed Judge and Diesel of what he had found. "It's not good, my friends," Saint had commented finally.

Diesel had listened intently as Saint had filled them in on Konstantin's past and present. His association with the Russian mafia stuck out with every word Saint had uttered. Extortion, drugs, gambling, prostitution, the list went on.

"Fuck!" Diesel yelled. "How the hell am I going to get Ciara back from him, and why the hell does he want her in the first place?"

Judge had listened to what Saint had said with a clearer mind set. "I can't answer you, Diesel, but what I *can* tell you is the club is with you. If you want to ride up there and find out what the hell is going on, we'll ride with you."

Diesel looked around the clubhouse, packed with members and prospects, all nodding in agreement to ride with him. Diesel looked back at Judge, telling him, "I appreciate the offer, but having Ciara in danger is bad enough. I don't want anyone else to get hurt."

Judge looked over his shoulder as every man paused in what they were doing. Most of them were making sure they had enough ammo. He then slowly turned his head back to face Diesel, announcing with the rest of his brothers, "Fuck with one, fuck with us all!" Every man there shouted in unison.

Diesel bowed his head, humbled by their desire to help.

"Now that we know where she is, how do we get her out?" He looked Saint's way. "How do we do it and keep her safe? There is no fucking way we can pull this off." He ran his fingers through his hair as he paced back and forth.

"Calm your ass down, Diesel." Yankee raised his voice. "We will figure it out. We always do."

"But the place is a fucking fortress, from what Saint has shown us," Diesel complained.

"When has that ever stopped us, brother?" Judge questioned, putting his hand on Diesel's shoulder. "Besides, we have the element of surprise. Grave Digger and Shadow will map out the ride. Once at the house, we'll divide up. Yankee will take half of you to do surveillance. The rest of you will stay with me. If necessary, we will storm the gate and take Ciara back." Judge squeezed Diesel's shoulder reassuringly, then raised his voice for all to hear. "Kickstands up in twenty minutes."

The clubhouse started emptying as each man started moving to his motorcycle. Before Judge could move away to join them, Diesel stopped him, "Thank you, Judge. I don't think I could handle losing her. I think it would be my breaking point."

"We're going to get her back. Now, shut the hell up and get on your bike. You're with me, understood?"

"I don't need a babysitter," Diesel complained to Judge.

"Nope, you don't, but I'm going to make sure of it. Now, let's go bring your girl home." Judge threw his arm around Diesel's shoulder and dragged him out of the clubhouse to a parking lot of roaring motorcycles.

Diesel ran through the five stages of dying and got stuck on anger. He had lost his sister and emotionally was still processing that. Now, Ciara was missing, and again, he felt like he had no control over the situation, pushing his anger even further. No woman had ever affected him the way Ciara did.

It was like he couldn't take a full breath without her. His brain took a break as he got on and started his motorcycle. Judge gave the signal, and by the time they hit the highway, the sun was coming up. As Diesel rode, his brain went from feeling sorry for himself to realizing he was in love with Ciara. And then his fears turned to her. He had been held captive and knew some of the horrors she could be facing. He was grateful he was riding on his motorcycle, because until Ciara had come into his life, riding was the only thing besides medication that held his PTSD in check. Clearing his mind, he relaxed and let the ride give him the clarity he was going to need.

The ride took them about an hour, but they had finally made it to Hampton Way, the street that held the estate house that could be holding his old lady. Yankee and his group of men had split off and were coming up the road toward Judge and Diesel when the gates to the enormous house opened. Yankee held his group of men in place as a black Bentley left the driveway and turned toward a wall of motorcycles, with Diesel and Judge leading the way. As the gates closed, Yankee moved his group up behind them, making it impossible for the Bentley to move in either direction.

Diesel shut his motorcycle off in the middle of the roadway, put his kickstand down, and was about to make his way over to the now parked flashy car, but Judge stopped him and suggested, "Let's wait on them, brother."

As much as Diesel wanted to shrug Judge off, he knew his president was right. Judge joined him as they stood and waited to see what the people in the car would do.

"It seems your boyfriend has found you. Should we go see what it is they want?" Konstantin passively asked.

Ciara had her hand on the door handle and was ready to

make a mad dash, but Sasha kept her door locked from the controls at his fingers on the driver's door, forcing her to follow Konstantin out of the car. When they emerged from the vehicle, again, Ciara was ready to flee, but Konstantin wrapped his fingers around the upper part of her arm, holding her in place.

"Let go of me," she ground out between her teeth.

"Not yet, daughter, I want to know his intentions toward you first."

Ciara stopped trying to break free and looked up at Konstantin. "His intentions, I assure you, are better than yours."

Konstantin took his eyes off the group of men before him to look down at her. "Ciara, you hurt my feelings."

"I really don't care. I hardly know you. Hell, I don't even know if any of what you told me is even true."

"Oh, and you know him so well?" Konstantin countered, sounding like a spoiled child.

"I've known him longer than you, and yes, I know that right now he would like nothing more than to put a bullet between your eyes. But he won't, for fear I may get hurt."

"Then he's a very smart man. Because if you look over my shoulder, you'll see that he and his friends would not survive an attack on me," Konstantin said with unrelenting confidence.

Ciara took a moment and looked over his shoulder. What she saw certainly confirmed his statement. "If you hurt any of them, you'll never see that key," she sneered at him.

"You should never show your weakness to your enemy," Konstantin warned her. "When you do, you lose your leverage."

Diesel had had enough of this standoff and yelled to Ciara, "Are you all right?" He began moving forward with Judge by his side.

Judge mentioned offhandedly to Diesel, "You did see the arsenal facing our way, didn't you?"

"Yes, I saw them, but I believe they wouldn't want to take a chance and hurt her," Diesel responded to Judge quietly.

As they drew closer, Sasha got out of the car, and Konstantin tucked Ciara behind himself. And although Diesel and Judge were tall and built, Sasha dwarfed them. Sasha did nothing but create a barrier between Konstantin and the two men approaching.

Ciara shouted around Konstantin, "Yes, Diesel, I'm fine."

"That's far enough, gentlemen," Konstantin warned. "If you don't mind moving your motorcycles to the side, we need to be on our way. My daughter has a court appearance she is desperate to make."

Diesel and Judge stopped their advance and looked at each other, saying at the same time, "Daughter?"

"What the hell is he talking about, Ciara?" Diesel yelled to her. Then he thought to himself, *who kidnaps their own daughter?*

"Apparently, that DNA test I did has found this man, Konstantin Stepanov, to be my father," she said, adding quickly, "according to him."

Diesel realized that this definitely threw a wrinkle in his plans of taking her home. "What the hell does he want with you now, after all these years?"

"I want a chance to get to know my daughter," Konstantin answered for her.

"Bullshit," Ciara shouted. "He wants the key from my locket, so he can return to Russia and take his father's place as 'Pakhan', whatever the hell that is." She had air quoted when she said Pakhan.

Again, Diesel and Judge looked at each other. "If what they are saying is true, Diesel, you got yourself a Russian Mafia princess," Judge teased him in a lower voice.

Diesel's face lost all the color and he started to feel light-headed. He already didn't feel he deserved her. Adding a royalty status only made matters worse.

"You okay, Diesel?" Judge's voice was filled with concern for him, as he grabbed Diesel to steady him.

It took a minute or two before Diesel felt like himself again. "Yeah, Judge, I'm good." His attention then turned to Konstantin. Diesel would not lose the best thing that had happened to him in a long time. Nor was he going to let this woman he loved be intimidated by anyone. "Ciara, do you want to stay with him?"

Ciara looked up at Konstantin. "I'm going with Diesel. If you want any kind of relationship with me or to gain that key, you will let me go now." She then stood her ground.

Konstantin knew if he wanted the key, he was going to have to bide his time, time that he didn't really have. "I will allow you to go with him, but I'm not going anywhere. I've decided to stick around for a while and get to know my daughter." Konstantin looked in Diesel's direction, raising his voice. "Hear me well, biker man. If you hurt Ciara, I will have to kill you." Konstantin didn't flinch when he made his promise.

Ciara began walking toward the group of men as Diesel stated his promise, "Believe me, I have no intention of hurting the woman I'm going to marry, that is, if she'll have me." Diesel spoke the words from his heart. He watched as her steps faltered, but she continued on until she was standing in front of him. Reaching out, he pulled her into his arms, holding onto her like a lifeline. He quietly told her, "You have no idea how scared I was when I found you missing." Louder, he expressed his feelings to Konstantin, "You could have knocked on the fucking door like a normal person instead of dragging her out of her house in the middle of the night." His attention returned to Ciara. "I love you. I think I've loved you since the day I met you, I was just too stubborn to believe I could fall for someone so fast. Now, I know this is not how you dreamed of being proposed to, but I can't wait any longer. Ciara, I want you to be my sub, my old lady, but more importantly, I want you to be my wife. Will you marry me?"

Ciara couldn't believe this was happening right now. She had finally met the man who understood and accepted her as she was. A man who checked off all the boxes on her list of qualities. The man she had dreamed of meeting one day, and yet she couldn't say yes. A beautiful smile appeared on her face, as a lone tear slid down her cheek. "I want to say yes…"

"But?" Diesel added, never expecting her to refuse him.

"But if he is who he says he is, and from what I have gathered of the man," she leaned in close and whispered, "he's not a nice man." She leaned back and finished her reason. "I don't want you to be a part of that, and if you married me, it would put you right in the middle of everything." She reached up and placed her palm on his cheek. "Let's find out for sure if what he says is true before we decide anything." *They say people can wait a lifetime to find their soulmate. That one person who turns your world upside down. One person, who would fight to the death and sacrifice all they had for you.* Ciara knew she had found hers, because she would do anything to protect Diesel, even if it meant hurting him to keep him safe. It was tearing her heart apart to reject his marriage proposal, but until she knew the facts of her paternity, she couldn't say yes. "I love you, Diesel, I really do. Can you give me some time to figure all this out?"

"Ciara, I don't give a shit who your father is or what he does. Believe me, we aren't boy scouts, either," Diesel admitted, waving his arm back at the men behind him. "But if you need me to be patient a few days more, I will, but you are staying with me at the loft," he declared, not wanting a repeat of last night. He took her hand from his cheek, wrapping it in his. He brought it to his lips and kissed the back. "Let's go home."

He shifted to her side, his arm snaking around her waist.

He held her close to his body as he addressed Konstantin, "I will take Ciara to get another DNA test." He looked down at her, to confirm she agreed to what he had said. She gave him a slight nod of her head. Diesel then focused back on Konstantin. "Until then, Ciara will stay with me, and I will be joining her at every get-together the two of you plan. After all, if you are her father, you will have to get to know me as well, since I will be marrying her."

Konstantin glared at the biker standing in his way. When he had first found out that they had found a match to his DNA, he thought little about the woman the test had found. All he required from her was the key inside the locket. Yet, after seeing her, all the memories of his time with Joslyn came flooding back. Although Ciara had his eyes, she had her mother's wavy auburn hair and features that mimicked her mother. She was almost a perfect replica of Joslyn, at least what Konstantin remembered of her. This realization had changed his plans entirely.

In the small amount of time Konstantin had spent with Ciara, he had found her to be feisty, independent, fearless, and strong. She was also willful, a trait that could land her in trouble one day, especially if she was his daughter. He agreed with the biker on one thing. Konstantin would need to spend some time getting to know the man, so he could make sure this biker had what it took to keep his daughter safe. Konstantin needed to know he could trust this man, mainly because once the other mob bosses found out about her, they would have a target to use against him. "I agree to your terms," Konstantin hesitated a second to remember what his name was, "Diesel, and your promise to keep her safe. However, I am here now, and as much as I avoid courts at all costs, I would like very much to see my intelligent, successful daughter do her thing in court. So, Sasha and I will be seated in the courtroom today." He looked at his Rolex. "That, however, will not happen if we continue to stand here debating."

Ciara looked at Diesel. "He makes a good point. We really need to go. We might just make it for opening statements if I don't shower." She tried to lighten the moment by joking about not showering.

"Ciara, I could give two shits about court," Diesel shot back at her.

She stood away from him, with a touch of anger on her face. "You may not give a shit, but my reputation is on the line. This will be the first trial I testify at since I took my position. I need to be there so the prosecutor knows he can count on me."

Diesel hadn't looked at the situation the same way she did, but she had made her case. "Fine," he grudgingly expressed. "I will get you to court. Let's go." His next statement was meant for Konstantin. Taking a cheap shot at the man, Diesel added, "Had someone not taken you from your bed in the middle of the night, you would already be there."

"I deserve that, biker man." Konstantin tried to hide his anger toward Diesel, but the contempt seeped through his words. Konstantin then politely offered Ciara a ride. "If you'd like, Sasha and I can drive you." When she gave him a negative response, he added, "We will see you there then." Konstantin then got into the Bentley with Sasha sitting in the driver's seat.

"Boss, what are you planning?" Sasha questioned after starting the car.

"Well, Sasha, I can't get the key from her unless I play nice, so that's what we are going to do." A part of Konstantin wanted to tell Sasha that it was a lie, and he didn't care about the key any longer, not now after meeting his flesh and blood. He really wanted to get to know his daughter, but he also knew Sasha wouldn't understand.

"Yeah, but that doesn't mean we have to go to court. You're putting yourself into a vulnerable position," Sasha warned him.

"No one knows that better than I. But, no one knows we are here. We should be fine. Now, let's go before I change my mind," Konstantin demanded.

Ciara watched the two men get back into the car and wait for the motorcycles to move out of the Bentley's way. "We should leave as well. At this rate, I'll have time to change my clothes and get there," she groaned as she grabbed his hand and dragged him back to his motorcycle.

Diesel went with her easily, and Judge filed in next to him. "Thanks, Judge."

"For what? You did everything; we just had your back if you needed our help."

"I still have to get her to court."

"Don't you need to be there as well?" Judge reminded him.

"Yeah, but if I'm not there, my dad can handle Derek's preliminary trial," Diesel countered.

"But according to what you said, your sister requested you be at the table as well."

Ciara listened as the two men were talking, chipping away at what little patience she had left. "Could we please leave? You can just drop me off and I'll drive myself," she stated with a touch of attitude to her voice.

Diesel and Judge looked at each other. "Let's head back. You can decide what you want to do with that attitude later tonight," Judge hinted.

"Yes, I believe someone needs a lesson in manners," Diesel said as he slapped her ass. Ciara yelped and grabbed her ass to soothe the sting of his swat. "But she's right, we need to go."

The two men separated and got on their motorcycles. When Diesel was ready, Ciara climbed onto the back, wrapping her arms tightly around his waist. When Judge started his motorcycle, the thunderous sound of the other bikes followed.

Judge led the group of motorcycles around the Bentley, picking up the rest of the club with Yankee, and headed back to Hog Inlet. Judge knew Diesel and Ciara were racing a clock, so the trip back was faster than Judge's comfort level, but the club fell in line and rode.

Diesel and Ciara had made it back to her townhouse in record time. Rider pulled his motorcycle into the space next to Diesel.

"Why is he here?" Ciara asked.

"Rider will be your shadow from now on." Ciara was about to protest, but he stopped her. "This is non-negotiable, Ciara. However, right now he's going to go to my loft and get my gray suit from my closet and my briefcase near the couch."

"On my way, Diesel." Rider started his motorcycle again and left.

After Rider left, Diesel wrapped his arm around her waist and guided her to the front door, opening it, using his own key. Ciara gave him a curious look. "I had one of the prospects change the locks last night, and a few of the old ladies came over to put your place back in order for you." Diesel pushed the door open for her to walk in before him.

To Ciara's amazement, the townhouse was immaculate. She took a moment to look around. There was no blood on the floor, the books were all put back, even the plant that had gotten flipped over was back in place. When she turned around, her eyes were filling with grateful tears. "You did all of this? Thank you."

Diesel's eyes glowed with pride from her admiration. His phone started ringing and he pulled it from his pocket. "Hey, Dad." He paused, listening.

"Where the hell are you? The trial is about to start."

"We had a slight snag, Dad. However, I believe if you ask Moore for a delay until after lunch, he will agree."

"Seriously, you honestly think the court is going to wait on you?"

"No, Dad, but as we are speaking, Ciara is presently on her phone explaining how she was kidnapped by her father last night and requesting a postponement until after lunch." There was a long pause. "Dad, you still there?"

"Son, I need to go, Anderson Moore would like to talk to me." The line went dead on Diesel's phone in his hand. "I believe you just earned us a few more hours before we need to be in court." His cellphone buzzed in his hand. Opening the message from his dad confirmed his statement.

Ciara's phone vibrated as well, and she read the message to Diesel. "Moore asked the judge for more time, and it was granted. Apparently, the judge wants this case off her docket." She placed her phone on the organized counter and then walked over to him. Her arms encased his waist, as she pulled her body up close to his and let the tears flow.

Diesel didn't say a word, he just stood there and let her cry out all her frustration, anger, fear, and a host of other emotions he could sympathize with. One hand held her tight while his other rubbed her back. "Baby, it's okay, you're safe." But her tears continued. He stood there for as long as she needed him and held her tight until her tears subsided. "Feel better?" Diesel didn't want to trivialize her feelings. He knew the trauma she had experienced and wanted her to know she could trust him to be there for her.

"Yes, thank you, I do feel better." The tension that had riddled her body was nearly gone. Ciara tilted her head up and gazed into his eyes. "Thank you for coming to find me."

"I would have scoured the world to bring you back." He leaned down and touched his lips to hers. He barely removed his lips to confess, "You have stolen everything from me, my heart, my mind, my soul. I don't think I would be able to breathe without you." He kissed her cheek, then her neck, then whispered in her ear, "However, there will be a punishment at a later date, for scaring the shit out of me." He pulled her even closer. "I thought I had lost you for good when we arrived at your townhouse and found it torn apart. Thankfully, Saint pieced together what happened to you." He pulled back, and she glanced up. "I don't think I'll ever be able to pay him back for finding you."

"I don't think he expects anything in return; he doesn't seem that way to me. Now, I, on the other hand, owe him big time."

"We have a lot of time to talk about this, but right now, I'm taking you upstairs and washing this night off us." He swept her off her feet and headed up the stairs to her room. "I need my old lady."

Ciara settled comfortably into his muscular arms with her arms wrapped securely around his neck. She nuzzled her head against his chest, listening to his steady heartbeat. "Any other day, I would argue to walk on my own, but today, I'm grateful you're my legs." Memories of the night before flashed through her mind, and her body trembled.

Diesel carried her to the bathroom and sat her on the double sink vanity. He left her there and went to turn on the water, setting it to an agreeable temperature. Then he returned and pulled her sweatshirt over her head along with the skimpy satin pajama top that did nothing to hide her hard nipples. Diesel tossed them to the floor, kissing each bruise he saw highlighted on her body. "I will make sure Sasha pays for every bruise on your beautiful body." He reached for the waistband of her sweatpants. Ciara raised her butt up off the vanity, adding her assistance. He tossed her clothes to the growing pile, then took off his cut and hung it on the door.

The rest of his clothing joined hers on the floor. His hard cock, freed from the confinement of his jeans, was begging for her attention. He moved back and collected Ciara from the vanity; her legs immediately wrapped around his waist. Diesel walked them over and into the large stand-up shower. Still in his arms, Ciara closed the shower door.

She felt the hot water pulsing along her back and leaned her head back for the water to rush through her hair. As she allowed the water to wash away more of the tension she had felt, it left her neck exposed for Diesel to take full advantage of.

He pressed his lips to the side of her neck. The water splashed off the top of his head as he kissed and nibbled from one side to the other. His hand latched onto the cheeks of her ass, kneading the handfuls of lush flesh. "Ciara, I have been through a lot of shit in my life, but none of it could ever compare to the soul sucking agony I felt when I found you gone." He paused, allowing her legs to slide against his until her feet were touching the floor. "I made an error in allowing you to leave last night. I should have followed my instincts and told you to remain at the loft. I didn't want to deny your request, a mistake I will not be repeating."

"What you need to understand is I visualized the trial like a marriage. You know how the bride doesn't see the groom the night before? Well, I figured the prosecution's witness shouldn't sleep with the defense attorney the night before the trial. I know it's stupid, but who could have known that I would turn my life upside down by leaving? Rider had informed us that there had been no activity. I really thought it was safe."

Diesel pulled her close and held her. "Are you sure you're up to testifying in court today? I'm only concerned for your state of mind. You've been through a hell of a night."

Ciara smiled up at him. "I love you for your concern, but I

feel much better after my meltdown." She stepped back out of his arms and retrieved a bottle of body soap, pouring a healthy amount into her hand. Replacing the bottle, she rubbed her hands together. The aroma of coconut filled the surrounding air. Ciara placed her hands on his chest and lovingly floated her hands over his scars. She then began spreading the soap. Diesel stood as still as a statue, allowing her to lather the body wash onto his tight muscles. Moving her hands in a circular motion, she spread the soapsuds down his left arm, then his right. She stepped around him, her hands gliding over his stomach and obliques. Standing behind him, she started with his neck, her thumbs massaging the stress away. Her hands separated and floated to each shoulder, drifting down over his traps to his lower back. When they skimmed over his ass cheeks, she couldn't help but give each a little pinch. She kneeled behind him, her hands sailed down then back up, first the right, then the left, and each time, her hands grazed against his heavy balls. Ciara rose and continued rubbing the soap over his other oblique, dragging her hands to his long, hard cock. She wrapped her fingers around it, lathering the soap with each stroke she made. She slipped her other hand down between his legs, taking hold of his hefty sac. Squeezing and releasing in the same rhythm, she was manipulating his cock.

Diesel had withstood all he could handle. He had allowed her the freedom to relax, however, his body was now demanding an outlet for his adrenaline rush and all the pent-up fear, indecisions, and insecurities. He placed his palms over her hands, removing them from his body. He guided Ciara around him, placing her in front of him. He took her face in his hands, tilting her head up to look at him. "You have had your release of tension, it's my turn now." He watched a sly smile creep across her face before he picked her up. Her legs immediately wrapped around his waist. With his hands latched onto her ass again, he walked them through the water stream, rinsing the soap from their bodies. Ciara's back hit the shower wall, her head and body out of the water spray. Diesel's body pressed into hers as the water splashed off his back. He leaned forward and whispered in her ear, "I need to be deep inside you."

Ciara could only nod her head in agreement. The same adrenaline that drove her fears also navigated her desire to please him. The urgency that raced through her body was such a foreign feeling to her. The need to feel his rigid cock pushed deep inside her drove her desire. Her tight channel expanded to accommodate his size. Ciara closed her eyes, letting her senses absorb the ecstasy of the moment. A moan of pleasure sprang from her mouth when he was fully seated inside her.

Diesel pumped his hips, driving farther into her. This strong, beautiful little slip of a woman had been the final piece of the puzzle that was his life. The feelings that had plagued him when he had found her missing spurred him on, branding her as his own. "Ah, Ciara, this is going to be fast and hard."

Ciara latched her hands on his shoulders for balance, as Diesel ramped up his movements. She knew they had some-where to be, but she didn't care. She needed this as much as Diesel. Maybe more. For this moment, they were one and nothing else mattered. She felt him to her core, his need, his desire, and his love. All of it pouring out with every urgent stroke of his cock, each time hitting that magical spot, claiming what was his. And she was all his.

Diesel had held off as long as he could. He shoved into her a few more times before he exploded. He couldn't contain the growl that accompanied his release. The feel of his cock buried deep within her pussy was something he knew he would spend a lifetime taking pleasure in.

Ciara's body reacted to his touch like a puppet, manipulated by the puppet master. "Oh, my God, Diesel." She came apart, as the walls of her channel rippled along his shaft.

He stood holding her against the wall, resting his forehead on hers, allowing his breathing to regulate before softly speaking to her. "Ciara, I was serious when I proposed. I want you as my wife. When all this drama is put to bed, we will readdress this matter." He lifted his head to look into her eyes.

"Let's get through one thing at a time," Ciara expressed.

Diesel stepped back, pulling out of her, holding on to her until her feet were grounded on the floor and made sure her legs were steady. "I'll ask you one more time. Are you sure you want to testify today?"

Ciara grinned at him before she joked, "Are you afraid you might lose if I show up?" Her expression changed when she saw the serious look on Diesel's face before he responded.

"No, we believe your testimony will, in fact, help our client."

As much as Ciara wanted to understand the meaning of his words, she had no intention of prying further. "We'll know soon enough, now won't we?" She stood on her tippy toes and kissed his nose. "Either way, we will find out today." They finished their shower and prepared for court.

Chapter 8

Diesel and Ciara both changed into their court clothing. Diesel's three-piece, gray-colored suit intensified the blue in his eyes. His black shirt fit snuggly across his barreled chest. A blue Hex tie ran down the front of the shirt, covering the buttons. While his attire gave him that of a GQ look, his boots and cut showed an entirely different side of him.

"You're seriously riding your motorcycle? Do you even own a car?" Ciara teased as she walked into the living room.

Diesel couldn't help but stare at the stunning beauty approaching him. Ciara's black three-inch pumps were the only noise heard as she walked toward him, wearing a burgundy pencil skirt with a matching jacket over a sheer black, neck-tied blouse. The suit fit all her curves perfectly, in Diesel's opinion, and his growing cock also agreed. "I am in awe every time I see you." He took her in his arms and hugged her close. "And yes, I own a cage, but if the sun is shining, I am riding." He swatted her ass and gave her a quick peck on her cheek. "You're sure you still want to do this?"

"Yes, Diesel. I'll be fine."

"Well then, get that pretty ass moving. I think we've made them wait long enough." They rode the elevator down together and walked to their vehicles. Diesel placing his briefcase, jacket, and dress shoes in the trunk of his motorcycle. Ciara tossed her bag and briefcase onto the passenger seat of her Mustang that Rider had parked at the far end of the lot. She turned and gave him a wave before she got in her car and left for court.

They arrived within minutes of each other. Ciara joined him by his motorcycle as he changed into his shoes and put on his jacket. Then, together, they walked into the courthouse. After placing their belongings on the conveyer belt to pass through security, they then walked together to their appointed courtroom. When they reached the door, he looked at her. "Take a deep breath." She followed his instructions. "Release it." Again, she followed his direction. "Don't ad lib or add anything not asked of you. Do that, and you'll do just fine." He gave her a peck on her temple and grabbed the handle of the door.

"Thanks for the pep talk. I'll keep your advice in mind. And... Diesel, good luck."

"You too, Doctor O'Malley." He opened the door and disappeared.

Ciara watched him walk through the door and went to sit on one of the benches set against the wall outside the courtroom, to await being called in to testify. She opened her briefcase and withdrew a folder. Rifling through the pages, she reacquainted herself with the case. While she was sitting there, Konstantin and Sasha walked over to her before entering the courtroom. "Would you like some company while you wait?" Konstantin volunteered.

Ciara still didn't know how to react to the man claiming to be her father. And as much as she would have liked some company, she wasn't ready for his. "No, thank you. I think I should concentrate on my notes before I go in."

"I understand. We will go in and take our seats. There will be time to talk afterward." Sasha held the door open as Konstantin preceded him through the entryway.

Patience had never been a good virtue for Ciara. So, to help her pass the time, she got up and walked around then sat down again. Over and over, she did this, waiting for what seemed like hours before she was finally called to the stand. She walked into the courtroom and down the center aisle, passing Konstantin, Sasha, Josie, and Jacob, along with Judge, Yankee, Viking, Saint, and Ace. She wasn't sure if the Celtic Demons were there for moral support of Diesel, or if they were there to see Derek go to jail.

Gliding through the swinging doors that separated the lawyers and judge from the gallery, she proceeded to the witness stand. She stood next to the chair as the bailiff swore her in. Ciara then climbed the two steps up to the chair. Once she was settled, Anderson Moore, the prosecutor, began his examination. He asked her a normal range of questions, establishing her credibility. He then moved to the night Isabella Diaz was brought into the morgue. Ciara answered all of his questions without hesitation, confirming Mr. Moore's theory that Derek had indeed played a role in Isabella Diaz's suicide.

Inside, Ciara shrunk a little, feeling as if she had betrayed Diesel with her testimony. That was until his father began his cross-examination. He ask her similar questions, just worded them differently from Mr. Moore's. Ciara answered all of them honestly and to the best of her knowledge. He then asked her the process she followed when a body was delivered to the morgue.

Ciara listed the steps she followed to conduct an autopsy,

describing everything she did before, during, and after a body arrived at the morgue.

"Now, Doctor O'Malley, you've explained that you did the autopsy on Isabella Diaz alone, is that correct?" Javier asked.

"Y-yes," she stammered.

"But you weren't alone, now were you?" Javier posed the question to her.

Ciara's eyes shot to the gallery, catching Josie's eyes. Flicking them quickly over to Mr. Moore, she straightened her back and raised her chin slightly, looking at Javier. His face wore a slight grin as he waited for her response. "No, I was not," Ciara admitted. "But I was the only one in the room during the autopsy."

"Is that so, Doctor O'Malley?" His grin grew into a sly smile. "Then can you explain this?" Javier pressed the play button on the remote in his hand.

Ciara immediately heard Josie's voice, 'Hey, Doc, starting without me?'

Ciara's voice responded, 'What the hell, Josie, you were supposed to be off tonight.'

Javier hit the pause button. "Your report did not indicate anyone but yourself doing the autopsy. Who is Josie Lopez?"

"She's an intern," Ciara said softly.

"Doctor O'Malley, could you please tell the court why the recording device was shut off shortly after her arrival?"

"Because our conversation had nothing to do with the autopsy," Ciara shot back.

"Oh, but it does. Doctor O'Malley. By you shutting the recording device off, we lose the actual timeline for Isabella Diaz's autopsy, don't we?" Javier placed the remote on the table where Diesel and Derek sat, replacing it with two pieces of paper. "Because it shows on the chain of command form, you received the body at one o'clock in the morning. However, the report filled out by you says you finished at six o'clock in the morning. How long on average, Doctor O'Malley, does an autopsy take to preform?" He handed her the two pieces of paper, confirming the times.

Ciara relieved him of the two pages, seeing what Javier had announced to the court. "On average, two to four hours." She bowed her head slightly, knowing she had screwed up by not addressing the recording device before she started. She now realized where Javier was going with his line of questions.

"So, why, Doctor, did it take you five? Could it be that Miss Lopez distracted you while planting evidence on the deceased?"

"Objection, Your Honor, Mr. Diaz is conjecturing his own scenario," Anderson Moore argued.

"Sustained," Judge Morgan Asher admonished him. "Mr. Diaz, ask your next question," the redheaded, forty something, attractive judge urged him on.

Javier nodded his head in agreement toward the judge, "Yes, Your Honor." He turned his attention back to Ciara. "Doctor O'Malley, is it plausible to say Miss Lopez's visit extended the time to perform the autopsy on Isabella?"

"Yes," Ciara answered. She then spoke, defending her actions. "But she did not remain in the morgue. She viewed it through the glass window of the gallery."

"Doctor O'Malley, are we to believe that at no time Miss Lopez was near the deceased body before you turned on the recorder? That during the time the device was turned off, she didn't contaminate any samples taken?"

"No, she didn't. She wouldn't. She knows how important the chain of command is. She wouldn't do anything to hinder the investigation."

"And why is that, Doctor O'Malley?" Javier knew Josie and Isabella were friends. He knew Josie would not want to be the reason they didn't put away the person who helped her friend end her life. Yet, he knew if he pushed Ciara hard enough,

Doctor O'Malley would admit she knew about the friendship between the two women.

"Because she is an intern and knows the rules," Ciara stated.

"Is that all?" Javier prodded her.

"No," Ciara growled out, knowing what he was getting at. He was placing the seed of doubt.

"Could you please elaborate?" Javier requested. He knew the moment Ciara admitted she knew about the friendship between Josie and Isabella, the court would have to throw out all the evidence collected.

Ciara sat quietly, her eyes flashing around the courtroom. First to Anderson Moore, knowing that he was going to lose this case. Next, her eyes found Konstantin and Sasha. Although they had just met, she craved his approval for some reason. Finally, her gaze landed on Diesel. Her answer would likely win the case for Derek, enabling Diesel to fulfill his sister's request.

"Doctor O'Malley, would you explain?" Javier insisted.

"Miss Lopez and the deceased were close friends," Ciara finally admitted.

"Close enough that she would want whoever was responsible for helping Isabella to be punished for their role in her death?" Javier poked at her.

"Honestly, I don't know how deep their friendship ran. But I know the deceased played a role in Miss Lopez's life. And I believe Josie did nothing to interfere with the results."

Javier had his answer. "Your Honor, the defense would like to request all evidence collected and tested by Doctor O'Malley in this case be deemed inadmissible. Including all DNA samples. Hence, no DNA sample means no legitimate reason to issue a warrant for my client. Which, in turn, indicates a lack of evidence against our client. Your Honor, I request the charges against Derek Mancini be dismissed."

The court was silent for a few moments. Judge Asher then turned to Ciara, posing one question to her. "Doctor O'Malley, can you assure the court that Miss Lopez in no way obstructed the results of Isabella Diaz's autopsy?"

Ciara took a moment before she answered. She knew in her heart that Josie had in no way impeded the autopsy. At the same time, Ciara knew if she said she was unsure, the judge would have to throw out the evidence, ensuring a win for Diesel. It would also help with not placing blame on Josie's shoulders. However, she could lose her position. In the end, Ciara simply told the truth and prayed for the best. "Your Honor, I believe Miss Lopez played no role in contaminating any evidence gathered. However, there was a brief moment when my back was turned away from Miss Lopez and the deceased." Ciara bowed her head slightly and looked down at her fidgeting fingers on her lap.

Once again, the courtroom was silent while they waited on Judge Asher's ruling. "Are there any more questions for Doctor O'Malley?" When both men answered "no," Judge Asher turned to Ciara. "You're free to go, Doctor O'Malley. Thank you for your honesty." The judge waited until Ciara was seated in the gallery. She focused on the prosecution. "Mr. Moore, do you have any more witnesses?"

Anderson stood to address the court. "No, Your Honor." There was a slightly dejected tone to his voice as he sat back down.

"Mr. Diaz, do you have anything to add?"

Javier stood from his chair. "No, Your Honor. The defense rests."

Judge Asher took some time before she cleared her throat and addressed the courtroom. "Mr. Mancini, please rise." She paused, waiting for him to comply. "Considering Doctor O'Malley's testimony, I have no other option but to find all evidence collected from the autopsy of Isabella Diaz be deemed inadmissible. And since Mr. Moore has no further proof that Mr. Mancini played any role in the death of Miss Diaz, I hereby find Derek Mancini cleared of all charges." The judge then picked up her gavel and hammered it down, sealing her decision. "Court adjourned." She then stood as the bailiff yelled out over the noise, "All rise," one last time, and Judge Asher left the courtroom.

Once the judge left, Ciara made her way over to Mr. Moore. "I'm sorry I'm the reason you lost this case."

Anderson latched the two gold locks on his briefcase, stood it up on the table, and turned to address her. "No need to apologize, Doctor O'Malley. I knew this was a weak case when I took it on. I should have passed on prosecuting the case. On a personal note, you did well today, just make sure the next time you take the stand in a case for me that you have no holes in your testimony." He picked up his briefcase with one hand and the other, he extended toward Ciara. She grasped his hand as he expressed to her, "I look forward to working with you in the future." He leaned in so only Ciara could hear him. "My own opinion, I believe a person has a right to choose how they leave this world, when given a death warrant as a diagnosis. So, you see, Doctor O'Malley, my drive to win took a back seat today."

Ciara was grateful for Anderson's explanation. It took a weight of guilt from her shoulders. "I will come better prepared next time, Mr. Moore," Ciara promised, then gave him a knowing smile.

"I know you will, Ciara, you don't seem the type of person to make the same mistake twice." Anderson gave her a nod of his head and stepped around her. "Congratulations, old man." He walked over to Javier and held his hand out.

Javier smiled and accepted Anderson's praise. "Who are you calling old, Moore? The word is distinguished."

Anderson laughed, before filling Javier in on the joke. "You sound exactly like my pop." They released their hands, and as Anderson turned to leave, he advised him, "Give my dad a call sometime; he's always looking for someone to play golf with."

"I'll do that," Javier yelled to Anderson as he left the room. Javier then turned his focus to Derek. "Well, son, you're free to go." Javier tilted his head down, gathering his words. He lifted his head and added, "I believe I owe you an apology. I needed someone to blame for Isabella's death, and you were it. I know now you were only abiding by my daughter's wishes, even though the ultimate outcome here today could have landed you in jail for a very long time."

"I loved your daughter very much, Mr. Diaz. You raised an extremely rare woman. I would have done anything she asked." Derek's eyes welled with tears. "She took me in when I was beaten and broken and living on the street. She did not know what kind of man I was, and yet she didn't care. She treated me just like she treated everyone else. When no one gave a shit whether I lived or died, your daughter was my light to a fresh path, a path on which I'd like to continue, Mr. Diaz. I know I must prove myself to you, but I intend to carry on with what Isabella started. She had so many dreams, and I hope with your help, we can make them come true." Derek wiped a stray tear that slipped down his cheek.

While Derek had been speaking, Diesel made his way over to Ciara's side. He slipped his arm around her waist, pulling her close, not caring who saw them together. The loss he felt when she had gone missing was still too raw. He glanced toward his father as he spoke to Derek. "I think I speak for the both of us." He waited for his father's approval, by way of a head nod. "We have no plans of changing anything down at the mission. In fact, we would like to sit down and talk to you about some things Izzy wanted to implement, and if it wouldn't be too awkward, Judge and Yankee would like to join the meeting."

At that moment, the members of the Demons joined the group. Judge interjected his thoughts. "The Celtic Demons would like to renovate one of the nearby warehouses into a shelter."

"I would also like to contribute to this good act of charity. How does one million dollars sound?" Konstantin volunteered, as he and Sasha walked from the back of the gallery, joining the group. They all turned to look at Konstantin as he elaborated on his pledge. "I would very much like to start a business relationship with the Celtic Demons. This could be the start of a very prosperous and lucrative arrangement."

Javier and Derek looked at Diesel for some form of explanation. "Dad, Derek, meet Konstantin Stepanov. The man who claims to be Ciara's father."

"Javier Diaz, nice to meet you." Javier extended his hand in greeting. "That's very generous of you."

Derek, in turn, introduced himself as well. Having no clue as to the reputation of the man whose hand he was shaking, Derek blurted out, "Oh my God, that would be amazing." He then smiled from ear to ear.

"Before we accept any money from Mr. Stepanov, we need to sit down and discuss the terms of his donation." Judge made his opinion known that the Celtic Demons would not simply jump on the Konstantin Stepanov freight train.

Sasha stepped up to defend his boss, but Konstantin put his hand on Sasha's chest, stopping him. "Relax, Sasha, remember where we are." Sasha stopped in his tracks, glancing at the courtroom officers. "You hurt my feelings, Mr. President," Konstantin poked at Judge. "My money is as good as yours and it comes with no strings attached. It is strictly a gift to help the needy."

Judge had no intention of indenturing his club to the boss of one of the biggest Russian Mafia gangs. "Konstantin, it appears we have gotten off on the wrong foot. Kidnapping one of our member's old ladies will do that. However, you seem determined to be involved in a monetary way. I have some free time tonight. Let's sit down and see what you have to offer. If the DNA test, you are undoubtedly going to be taking today comes back as a negative reading, all cards will be off the table." Judge was letting Konstantin know there would be no partnership.

"Have no fear, Mr. President, the test will come back positive, but in the meantime, we can sit and speak about a legitimate venture." All the Celtic Demons, Ciara, and Javier looked at Konstantin as if he had two heads. "What?" he drew out. "If I'm going to begin a life with my daughter here in America, I want it to be one she can be proud of."

Even Sasha looked at Konstantin as if he had lost his mind. "Boss, what are you talking about?" He tried to keep his voice low. "I thought we were here to get the key and then go home. Now, you're talking about planting roots and partnering with a motorcycle club. What's happening to you? You said it yourself. With you around, that puts Ciara in danger."

Diesel pulled Ciara even closer. "Ciara will be safe with me."

Ciara basked in the feeling of being tucked securely against Diesel's warm body, daydreaming in her own world. Until Konstantin interjected himself into the conversation, she had pushed him from her mind. Now that they were finished with the trial, she needed to address the matter of her paternity. She tilted her head up to look at Diesel. "Can you take me to get my DNA test done, so we will know for sure if he's really my father?" She looked at Konstantin and Sasha. "If you follow us," she volunteered, knowing Diesel would want to be there, "we can get tested together. Hell, you could be volunteering your money for nothing."

Konstantin zeroed his whiskey-colored eyes on her. "Either way, I would still like to contribute to the mission, and I would like to sit down with Mr. President here to see if there is a way we can work together." His gaze rolled to Judge.

"Damn, we have connections with the Italian and Irish mafia, why not Russian? My decision will strongly rely on the type of business you're looking to be involved with," then he added, "and call me Judge."

Diesel was the first to break up the gathering. "We should leave if we want to get to the clinic before they close." His next statement was directed at Judge. "After we're done, do you want me to bring him back to the clubhouse?"

"You know we won't get the results back for a few days. You might want to hold off on any deals until then," Ciara informed them.

"You may not believe this, but I have no doubt that you're my daughter. However," he looked at Judge, "Ciara being my daughter should have no bearing on whether the Celtic Demons do business with me. Am I correct in assuming that?"

"You are correct," Judge agreed with him. "Diesel, after the test, bring Konstantin to the clubhouse. Let's see what he has to offer." Judge's next order was directed toward Saint. "Get ahold of the board members, I want them to attend this meeting. After we hear what he has to say, we'll bring it to church." Finally, he turned to Derek. "You have the opportunity to prove us all wrong. Don't blow it." Judge extended his hand to him.

The look of pure disbelief crept up Derek's face. Hesitantly, he reached for Judge's olive branch and shook Judge's hand. "Does this mean I won't have to look over my shoulder anymore?" His green eyes flashed over to Yankee as he spoke. "Because you do not know how much I regret my actions toward you." His eyes switched back to Judge. "And your club. I really was messed up; Vito wasn't the best brother." Derek released Judge's hand.

Judge looked over his shoulder in Yankee's direction, asking the silent question. 'You're good with him, correct?'

Yankee stepped forward, "Obviously, if the club is going to invest a substantial amount into the mission project with you, we will cross paths. I will never forget that you pulled a gun on my wife, but even a halfwit like you deserves a second chance." Yankee offered Derek his hand, which Derek accepted. As Yankee shook his hand, he quietly added, "But there won't be a third. Don't fuck this up."

"You have my word; I will not screw up again. Isabella gave me back my life, and I'm going to do everything I can to live up to her standard."

Javier had been standing by Derek while the Celtic Demons gave Derek a pass on his transgressions. "That's very admirable, my boy, and with all this help," Javier waved his hand at their audience, "I'm sure you will succeed and make my Izzy proud. Nevertheless, I believe it's time we vacate this courtroom and go enjoy a celebratory drink." His next comment was directed at Diesel. "I'll let you all sort this out and look forward to the outcome." Lastly, Javier spoke to Ciara, taking her hand in his. "It's my pleasure meeting you, sorry about the inquisition on the stand, I was only doing my job."

"I understand, Mr. Diaz."

"Javier, please."

"Javier, it's my pleasure to meet you as well. No hard feelings. You had a job to do, and you did it well." She then dazzled him with a lovely smile when she released his hand.

"I imagine we will be seeing more of each other if I know my son."

Ciara spoke up before Diesel could say anything about his proposal. "I'd like that very much, Javier. I look forward to getting to know you better." She then placed her palm in the middle of Diesel's chest, patting it gently as she advised him, "We need to go."

Javier and every Celtic Demon glared at Ciara as if she'd committed murder. All of them waiting for Diesel to recoil and withdraw. But that didn't happen. Instead, he took her hand in his, bringing it to his lips, kissing it, and agreeing with her. "You're absolutely right." He looked up from her face to tell Konstantin and Sasha to follow them. He stopped short when he saw the faces of his family. "What?" he posed the question, knowing exactly why they looked so shocked. "Now you understand why I want to keep her." His eyes looked to Judge. "See you back at the club. Have Rider pick up my bike, I'll get it later." Diesel's next comment was directed at the two Russians. "Let's get going." His last goodbye was to his father. "I'll call you tomorrow." Still holding Ciara, he turned them to leave, but Derek stopped them before they got four steps away.

"Diesel, is there any way you and your father have some time to talk tomorrow?" Derek spit out. "I have something I need to speak to the both of you about, but I would rather do it in private."

Javier responded, "Stop by the office around eleven, that good for you, Diesel?"

"I can make myself available, mind if Ciara sits in?" Diesel wanted to clarify.

"That's fine, it will give us a chance to get to know each other," Derek remarked.

"We'll be there," Diesel announced. "See you then." Still holding Ciara's hand, he led her from the courtroom, with Konstantin and Sasha trailing behind.

Chapter 9

The meeting between the Celtic Demons and Konstantin went smoothly. Both parties decided on building and running a casino. However, since gambling was illegal in South Carolina, they agreed to build in West Virginia where it was legal. Konstantin decided to reside in the mansion on Myrtle Beach and maintain a secondary home in West Virginia.

When Judge mentioned hiring a construction company, Konstantin cut him down, showing his interest in starting his own construction company that would provide the crew and materials for the building of the casino. The club and Konstantin discussed each of their roles in the purchase and refurbishing of the warehouse for the mission.

Diesel wanted to kick the shit out of Sasha after seeing the bruises he had inflicted on Ciara, but he kept his shit together. There would be another time to express his anger at the man. Instead, he drew up all the paperwork, which would be signed after the DNA report came back.

Ciara sat and listened as the club and Konstantin made each deal. Although Judge had set things in motion with

Konstantin, it all hinged on the results of the DNA test. If Ciara was, in fact, Konstantin's daughter, all things would go as planned. However, if she wasn't, all deals would be off. The Celtic Demons could look past the fact that Konstantin had taken his daughter against her will; what they could not abide with was Konstantin kidnapping an innocent woman.

Ciara and Diesel returned to the loft after the meeting at the clubhouse. The worries of the trial were gone, only to be replaced by the anxiety of a four day wait for the test results.

As soon as they stepped off the elevator, they kicked off their shoes and dropped their belongings on the floor. Diesel took her in his arms and simply held her. He needed to feel her, know she was safe, and let her know she could lean on him.

"I need to go wash this day away. Care to join me?" Ciara asked.

"I wouldn't want to be anywhere else." He unfolded his arms from around her, his fingers grazing down her arm to take her hand in his as he led her to his bed. There, he began undressing her. His hands swiftly slipped the jacket from her shoulders and his fingers hastily released the buttons on her blouse. He looked at the bruise on her ribcage that had changed to a darker shade from earlier. "Does this hurt?" He pressed against the discolored flesh. Her quick intake of breath confirmed his suspicion. "I will let this go for now, but the next time I see Sasha, I will make my displeasure known." He spun her around slowly, releasing the hook and lowering the zipper of her skirt, letting it slip down her legs. He freed the fasteners of her bra, gliding the straps down her arms to the floor, and finally slipping her panties down her legs. Again, he kissed the soft skin of her neck and shoulders. Rotating her back around, she stood before him. "God, you are stunning. How the hell did I get so lucky?"

Ciara beamed at his words of praise. She raised her arms

up to his shoulders to commence removing his courtroom apparel. Pushing the jacket from his body, she told him, "I'm the one who should be thanking the stars for sending you to me." Her fingers made quick work of removing his shirt, leaving his exquisite chest, scars and all, exposed to her. Ciara then grabbed the waistband of his slacks, opening and shoving them down his legs to the growing clothes pile, freeing his stiff cock.

Diesel effectively shed both socks from his feet. He then stepped up to her and swept her into his arms.

Ciara waited patiently for him to prepare their shower, her body raging within itself. Part of her wanted to be romanced and pampered. The other part wanted him to press her up against the wall and push deep inside her. Ciara felt like a small child in his strong, capable arms. She slipped one arm around his neck and laced her fingers together, placing them on his shoulders. Her head moved forward, spreading little kisses on his exposed neck. Ciara meandered her way up to the outer rim of Diesel's ear, as he climbed the stairs to the open shower. She slid her tongue along his ear, opening her mouth and releasing a warm breath of air, as she gently teased him. She felt the low growl against her chest, bringing her nipples to hard little nubs. An overpowering need to have him deep inside her seeped into every molecule in her body.

Diesel climbed the stairs, holding her close, as she continued her assault on his ear and neck. He resisted every urge to press her against the wall and fuck her hard. He knew as her Dom that tonight, she needed to be cherished. He reached the top of the stairs and walked to the vanity, sitting her down. He proceeded to the shower faucet, setting the temperature, then retrieving three towels and placing them on the freestanding cabinet. Diesel finally sauntered back to her, walking into her open arms and legs. He picked her up off the vanity; her ass in his hands, her legs wrapped around his waist as he lifted her up and carried her into the shower. Diesel backed her into the waterfall of steamy water, and her body melted into romance.

She dropped her head back, allowing the water to flow through his cascading hair. She let go of his neck and raised her arms to pull the rest of her hair back into the flow of water. The movement pushed her breasts up and her wet pussy against him.

Diesel shifted one hand from her ass to the center of her back, supporting her body. Once her hair was wet, as much as Diesel didn't want to, he let her legs slide to the floor. He held her arms for a few moments to make sure her legs were underneath her. He reached for the shampoo on the ledge and poured some into his palm. Rubbing his hands together, he told her, "Turn around and let me wash your hair."

Ciara did as she was told while commenting, "That smells exactly like my shampoo."

"It should. I had Colton do some shopping for me. I wanted you to have all the things you prefer when you're here. Now, be quiet and do nothing but feel my hands on your body."

Ciara closed her mouth along with her eyes. She stood before him while his fingers massaged her scalp, lathering the shampoo in her hair. He instructed her to rinse the soap from her hair and repeated the process with the conditioner. It had been a long time since someone had washed her hair for her. Diesel's fingers were like pure magic. Anytime they touched her, her body fell under his spell. This time when she rinsed the conditioner from her hair, she allowed the stress of the day to trickle away. Ciara picked her head up out of the water and opened her eyes. "You have no idea how incredibly relaxed I feel." She lifted up on her tippy-toes and gave him a quick kiss. "And if I feel this good now, I can only hope to be standing by the time we are finished." Ciara purred as she clasped her hands behind his neck, but he stopped her.

"If you should begin to fall, I will be right here every time, to catch you." He leaned down and kissed her lips, sealing his promise. He pulled his head back and whipped her hair from his face and then swiped the leftover water away. "For now, let's finish here so I can ravish your magnificent body." Diesel picked up the bottle of shower gel, pouring some out in his palm, with the aroma of coconut surrounding them. "Turn around," he instructed her.

Ciara followed his direction, spinning around to face the wall. The water flowing from the shower faucet bounced off her sensitive chest as she stood waiting for Diesel to continue. And continue he did. He started with her shoulders, massaging any residual tension that still lingered. Ciara rolled her neck, giving Diesel better access to the tightened muscles. She raised her arms away from her side while his hands spread the lather down to her fingers. Repeating the process on the opposite side, his soaped hands resumed their exploration of her body, widening his fingers, spanning them across her back. Down to her heavenly ass they crept, molding each orb into his hands. The friction was creating more lather. Diesel stepped closer behind her, pressing his painfully hard cock against her. He slid his hands under her arms, circulating the shower gel across her chest. He stopped to tug on each of her erect nipples, before scooping both breasts into his hands, pulling her body back against him. His hands drifted down to her abs as suds followed along.

Ciara rested her body against Diesel's muscular chest, letting him bear her weight. When the fingers of his right hand slid between her legs, she was grateful for his support. Her head lolled to the side, then closing her eyes, Ciara cleared her mind of all thoughts except the sublime feeling he was building. She reached her hands back, latching them onto his ass cheeks, digging her nails in and out of his fleshy skin.

As soon as Ciara moved her arms back, Diesel took full advantage, placing his left hand across her body, encircling her breast. His hands worked in unison as his index finger pushed inside her and his other hand began tweaking her hard nipple. Diesel then added his middle finger inside her, to tease and awaken her desire. He leaned his head down, kissing her collarbone and then whispered in her ear, "I was so scared when I found you missing. My mind immediately went to the worst scenario, but my heart, my heart knew you were alive because it continued to beat. I don't understand how I could fall so deeply in love with you, nor do I want to understand, but I have. You have stolen everything from me, my mind, heart, and soul. I want to hold you like this forever and never let you go. I promise you here and now, no matter what happens with the DNA results, you will be my wife, my sub, and my old lady." His fingers continued to heighten her need to come. "Tonight, I want you to be my lover. I'm going to take you in this shower, then on the balcony, and finally in our bed."

The more Diesel talked, the closer Ciara was to tipping over the edge. She moved her hands to cover his, squeezing them as she spoke. "I was just as scared that I'd never see you again. But can we talk about all this stuff later? Right now, I just want to feel alive." She moved his hands away and turned around. Placing both her hands around his neck, she stepped closer to him. "I need to be with the man I love."

Her words of love pushed Diesel beyond his limit. He removed her hands and spun her body around. Bending Ciara at the waist, he stepped behind her. His throbbing cock slid between the apex of her legs. He left one hand on her waist. With the other, he guided his aching cock into her waiting body. Shoving his dick in until it could not push in any farther, he then waited, allowing her body to adjust.

Ciara had placed her palms on the glass wall overlooking the loft, dipping under the stream of water that was now bouncing off her back. This position gave Ciara the ability to counteract his movements so that when Diesel shoved his hips forward, she could push back, impaling herself farther on his cock and creating a friction that drove their pleasure beyond the stars. She cried out, "I can't wait any longer." And with that, an uncontrollable surge pulsed through her body, releasing an ear-shattering scream. All the problems of her day were finally gone, leaving her satisfied and tired.

Diesel grabbed onto her hips with an urgency he'd never experienced. His need to come with Ciara had him plunging into her faster. The low growl that grew while he drove into her turned into a howl when his body rocketed off the charts. Reaching his pinnacle, he pinned his cock deep inside her, reveling in Ciara's surging walls as they milked the cum from his body.

Ciara's head sagged down between her arms that were still fixed on the wall. Breathless, she filled her lungs with air as she picked her head up and set it on her outstretched arm. Forming a sly smile on her face, her satisfied eyes gazed at him through small slits. "I don't want to move, but if we stay here, at some point we are going to run out of hot water."

Diesel took his cue from her. Pulling out of her, he kept his hands locked on her hips, making sure she was steady on her feet. "As much as I'd like to test that theory, we have both had a long day and I do believe I hear the bed calling our names," he teased with her, then presented her with a brilliant smile. He guided her body up into a standing position, pulling her back against him. Diesel wrapped his arms around her waist and leaned his chin on her shoulder, whispering in her ear, "I want a lifetime of theories to test with you." He then placed a kiss on her neck. "Let's get dried off, and I don't know about you, but I could sure use a drink."

At the mention of the word drink, Ciara relaxed against Diesel, mumbling, "How do you always know what I need?"

Diesel moved her to the side and rinsed his body off in the water spray before shutting it off. Grabbing a towel from the stack, he opened it, and Ciara walked right into it. Securing it on her body, he handed her another one. "Here. You can tackle that head of hair. I'm going to grab our drinks." He pulled the last towel off the stool and closed it around his waist, leaving her to finish drying off. By the time he returned, Ciara had wrapped her hair in the towel and had climbed into bed. She was raised up on the stack of pillows behind her. She reached and took the drink from his hand. He dropped his towel and carefully got in next to her with his drink intact. She waited for him to get comfortable, then snuggled in next to him and sipped her drink.

Holding her in comfortable silence, his mind drifted to the earlier conversation with Derek. Breaking the silence, he said out loud, "You know, ever since Derek asked to meet with us tomorrow, I've been trying to figure out what it could be about."

"Maybe he wants to talk about Isabella now that he knows he won't get killed for it," Ciara hinted at the conversation back at the courthouse. "Whatever it is, you'll find out soon enough." She finished her statement with a yawn. She then put the glass to her lips, finishing her drink in one swallow. She sat up and twisted her body to place the glass on the night-stand and slumped back onto the bed. Resting her head on his chest, she glided her hand over his scarred chest and left it there. "Konstantin feels confident that I am his daughter." She paused and tilted her head up to look at Diesel. "Why does life have to be so damn unpredictable?"

Diesel downed the rest of his drink, leaned over, and

placed his glass on the other nightstand. Resetting his position in bed, he held her in his arms. "I guess that's how God wanted it. If you knew what was coming, your fears would stop you from experiencing life to its fullest. Because along with all the bad, there is always good. Try not to stress too much about it. Besides, I wouldn't mind being married to a mafia princess, and a Russian one to boot."

Ciara smacked his chest before saying, "Cut it out! I'm not a mafia princess. Although, I did dream of being a princess one day and that a handsome prince would rescue me."

"I believe I fit the bill of the part for handsome prince since I've already saved you once."

Ciara giggled at how nonchalant he was about the entire ordeal with her paternity. "Indeed, you have." She covered her mouth as another yawn escaped.

"Close your eyes and get some sleep. I have a feeling the next couple of days are going to be filled with a few more unpredictable things." He pulled her closer, needing to reassure her he'd be right by her side. Ciara listened to Diesel and closed her eyes. Within minutes, she was fast asleep. He lay awake, watching her sleep. He placed a kiss on her head then whispered, "Mafia princess or not, you are mine, and I will do anything to keep what's mine." Snuggling farther down, he fell asleep with his keepsake in his arms.

Chapter 10

The next morning, Diesel woke before Ciara and gazed at the stunning beauty lying next to him. He watched the REM movement of her eyes and knew she was dreaming, and by the slight smile on her face it appeared to be a delightful dream. Diesel gently pulled the covers from her naked body, admiring her taut nipples that reacted quickly to the cold air brushing on them. Lying beside her, he leaned his head down, sucking her nipple into his mouth. A moan of need sounded deep in her throat. While Diesel assaulted her nub with his tongue, his hand slid down her stomach to the apex of her legs, slipping his index and middle finger through her wet lips. This time it was Diesel's turn to moan. Her legs dipped slightly open, allowing him better access, and his fingers crept lower, to her entrance. Diesel then dipped them within, pushing farther in as Ciara's body involuntarily acted on its own, her pelvis rocking forward, striving for more. Diesel raised his head to find her sleepy eyes gazing at him.

"What a delightful way to wake up. Please continue." She

stretched her arms above her head, giving him complete control of her body.

Diesel switched his position, holding himself above her, leaning his weight on his elbows. His cock pressed against her opening; he began guiding it into her. "If we had more time, I would ravish every inch of your body, all day. But since we need to be somewhere in a few hours," once he was fully seated within her, he finished his statement, "this will be quick."

"Fast or slow," she latched her legs around his, and twisted their positions so that she was sitting on his cock looking down at him, "bottom or top, it doesn't matter to me, just as long as it's with you."

A grin spread across Diesel's face, while his hands clasped onto her hips, holding her in place. He lifted his pelvis up from the bed, pressing his cock into her until he could push no more. "Hold on, Doc, and ride my cock."

Ciara leaned forward, placing her palms on his chest, while she ground her hips down against him. Once she was secure, Diesel held her hips and raised her up until just the tip of his cock was in her. "Do not come until we change positions." Ciara's face showed disbelief. "Your punishment for topping from the bottom." He yanked her hips down, impaling her on his cock, over and over, until he was deep inside her. Quickly, he shifted his hands, pressing one to her back, and the other to her bottom, flipping her over onto her back.

The moment her back hit the bed, Diesel began pumping into her, reawakening her senses, sparking the kindling back into a burning inferno. Within seconds, Ciara's body tipped over into the delicious burning pulsing through her veins. Diesel leaned his body to the side, reaching his hand between their joined bodies, pinching her clit and pushing her body farther over the edge. Ciara clawed at the pillows as wave after wave of pleasure washed over her. She pinned her shoulders to the bed and rode the exquisite feeling until she slumped onto the bed, spent from divine pleasure coursing through her.

Diesel dropped to her side on the bed, telling her in between sucking in gulps of air, "I think this should become part of our morning ritual." He turned on his side, his arm folded up to hold his head in his palm. "What do you think?" His face transformed into one of a child pleading for a treat.

Ciara shifted her head to look at him. "I do agree. It is a very pleasant way to wake up, but there's a lot to be said about spontaneity," Ciara pointed out as her eyebrows waved up and down.

Diesel couldn't help the laughter that erupted from deep within him. When he was finished chuckling at her comment, he blurted out, "Damn, woman, I like the way you think." He leaned over and gave her a good morning kiss.

Ciara brought her arms down from over her head, placing one on his shaved neck and the other at the back of his head. Her nails lightly grazed his skin and moved up to the hair atop his head. She let her fingers sift through the silky strands. Ciara tried desperately to deepen the kiss, but Diesel pulled back away from her. She gave him a curious look but suggested to him, "Kissing should definitely be a morning ritual."

"I can agree to that." Diesel gave her a quick peck on the forehead and moved to get out of bed. "But as much as I would like to stay right here with you all day, we have a meeting to attend in an hour and a half."

That got Ciara's attention. She had forgotten all about the meeting with Derek at his father's office. "Shit, I totally forgot about that." She sat up in the bed and threw the covers back over a chuckling Diesel. She gave him a death stare that paused his laughter but left a natural smile on his face. "Stop laughing; you have no idea how long it takes me to tame this head of hair." She slapped both hands on her head, clumping fistfuls of her frizzed out, knotty, unruly hair. "This is what happens when I fall asleep with wet hair." She heard him chuckling again and yelled at him, "Oh shut up, you'll go get a pair of jeans, a tee shirt, your boots, and cut, and you'll be ready to go." Tossing a pillow at his head, she swung her legs off the bed and stood by the side. "Would you please make coffee while I get ready?" Her voice sounded a little more humbled.

Diesel tossed the pillow to the side and got out of bed, telling her, "It will be brewed and ready when you are." He didn't have the heart to tell her he had set the pot up last night, and it was probably already brewed.

Ciara had finished her hair in record time. She applied some makeup and chose a pair of black capris and a purple short-sleeved blouse with black-flowered print. She slipped on her three-inch wedge sandals, grabbed her bag, and was soon sipping her freshly brewed coffee as Diesel drove his Audi A8 to his father's office. He pulled his car into the spot next to his father's Mercedes. By the time Ciara finished her coffee and gathered her purse, Diesel was holding the door open for her. "You're such a gentleman. Your parents raised you with good manners," she complimented as he helped her from the car.

"More my mom than my dad," Diesel confessed. "Dad was always working." He closed the door and guided her to the entrance.

Ciara hesitated a moment, reading the name on the door. "It says Javier Diaz and Son. I thought you worked for the club?"

"I do. My father changed the name and added son when I passed the bar. I told him at the time that I wasn't going to be a part of his firm. I wanted to make a name for myself, not live in my father's shadow."

"I really can't comment on that subject. I recently found out that I might have a dad with a reputation that has shadows I'm not sure I want to be a part of."

Their conversations dropped when they entered the office. Carol greeted them with a good morning and asked if they'd like coffee, to which both responded with a quick "yes."

"Your father and Mr. Mancini are in the conference room if you'd like to join them. I'll bring your coffee in when it's ready."

Ciara and Diesel greeted Carol accordingly, then following her directions, they joined the men in the conference room. Both rose from their seats as Ciara walked into the room. Once everyone had said their hellos and Carol returned with their coffee, they all took their seats around the table.

"Okay, Derek, the floor is yours," Javier prodded.

"That's kind of you, sir, but it will be Izzy who will be telling you." Derek reached into his jacket pocket and pulled out a white envelope, handing it to Javier.

The heading on the envelope read, *After court, for Dad and Romeo.* Javier's hand shook slightly as he peeled open the envelope flap. Sitting back in his chair, he began to read aloud.

'Dear Dad and Romeo,

If you are reading this letter, it means Derek is safe from any formal charges, or they found him guilty and they have decided the outcome of his future. As I write this, I pray you have been successful in gaining Derek's release. And for the rest of this letter, that is how I will believe the future will be.

I'd like to start by saying thank you. I knew you guys would save his ass from jail. What I have to say next will come as a complete shock, but since I could not be there to say it in person, this is the next best thing. Dad, Romeo, I'd like to introduce you to Derek Mancini, my husband.'

Diesel and Javier turned to look at Derek, sitting in his chair ready to produce whatever documentation they needed for clarity. Yet, all he said was, "We eloped six months ago when she received her diagnoses. Please read on; we can discuss everything when you're finished."

Javier continued to read.

'I know you might be disappointed with me for not telling you. I wanted to, but I knew if I did, what little time I had would have been filled with anger and yelling. And that's not what I wanted. I desired a much calmer atmosphere for my last days and believe me, they were exactly as I hoped. I would like both of you to get to know him as the man he is and not the man he was. Believe me when I say he is the love of my life and I will be right here (wherever here is) waiting for him.'

Diesel glanced at Ciara when he heard a sniffle come from her direction. He got up from his chair and retrieved a box of tissues, setting them down in front of her. She gave him a grateful smile as she snatched one from the box.

Javier waited until Diesel was settled back in his chair before he continued.

'He is part of the family, please treat him as such. Now, for my most important request from the both of you. Do you remember when I was a little girl, and all I wanted was to be a wife and mother? Then the years went by, and my focus changed to helping others. The desire for a family never left my mind. When I met Derek, for the first time in my life, I

believed my dream would come true. However, cancer had another plan for me. It crushed me. I had finally found the love of my life and I would never be able to share that with him. That was until I had a brilliant idea, but first we needed to be married.

I started researching and discovered I could leave a little piece of me with you. I made an appointment and had my eggs extracted. Derek and I then interviewed several women until we found the perfect surrogate. If you haven't figured out what this is leading up to yet, I will tell you. Dad, your grandchildren should arrive sometime in October. Romeo, I hope you will agree to be Jasper and Alisa's godfather? I want you and the love of your life to be a part of my children's upbringing. Jasper is going to need your athletic skills, and Alisa, your soft yet protective sides.'

The men looked at each other in stunned disbelief. Then at the same time shouted, "Twins?" each glancing Derek's way for confirmation.

With a slight nod and a beaming smile, Derek corroborated what Isabella had written.

Javier returned to the letter.

'Derek will need your support and help. I'm not telling you to move him into the house, but if he would agree to it, my childhood home is exactly where I would like my children to be raised, with family all around them. I want you to tell them stories of me and tell them every day that their mother loved them, even though she never had the chance to meet them. Jasper and Alisa are the two little pieces of me that will live on.

So, as I say my last farewell to you all, know that I was truly blessed to have parents who cherished me, a brother who protected me, and a husband who filled the last few months of my life with unconditional love. Pass these traits on to my children, so they may experience a life full of wonder and laughter, with the abilities to decipher between right and wrong, to live a life of stability, and have an understanding of compassion.

I love you all so much, and I know I will rest easy because I have completed God's plan for me. It's up to the three of you to follow through now and work together, so Jasper and Alisa never forget their mother.

With all my love,
Isabella'.

The room remained quiet except for Ciara's sniffles. Derek stood up from his chair, accepting the fact that his father-in-law and brother-in-law needed more time to adjust to the news, but before he took one step away, Diesel spoke up. "Where do you think you're going?"

"I assumed you needed time to digest that you are soon to be an uncle and," Derek shifted his eyes Javier's way, "you, a grandfather." He turned to leave again.

"No, Derek, don't leave. Sit back down, please." Javier stopped him this time and waited for him to return to his chair.

"I'll be honest with you. Never in a million years would I have thought I'd be having this conversation. The notion that my daughter's children will be born months after we buried her sounds like something straight out of a sci-fi movie."

"In-vitro fertilization has come a long way, sir, and our surrogate has had two natural births with no complications. That was one reason we chose her, beyond the fact the woman's whole aura is all about helping people."

"Where is she now?" Diesel asked.

"She has a two-bedroom apartment off Shorehaven Drive."

"I'm assuming you have a contract with this woman?" Javier inquired.

Derek produced another envelope containing the legal

documents in question, along with his and Isabella's marriage certificate, and a flash drive. "Isabella and I had Neil look over the documents, and the flash drive is Amiee's resume. Your daughter felt a connection with her immediately, and vice versa with Amiee. Would you like to meet her?"

"Yes, I would," Javier's answer was instantaneous.

Derek played with the screen on his phone, and when he found what he was looking for, he handed the phone to Javier. Diesel's father looked down, and what he saw brought tears to his eyes. On the screen was a sonogram photo of the twins. "I buried the original with Isabella," Derek explained.

"That was what you slipped into the casket when you said goodbye, isn't it?" Diesel wanted to know.

Derek nodded his head as Diesel pick up the phone his father had pushed across the table. A proud grin slid across Diesel's face when he looked at the picture. "Who is Neil?"

"Neil is one of the homeless people Izzy helped get back on his feet. He was so happy to help her after all she had done for him. He was very thorough. You will not find any loopholes. He wanted to guarantee to Izzy that after she was gone, I would have no problems retaining custody of our children."

"I'll feel better after I look them over," Javier announced as he removed the documents and spread them out on the table.

Ciara had sat and listened to the exchange between the men. She glanced Derek's way, to see the apprehension written all over his face, and took it upon herself to try to cut through the tension growing in the room. "Derek," she spoke up, gaining his attention. "I'm sorry for your loss, but on the other hand, I'm elated that you're going to be a dad." She then pinched Diesel's thigh, inducing a quick yelp. "What are you waiting for? Congratulate your new brother-in-law and welcome him into your family."

Diesel focused his attention on her. "Will you be as agreeable when we receive your DNA reports back?" he snapped at her.

"That's totally different. My father walked out on me. Derek is doing everything in his power to cement his paternity for those children." Ciara was angry that he would compare her situation with Derek's.

She rose from her chair, but he stopped her. "I'm sorry. That didn't come out the way I meant it."

"What did you mean then?" Ciara poked at him.

"We've had ten minutes to digest this information. You, however, will have a few days to get used to the idea that Konstantin is your father."

Ciara darted her gaze toward Derek. "I think I understand why Isabella wanted to avoid this conversation." Shifting her glare back on Diesel, she added, "You will have a lifetime to love and cherish these babies. I may only have a few months or even days to get to know my father, given the profession he's in." She flashed her eyes to Javier. "Think about this. If you let how this whole situation came to be make you alienate Derek, you will miss out on getting to know the one, excuse me, two babies Isabella will never get to see. She'll never get to hold them or be there to pick them up when they fall. She will never get to hear them laugh or teach them to ride a bike. She will never get to love them. She left that job to the three of you."

Her eyes watered when she swung her gaze to each man, finally landing on Diesel. "So, I suggest you work as a team to give those twins the love their mother so desperately wanted to give them." With that said, she rose from her chair. "I'll wait for you outside." She leaned down and gave Diesel a kiss on the cheek, and whispered in his ear, "Give him a chance."

Standing up straight, she looked back and forth between the two. "Congratulations, Derek, I think you'll be an exceptional dad." Then to Javier, "You, as well, Mr. Diaz. Those children will need their Poppy to tell them about their beautiful mother." Ciara held back the tears that threatened to fall until she left the office. As soon as the door closed behind her, with the blink of her eyes, they fell freely down her cheeks. Before she walked any farther, she wiped her cheeks with the backs of her hands, took a deep breath, and then walked past Carol, waving goodbye as she left the office.

Once she was seated in Diesel's car, she crumbled into pieces. She placed her hands over her face and let the tears flow as uncontrollable sobbing wracked her body. She leaned forward, bending at the waist, the backs of her hands resting on her thighs, her thoughts brought back to the times she had dreamed her father would return and that they'd finally be a family. Or when after her mother died, how she wished he'd magically appear to comfort her and promise her a life with him. But... none of that happened. Her father's only reason to be searching for her now was to retain ownership of a stupid key. Ciara cried a bit more, freeing herself from years of resenting, speculating, and sometimes downright hating her unknown father.

Her tears subsided. After reaching the pinnacle of her despair, she dug into the pocket of her capris and pulled out a tissue. Cleaning her face of any lingering tears, she fixed her makeup and took a deep cleansing breath. She then folded down the mirror, added some lipstick, and pinched some color back into her cheeks. She sat back as she struggled to tamp down her feelings of rejection, loneliness, and resentment. Instead, she decided to focus on what it could be like if she gave her father a chance to be in her life. She wondered if he would want to stay around to get to know her. Ultimately, everything still relied on the key. Should she hold the key hostage until she'd gotten all her answers? Or should she give it to him and let him be on his way? Diesel was right about one thing. She had more time to come to terms with the jaw dropping reality that Konstantin might be her father. Because she was going to need those days to decide whether to forgive him and move on or reject him and lose out on a chance of ever getting to know him.

It wasn't long after her breakdown that Diesel joined her in the car. Before she could apologize for butting into his affairs, he took her hand in his and spoke to her. "I had no right to attack you back there. Both Derek and my father laced into me after you left. I was projecting my own fears onto you, and for that I am sorry."

Ciara was still fragile with her tears. Even after she had pulled herself together, they still wanted to fall. She sat quietly, listening to his apology, holding her tears at bay.

Diesel continued, "You had a valid point. I wasn't looking at the situation from my sister's eyes. I was still looking at the man who helped Isabella take her own life. It's going to take some time and maybe a touch of therapy, but like you and my father so wisely pointed out, I will learn to look past who he was and try to give the man a chance. I want to live up to Isabella's expectations. That is why, tomorrow night, we will be hosting a party to introduce the new Derek and announce the expected births of Jasper and Alisa." He squeezed her hand and turned to look at her. "Will you help me with that? Because I have absolutely no idea about planning a baby announcement party." Diesel gave her a pleading face.

Ciara couldn't help the laughter that bubbled up when she looked at his face. His eyelids were droopy, his forehead was furrowed, and his lips were pressed together. A single tear slipped away, down her cheek at the bat of her eye, but this time it was a tear of happiness. He kept that face in place a few seconds longer as she giggled at his playfulness. Finally, she gave in and agreed. "Yes, yes, I'll help you plan a party. Now, stop doing that with your face." Diesel had succeeded in putting a smile on her face, and her mind was on something other than the results of the DNA test. "Thank you! I take it you're more accepting of being an uncle now?"

"It's growing on me." He brought her hand to his mouth and kissed her knuckles. "They say it takes a village to raise children, and I'm going to make sure Jasper and Alisa have a town." He released her hand and started the car.

Ciara reached back, grabbing her seatbelt as she asked, "Where are we going?" while she snapped the seatbelt in place.

"Back to the club." He hesitated, wondering if she caught his drift.

"You can't want to have sex now; we have a lot to do, and not a lot of time to do it."

Diesel rolled his head to the side to look at her. "I will always want your luscious body, anytime of the day. But I was referring to Delectable Desires. Why own a restaurant if you can't use it? Besides, we won't take up the whole restaurant, just part of it."

"So true, I'm sure Colton and Chef Declan will be able to help things along."

Diesel backed the car out and got on the road toward home. "Are you kidding me? The minute Colton and Chef hear the words baby announcement, get out of their way because they are very passionate about planning their parties."

Ciara laughed as she pictured the two men bickering over the pink and blue decorations. "I've been warned," she told him.

"You have nothing to fear. They both adore you, and that's why I'm putting you in change of Chef and Colton. I'll stick to inviting people." He glanced at her and flashed a Cheshire grin. Then, he turned his face back to the road and hit the gas.

At the speed Diesel drove, they made it to the club in no time. Diesel pulled Colton into the kitchen area to speak with him and Chef Declan. He explained what he wanted them to do, and as Diesel predicted, the two men were ready to start planning immediately. They had no problem incorporating Ciara's feminine advice, especially since they had a day to put everything together.

The threesome had worked well into the night, picking out shades of pinks and blues. Agreeing on the menu had taken most of the time, but they had completed it before Ciara left. Colton walked her to her car, asking, "Are you sure you want to go home?"

"Yes, I'm sure," Ciara told him as she stretched out her words. "Besides, Diesel's probably already sleeping because I confirmed with him earlier that I was going home. You're such a worrywart, Colton."

"I simply remember the last time you went home alone." He raised his eyebrows to emphasize his point.

"I remember, but nothing like that will happen, considering Konstantin and Diesel both have men following me everywhere." She nodded in the direction of the black car, where her bodyguard from Konstantin was waiting for her to leave, along with the lone motorcycle rider waiting for the same thing. "That's Rider; Diesel has made him my shadow."

"Well, to be honest, I feel better knowing that." She kissed him on the cheek and got in her car. "You'll see; everything will be fine."

"We'll find out soon enough." She started her car and Colton stood watching as she drove away.

Ciara stood looking at her reflection in the mirror. She had taken the front section of her hair and sectioned it off, weaving an intricate braid that flowed into the rest of her free-flowing hair. The creation highlighted the multi strands that made up her chestnut-colored hair. She wore a sleeveless, rainbow-colored, A-line maxi dress that displayed her ample chest and flowed down to her ankles, showing off her beige leather ankle laced three-inch heels.

She had done her makeup with care and put on her earrings before she slipped the chain of her necklace over her head. The locket landed in her cleavage. Ciara took it in her hands and snapped it open to look at the key she had picked up from the bank earlier. Diesel had commented that he'd invited Konstantin and that he had accepted. As she snapped the locket closed, she told herself in the mirror, "Tonight, I will give him the stupid key because daughter or not, he's eventually going to take it from me. I'll save him the trouble." Ciara took a deep breath and blew it out slowly. She picked up the bottle of Hypnotic Poison, spraying the perfume on her neck and wrists, then grabbed her lightweight brown leather jacket. She made her way downstairs to put her cellphone and keys in her evening bag and made sure she was ready when Diesel came to pick her up. As she got to the bottom of the stairs, there was a knock on her door. Changing directions, she answered it. Thinking it was Diesel on the other side, she opened the door, saying, "Give me a minute, I'll need to get my things."

Yet it wasn't Diesel on the other side; it was a courier. "Are you Doctor Ciara O'Malley?"

"Yes," Ciara replied with curiosity in her tone.

"I need you to sign right here." The courier turned his phone around for her to sign. After that was complete, he shoved his phone in his pocket and handed her a nine by twelve envelope, explaining to her. "I was supposed to tell you…" Reaching for his phone again, he went on, "Oh, I'm supposed to tell you that your friend Abagail put a rush on your results. Have a good day." He waved his hand and walked away.

Ciara looked at the envelope in her hand. Inside, were the DNA results. A shiver of unexpected excitement rushed through her body. She debated about whether she should open it or wait until later to find out the results together with Konstantin. She finally settled on waiting until later. Holding the envelope in her hand, she started gathering her things.

"Any special reason your door is wide open?" Diesel questioned her, standing in her doorway.

Startled by his appearance, she replied, "Oh, hi. Nope, I was simply waiting for you." Ciara folded the envelope and tucked it in the inner pocket of her jacket. She then turned and drank in the sight of him. He wore a black button-down shirt tucked into his black jeans. His cut rested on his shoulders, emphasizing the blue Hex tie down the front of his shirt.

"Whew, whew," he whistled her way. "Damn, woman, you are so fine." He approached her, taking her in his arms. "How did I get so lucky to have found you?"

"You look mighty fine yourself." She returned his hug, her arms snaking around his waist, and leaned back in his arms. "I don't believe in luck. I think our paths were supposed to cross, right now, at this time, when we both needed each other the most."

Diesel leaned forward and kissed her forehead, murmuring, "My mother would say our stars have aligned." He pulled back, looking down at her. "Are you ready to go?"

"Yes." She gathered her things, slipping her arm through his and commenting, "I have a feeling it's going to be an interesting evening." Then she allowed him to guide her from the house to his car.

Diesel and Ciara arrived at Demons' Dungeon before any of their guests got there. Ciara wanted to tie up any loose ends, to make sure the party was a success. She, Colton, and Chef Declan had decorated the entire restaurant in shades of pinks and blues. Some tables had pink table cloths and blue napkins, other tables with the opposite color scheme. Cooper, the maitre'd, had made the decision to garnish the entire area, although only a section would be used for the party. He thought to include the other diners in the festivities as well. There were balloons, streamers, and banners. In the center of each table, were three individual vase candle holders. Each cylinder was a different height, containing a cherry blossom stem of the following colors, pink, white, and blue, each one filled with fluid to keep the candles floating. The final decorations were tucked off to the side, to keep them safe until they were unveiled. On separate tables, were one pink and one blue four-tier cakes, with flowers flowing from top to bottom. Each cake had a cake topper with one of the children's names on it.

The bus boys were lighting the last of the candles when Ciara and Diesel walked into the restaurant. Ciara stood at the entrance, taking in the room's elegance. While she stood there, Colton came up beside her and whispered in her ear, "It looks beautiful, Ciara."

"I was just thinking the same thing." She turned and gave him a kiss on the cheek. "Thank you for all your help. I couldn't have done any of this without your and Chef Declan's advice."

Diesel came up on her other side, informing her, "My father called. He and Derek convinced Amiee to come tonight."

"That was very nice of you to include her. I'm looking forward to meeting her."

And with that said, their guests began arriving. Judge and Skylar were the first members of the club to arrive. Diesel introduced Ciara to Judge's old lady. He knew once they met, Skylar would take Ciara under her wing and acquaint her with the other women, which is exactly what she did as they arrived. Skylar introduced Ciara to Rachel, who was with Yankee, Willow and Saint, Hailey, and Viking, and so on. There were also friends of Javier's arriving, all wondering what the announcement would be about. They had been invited under the guise of a baby announcement, but none knew who the expectant mother-to-be was.

Ciara saw when Konstantin and Sasha joined the gathering. She watched as he greeted the members of the Celtic Demons and then as if sensing someone's eyes on him, he turned toward her, making eye contact. He gave his excuses and starting making his way over to her. His progress was halted with the arrival of Javier, Derek and Amiee. The threesome found Ciara and Diesel right away in the crowd and moved in their direction. Amiee was introduced to them, and then Javier quieted the crowd down.

Once Javier had gained the attention of the crowd, he announced, "I would like you all to meet Amiee Flores and Derek Mancini. On behalf of my son and son-in-law, we would like to thank you for joining us on such brief notice." There was a buzz of conversations around the room. "I know you are all wondering what our announcement is, so I won't keep you in suspense any longer." He waved his hand, moving Derek to his side. "Unbeknownst to Romeo and myself, Isabella took it upon herself to marry the love of her life." He waited for the murmuring to settle down, then continued. "She then took it one step further, finding Amiee here to carry her and Derek's child."

The crowd around the room started clapping, and someone yelled out, "Is it a boy or a girl?"

The servers then walked forward, pushing the tables holding the cakes on them. "Both," Javier answered. "In a few months, Amiee will give birth to Jasper and Alisa Mancini." The crowd again clapped and cheered, expressing their good wishes. "Now please, everyone, enjoy yourselves," Javier extended his warm invitation.

Judge and Skylar walked over to Diesel and Ciara. Judge was carrying two shot glasses of bourbon and handed one to Diesel. "Dude, congratulations! You're going to be an uncle."

Diesel accepted the shot and touched the glass to Judge's. "I'm going to be a godfather." Diesel continued, "Ironic, right?" Then he downed the shot with an "Ah."

Ciara stood to the side, half listening to the conversation. Her thoughts were focused on the envelope in her jacket. But before she looked at the results, she had to do something. She tapped Diesel on the arm to get his attention. "I need to go talk with Konstantin. I'll be right back." Straightening her shoulders, she left the group and made her way over to him.

"Good evening, my lovely Ciara. You look beautiful. That's such good news for your biker man, isn't it?"

"Hello, Konstantin. Yes, it is wonderful news for *Diesel* and his family." She stressed his name. "But that's not why I'm here." She reached for the locket, holding it in her hands. She snapped it open and removed the key, holding it between her thumb and index finger, "Here. You have more use for this than I do."

"I'm confused. Why are you giving this to me now?"

Ciara bowed her head, gathering her words, then looked back at him. "I know I said I was going to wait. However, whether you're my father or not, this does not belong to me." She reached out, handing him the key.

Bewilderment showed on Sasha's face as Konstantin took the key from her. "Thank you, Ciara. I will now be able to obtain the will and the Stepanov ring, the proof I need to shut my cousin Boris up." He took the key and stashed it inside his jacket pocket. Before Konstantin could say anything more, Chef Declan announced that dinner was being served. "I will talk with you more after dinner."

Although they were not sitting at the same table, Konstantin and Sasha sat at one in close proximity to her. Javier and his associates also sat nearby. Ciara, on the other hand, sat with Diesel and his brothers from the club. The rest of the evening was filled with festivities and good cheer. After coffee and cake were served, the party started to wind down as guests began to leave. Those who remained moved into the bar area of the dungeon, where they continued celebrating. When the clock struck closing time, the other patrons of the dungeon filed out the door. Konstantin and Sasha joined Derek, Ciara, and Javier after they put Amiee in a car with one of the prospects, so he could take her home.

"Thank you, Javier, my friend, for including us in on your special party, but it's time for us to take our leave." Konstantin slapped his hand on Javier's shoulder.

Ciara interjected before Javier could respond, "Could you wait a few minutes longer?" She waited until she received his affirmative answer, then ran and grabbed her jacket. She removed the envelope and returned, ready to share the results. "I received this earlier tonight, but I didn't want the results to overshadow the baby announcement." She shifted her gaze to Konstantin. "But I want to open this," she waved the envelope in front of him, "before you leave."

Judge, Yankee, and Saint, along with Skylar, Rachel, and Willow sat at the bar beside Diesel. All of them watched as Ciara ripped the envelope open and removed the single sheet of paper. Holding it against the envelope, Ciara skimmed the results, reading, "The alleged father is not excluded as the biological father of the tested child. Based on the testing results obtained from analyses of the DNA loci listed, the probability is ninety-nine point nine-six percent." There was more written, but Ciara didn't need to read further. "So I guess you were right. I am your daughter."

As she finished her admission, the double doors of the

club opened, and a group of five people walked in, three well-dressed handsome men and two beautiful women, one redhead and one brunette. All the members of the Celtic Demons stood from their seats and formed a wall, preventing the group from advancing farther.

"The club is closed, and this is a private party." Diesel's voice rang out in the quiet area.

The tallest of the three men stepped forward. "We're not here to make trouble, I'm here to meet my uncle. I heard through the Russian grapevine that he was here." He tilted his head of sandy-blond hair and swept his hazel eyes around the room of people.

Hearing the word Russian, the wall of Demons opened, and the Demons turned their attention Konstantin's way. "I suppose he's talking about one of you," Diesel commented as he stepped up to introduce himself to their new guests. "Diesel, and you are?"

Reaching his hand out, responding to him, the man said, "Dimitri Zilkin." He then turned to introduce the rest of his group, "Let me introduce Madison, Xavier, Cameron, and Sadie." They all waved or acknowledged who they were when Dimitri mentioned their names. "I apologize for crashing your party this late. However, the drive from New York took longer than we expected." He glanced at Madison and Sadie.

"It's not my fault your son keeps playing the drums on my bladder," Madison defended herself. "By the way, could you point me in the direction of the ladies' room?" she asked Diesel.

"I'll show you where it is." Willow jumped down from her stool, leading the way for a very pregnant Madison, and Sadie followed her.

Dimitri watched the women walk away then turned to Xavier. "I think we'll rent an RV for the ride home. That way, she'll have access to a bed and bathroom instead of being cramped in an SUV."

"I'll see what I can find tomorrow," Xavier volunteered.

Dimitri turned back to Diesel. "She has a month to go but insisted on coming with us," he explained.

In the meantime, Konstantin and Sasha moved closer to the new group. "Since Sasha has no family, I would think you were speaking about me, Konstantin Stepanov," he introduced himself. "But if that's the case, I don't understand how you could be my nephew."

"Yakov Stepanov had two legitimate sons and one bastard. Nikolay, your father, and Viktor, your cousin Boris's father. My father, Sergei, was his cast off."

The hair on the back of Konstantin's neck stood up. Here, he had just acquired the key to secure his seat as Pakhan of the Stepanov Gang, and now some unknown nephew pops up out of nowhere. "I vaguely remember that Yakov's second in command was named Sergei, but I never knew he had family. I assume you have proof of this claim."

Dimitri could hear the challenging tone in his voice. "Konstantin, I am not here to stake a claim in the Stepanov Gang. I want nothing to do with that life. That was my father's calling, not mine or my brother Sebastian's. I have my own successful business with my partner Cameron. Maybe you've heard of it, The Midnight Oasis Cruise Line?" He looked around the club, "We took all of this," pointing to the BDSM equipment in the exhibition room, "and put them on a cruise ship. In fact, the reason we were in New York was to finalize plans for a new ship leaving from the Big Apple. That's when I heard you had been in town. With the recent reading of my father's will, Sebastian and I found out we had an entirely new family. It was one thing to think my father worked for the Stepanov family, but to learn I was related by blood, stirred my curiosity."

"Well, your timing couldn't be any better. I am also finding out I have an entirely new family," Ciara butted into the conversation, stepping around Diesel. "And if he's your uncle, that would make you my cousin." She offered her hand to him. "I'm Ciara, by the way."

"Dimitri Zilkin." He took her outstretched hand. "Nice to meet you, cousin." He was about to introduce Xavier and Cameron until they all heard the women returning. They were laughing and talking as if they were old friends instead of new acquaintances.

Madison sidled up between Dimitri and Xavier. "So, what did we miss?"

"I was just getting ready to introduce Xavier." His hand swept toward the tall, olive-toned, brown-haired man on the other side of Madison.

Xavier's intense brown eyes had been inspecting the club while he had been standing there. Hearing his name mentioned, his attention was drawn back to the conversation. "Nice to meet you, Ciara, nice place you have here."

Ciara smiled at the compliment. "Yes, I agree with you, however, it doesn't belong to me. That honor belongs to Diesel and his club."

Diesel shook Xavier's hand. "It was a joint venture."

While the introductions were being made around the room, Konstantin stood and observed the two groups and his daughter. He could now say, without reservation, she was so beautiful. The way she laughed and got excited about the upcoming birth of yet another cousin and how comfortable she was, reminded him of her mother Joslyn. Konstantin was in deep thought when Javier nudged him in the arm.

"It's been a hell of a few days for us. First, I find out I have a son-in-law, along with grandchildren on the way. And if I know my son, I'll soon be adding a daughter-in-law to my family. Then, you learn Ciara is your daughter and meet a new member of your extended family in one night. I don't know about you, but I could use a shot," Javier offered his company to his new friend. "They'll be at it for a while. You'll have better luck talking to her tomorrow." With Derek sitting next to him, Javier ordered four shots of Beluga Nobel Gold vodka.

Konstantin swiveled his body toward the bar in response to Javier's invitation, at the same time telling Sasha, "Take a seat, my friend. We have time for a drink with our new friends, and I can observe my daughter a while longer." They took their seats and received their shots of liquor. Javier raised his in a toast. "Like Abraham Lincoln said, 'The best thing about the future is it comes one day at a time'." They then downed their drinks.

Ciara sensed Konstantin's eyes on her, and when she turned toward him, she saw he was drinking with Javier. She excused and extricated herself from Diesel's arm and walked over to him. She placed her hand on his shoulder, letting him know she was there. "I'm sorry we got interrupted earlier. I never got a chance to say although our relationship started out on a rocky road, I'm hoping we can start again. I'd really like to get to know my father." She wasn't sure, but she could have sworn his eyes had a sheen of wetness to them.

"Earlier, when you gave me the key, did you have the results then?" Ciara nodded her head yes. "Why?"

"Because as much as I'd like to believe, my mother took the necklace as a keepsake. I can also see her taking it out of resentment. Besides, the key meant nothing to me. It was the locket that mattered."

Konstantin smiled at her reasoning and hesitantly placed his hand on her shoulder. "I need to return to Russia to avoid a bloody power struggle with Cousin Boris. But when I return, can we spend some time together?"

Ciara was a little taken back by his nonchalant attitude, but she figured if she was going to be part of his life, she would have to get used to the business side of him as well. "Yes, I'd like that." She wasn't sure, but it seemed like he wanted to hug her but didn't want to overstep. So, she took the decision from him and reached her arms around and hugged him.

Taking his cue from Ciara, Konstantin wrapped his arms around her, holding her close. "In a very brief time, you have become an important part of my life. I don't want to leave you, but I know I am leaving you in good hands."

While Ciara had been saying her goodbyes to her father, Diesel had snuck up behind her. "You have nothing to worry about. I will make sure she remains in one piece and breathing until you return."

"I'm holding you to that, biker man," Konstantin threatened with a smile and then released Ciara into Diesel's arms.

"When are you leaving, Uncle?" Dimitri and the others had slowly worked their way over to the four men at the bar, Ciara, and Diesel.

"I'd like to sit with Judge tomorrow and sign some contracts before leaving the day after. That way, things can get started on our business ventures while I'm gone." He glanced Derek's way. "I transferred the money I pledged for the new mission. I can't wait to see the progress the next time I'm here."

"I look forward to getting started, sir. Thank you again for your generosity," Derek acknowledged him.

"How would you feel about dinner tomorrow night? I was serious when I said I wanted to learn more about the Stepanov family," Dimitri suggested. "Would you join us as well?" Dimitri extended the invitation to Ciara and Diesel.

Diesel answered for the both of them, "Let us know what time, I'll reserve the V.I.P table. Also, you mentioned you drove straight here. Do you have a place to stay tonight?"

"We figured we'd find a hotel in town to stay in," Xavier answered.

"Stay here. We have rooms upstairs that can accommodate you while you are here visiting. I'm sure the last thing Madison wants to do is get back into a car again tonight," Diesel offered.

"Are you sure it wouldn't be too much trouble?" Dimitri wanted to know.

"No trouble at all. Plus, Ciara and I will be around if you need anything."

"We'll be here too," Killian spoke up.

"Us, too," Hunter added.

"Wow, that's super nice of you," Sadie complimented.

Javier got off the bar stool, dragging Derek with him. "I think that's our cue to say good night."

Konstantin followed Javier's lead and said his goodbyes as well. After confirming their dinner plans, he walked with Sasha, Javier, and Derek out the door.

Ciara, Rachel, and Willow escorted their guests upstairs to get them settled, while the rest of the club members closed the club and locked up. When the women were finished settling in their guests, they joined their men at the bar. Judge and Skylar were finishing their drinks.

"You staying in Ace's loft?" Killian asked.

"Yeah, I let him know earlier that we would be using it. I had a feeling tonight's events would be interesting, and you didn't disappoint me," Judge flipped his comment Diesel's way. "If I wasn't here to witness it all, I don't know if I would have believed any of it." He stood from his bar stool, helping Skylar off hers. "But that's a discussion we can have tomorrow." He looked at his watch. "Well, later today. We're out of here, night everyone."

"I'm with Judge," Hunter agreed.

The four couples walked to the private elevators, saying their goodbyes as the doors opened for each couple.

Ciara and Diesel rode the elevator in comfortable silence. When the doors opened for them to exit, Ciara expressed her gratitude. "Thank you for letting my cousin and his friends stay here. You didn't have to do that." And before she could say another word, she heard music playing. Donny Hathaway was singing *A Song for You*. Diesel swung her up into his arms and carried her into the loft that was decorated with candles and flowers everywhere. "What's all of this?" Her voice was filled with wonder as the music played in the background.

Diesel carried her to the bed and sat her down. The bed was covered with rose petals in pink, white, and red, spread out in the shape of a heart. He then took a ring box out of his pocket and got down on his knees before her. "I asked you the other day. I was unprepared, and I kinda put you on the spot. But now, the trial is over, we know Konstantin is your father, and we are alone." He opened the box holding a two carat, white gold, marquise cut engagement ring "This was my mother's. When we were at my father's office, after you left, my father gave me this and told me, 'marry that woman.' Ciara, like the words say in the song, 'I love you in a place where there's no space or time.' I was broke, and you healed me. You are my present and future and without you, I have neither. Be my wife. Let me love you until my last breath. Marry me and together we'll ride the road of life."

Ciara had tears streaming down her face as he laid his heart bare to her. Listening to his declarations and promises, she remembered her grandmother's words, 'Men will come and go in your life. But when you meet the man you're meant to be with, it's like a switch flips, filling you with the light to feed your soul. Marry that man, Ciara.' Ciara wiped the tears from her face and smiled at him. She took a deep breath and released it before she gave him her answer. "It physically hurt me when I refused your proposal. I knew then, just like I know now, I love you. I don't need any more time to tell you that there is nothing I want more than to be your wife, lover, submissive, and the all-important 'old lady'."

Diesel took the ring from the box and placed it on her finger, kissing it in place. He then stood up, taking her with him. He took her hands and placed them around his neck, sliding his fingers down her arms. Then he wrapped his hands around her waist and leaned his head down, placing his lips to hers. Pulling her body close, they swayed to the music. He broke from the kiss, pressing his lips to her cheek, her neck, and ear, whispering, "You brought color back into the dark world I was hiding in. Your light broke through all the barriers I had put in place to protect myself from disappointment, rejection, and indecision." He pulled back to look into her beautifully watery eyes. "Your father may remember his mother when he sees your locket. My father may reminisce when he sees your ring. But you, Ciara, are my keepsake and I will cherish you for the rest of my life."

The tears returned to slip down her face. He bent forward, catching the salty droplet on his tongue. "Why are you crying?"

It took a moment to get control of her emotions before she told him, "You keep blindsiding me with a romantic side of you I did not see coming." She brought her fingers up to wipe the stray tears and makeup from her eyes.

He gave her a slanted smile before confessing, "You got me. Rachel, Skylar, and Willow did all of this." He spread his arm out, indicating the setting. "But the words were straight from my heart." He gave her a peck on the nose before he stepped away from her. "Go get comfortable, I'll grab two glasses and a bottle of champagne, and we will continue this celebration in bed."

"It's late. Are you sure you want to celebrate now?"

"I know it's late, That's why we are only going to celebrate with champagne. After that, I'm going to hold you until you fall asleep, and then hold you some more."

Diesel walked away to change and retrieve the items he needed. Ciara stood gazing at the beautiful ring wrapped around her finger, thinking, *who would have thought that in a matter of weeks after meeting Diesel, we would be engaged? You were right, Grandma, he flipped my switch.* She smiled to herself and went about changing into a lavender satin cami and shorts. When Diesel returned, she was propped up, sitting in the bed, and still gazing at the ring on her hand. "I can't stop looking at it. It's so beautiful." She looked up at him as he stood by the side of the bed. "Your mother had excellent taste."

Diesel handed her the glasses to hold as he poured the champagne, and then he placed the bottle on the nightstand and got into bed beside her. Once he was settled, Ciara handed him a glass. "Not Mom, Dad. My father had it made specially for her." He reached for her hand and held it up, showing her. "You see the diamonds on the side?" Ciara pointed to the eight stones, four on each side. "Yes, those. They were originally from my grandmother's ring. My dad had the jeweler cut and add them to my mom's."

"So, technically, I have a two-generation ring? That's amazing."

"Dad said if you didn't like it, you could always do what he did and design your own with these stones."

"Nope, I think it's perfect the way it is." She raised her glass and waited for him. "To a lifetime of new traditions." They both took a sip from their glasses.

Diesel looked over at her and saw two stray tears rolling down her cheek. Concern filled his voice. "What's the matter, Doc?" He put his glass down, then took hers from her hand, placing it next to his. "Come here, baby, tell me why you're crying now?" In their short time together, Diesel had viewed

Ciara as such a strong woman. To see her so vulnerable with him, only made him love her more. He tucked her in beside him, holding her close. "I have big shoulders, Doc. Let me carry your load; tell me."

As music played around them, Ciara settled into the comfort of his muscular arms. "I was just thinking that, in only a matter of days, I went from being alone to my life being filled with an abundance of people and family. You say I healed you. Well, you filled my lonely life with unconditional love. I know it was a sad day for you when we met, but for me, it was like my body had gotten a reboot back to life."

"Ciara, when I was lying in that hospital bed, barely holding onto life, I gave up on ever letting a woman get close to me. And yet, at another low point in my life, I met you. You're going to think I'm crazy, but I'd like to believe my sister played a role in bringing us together. The day will always invoke memories of Isabella, but she made it so the memories wouldn't hurt so bad."

"We've both been pretty blessed. Your family grew overnight, just like mine. I have a cousin who actually wants to get to know me." Ciara's joy overflowed in her words.

"How would you feel about getting married on Dimitri's latest cruise ship, the Blue Topaz? I'm sure we could get a good deal," he teased with her.

"I thought we'd get married here at the club. I believe we could get a good deal here as well," she countered, a sly smile forming on her face as she tilted her head up at him.

"Ciara O'Malley-Stepanov." He watched her nose crinkle. "Correction, the future Ciara Diaz," her face lit up, "I will leave that decision up to you because as far as I'm concerned, you are already mine, wedding vows or not."

"Stop, you're going to make me cry again," Ciara pleaded with him.

He placed his fingers on her chin, holding her face in

place. "I love you, now and always." He brought her face closer, pressing his lips to hers, sealing his promises. "Now, close your eyes and go to sleep. Tomorrow, we start a new journey together, and you're going to need all the rest you can get." Ciara followed his directions and closed her eyes, falling fast asleep.

He lay there watching her. *"Izzy, you rest easy, I will watch after your children and even your husband. These are my promises to you because you have sent me my perfect match, my perfect keepsake."*

If you or someone you know is struggling with thoughts of suicide, please contact the National Suicide Prevention Lifeline- 1-800-273-8255

Jill Shannon

Jill Shannon lives in a small town on Long Island with the love of her life and a very large dog. They've been together since high school where by the way, he received better grades on the stories she wrote for his classes. She has two professional daughters (one is an RN and the other is a Doctor of Psychology), a son-in-law, two very active granddaughters, and a beautiful grandson.

Jill has been reading romance novels since she was thirteen. The drama, suspense, and of course the love scenes all drew her in. Staying up till three in the morning just because she couldn't put the book down. Over the years Jill has expanded her genres of reading material. From historical, to paranormal, to sci-fi, and now BDSM, her dream was to write her own romance novel. She never thought it would happen with her busy life. However, Jill wanted to be able to do the same thing for others that her authors have done for her. For just a small time during your day, she would like you to be a part of the fantasy she creates.

You can email Jill at: jshannon7373@gmail.com
Follow her on Twitter: @JillCShannon
Or find her on Facebook
Visit her website.

Don't miss these exciting titles by Jill Shannon and Blushing Books!

Midnight Oasis Series
Onyx - Book One
Sapphire - Book Two
Black Diamond - Book Three

Celtic Demons Series
Killian's Masterpiece - Book One
Hunter's Treasure - Book Two
Diesel's Keepsake - Book Three

Blushing Books

Blushing Books is the oldest eBook publisher on the web. We've been running websites that publish steamy romance and erotica since 1999, and we have been selling eBooks since 2003. We have free and promotional offerings that change weekly, so please do visit us at http://www.blushingbooks.com/free.

Blushing Books Newsletter

Please join the Blushing Books newsletter
to receive updates & special promotional offers.
You can also join by using your mobile phone:
Just text **BLUSHING** to 22828.

Every month, one new sign up via text messaging will receive
a $25.00 Amazon gift card, so sign up today!